Doug and Carlie

By Lisa Smartt

www.lisasmartt.com

Copyright 2012

Library of Congress Control Number: 2012918527

ISBN 978-0-615-70358-9

Front cover photo by freedigitalphotos.net
Contributor: tungphoto

Back cover photo by Portrait Innovations

To Philip,

Your daily acts of kindness speak louder than words.

Table of Contents

CHAPTER ONE: My First Thirty-Two Years Condensed Into A Few Pages 'Cause Really...It Hasn't Been That Exciting

CARLIE

September 15, 2010

I ate a whole lemon meringue pie on May 12 of this year. I walked out of the Kroger in Athens, Georgia, sat in my '99 silver Camry, pulled a plastic spoon from my purse, and started in the middle and worked my way to the outside crust. It was good too. Well, good and terrible at the same time. The way a drunk feels after slugging back a half bottle of Jack Daniels. He doesn't know whether he's happy or sad. He's too intoxicated. I was sugar intoxicated the day I ate the whole lemon meringue pie. But thankfully, today I'm completely sober.

I'll graduate from the University of Georgia this December at the age of thirty-two. I first went to college when I was eighteen but I thought I was too brilliant to study and I made a mockery of the whole process. That's what my major professor, Dr. Sanders, told me. "Carlie Ann Davidson, you have made a *mockery* out of the scholarships that were entrusted to you because you were an honor student in high school. People had faith in you. They wanted you to succeed. They believed in you and this is how you have paid them back...with failure."

You may not know this or maybe you do. Failure feels, well, like a bad case of food poisoning. You promise yourself you'll do everything possible to never experience it again.

I don't know why I failed out of college. That's a lie. I do know. I didn't do the work. I hated going to biology lab because it stunk so bad and I hated actually doing experiments or lab work with my hands. I'm not a doer. I'm a thinker. Or that's what I told Dr. Billings when he asked me to carve up a dead rat. I calmly explained, "I just wrote a moving story about a rat who fell victim to America's prejudice against members of the rodent family. You certainly can't ask me to be a part of this rat's ultimate undoing. I have a moral obligation to opt out." Yeah, when an eighteen-year-old thinks she's brilliant she says really stupid things like that.

I thought I could opt out of the work part of going to college. But it just made people believe I was too immature to be there. They were right. I loved going to English classes because I got to write. They made me write. Someone has to make me write because I'm not a disciplined person at all. Hence, the pie episode above.

I dropped out of college at twenty and that's when I began my career as a cashier/stocker/finder of pork n beans at the Dollar General Store in Commerce, Georgia. I'm not all in love or anything. My parents are teachers and they're still in love after thirty-seven years. Sometimes I wish my family were more dysfunctional as that would make a good excuse for all my failures.

My two younger brothers, Sam and Bennett, are both married to beautiful women and wildly successful according to all-American standards. I think they succeeded because no one ever told them they were brilliant. They just worked hard and cut open the rat and did what they were told. Neither of them works at the Dollar General Store because they finished college and bought houses in suburban neighborhoods. All the normal stuff. Sam even got an MBA.

No. I don't know if they're embarrassed by their *brilliant* sister who works at the Dollar General. I try not to think about it. I'm sure they say what everybody says, "Well, did you hear? She's attending college now." Like that makes me a real person again. Going to college doesn't make someone a real person. Wiping an old lady's rear end at a nursing home makes someone a person. That's just my own opinion.

I love romantic movies and I pretend that someday I'll be starring in my own romantic movie. Except it will be for real. I mean, it will happen in real space and time. A tall good lookin' stranger will walk into the Dollar General Store and buy something really exotic. He won't be buying Wonder bread or Pop-Tarts or motor oil. No. It will be something like…well, I don't know. Something like a cheese grater or a cork screw. We don't carry cork screws, but maybe he'll buy a bread machine on sale for $39.99 because he wants to make his own wheat bread. I'll picture him going home to his perfectly-kept condo where he'll grate some kind of exotic cheese to put on a piece of fresh wheat bread because it's so much healthier than grabbing a burger at Burger Shack. He'll loosen his tie and sit down and have a drink out on his veranda. That's what all successful men do in movies. And yes, they have verandas…not porches.

I usually pretend that I'm too smart to worry about love. When Mrs. Grissom comes through the line every Saturday morning (senior citizen discount before noon) she always asks, "Carlie Ann, are you dating anyone?"

I say things I don't mean like, "Right now, I'm just concentrating on my studies." or "Men are all pigs." But I don't mean it. I just don't want to say what I really mean, "I desperately want a man to love me." or "I'm not sure there's a man who will love me." That seems a lot scarier than just pretending to be concentrating on my studies.

I'm majoring in English because the one thing I can do (other than tell you that toilet paper is on Aisle 9) is read and write. I know. English majors don't have any real job prospects. You think I don't know that? Sheesh. I know. But I had to major in the only thing I could do successfully. I couldn't risk another failure. According to the University of Georgia, in less than four months I will prove to the world that I'm brilliant again. Whew. I'm sure most people have totally forgotten my earlier brilliance at Commerce High School. After ringing up their Wonder bread and Pop-Tart purchases for the last ten years, I've become invisible.

But I'll be visible again soon. Just wait. My name and picture will be in the paper and everything. Commerce Woman Graduates from University of Georgia with Honors. Well, I won't actually graduate with honors. Biology and history and algebra and a few other classes stood in the way of that. I'm not sure I ever was brilliant. I was just really good at convincing people I was.

I weigh thirty-seven pounds more than the chart says I should weigh. I don't like it but every time I think about weighing thirty-seven pounds more than the chart says I should weigh, I want to eat a whole pie. Vicious cycle, y'know. My cousin swears up and down that there are men out there who like their women *chunky*. I don't see it. First of all, I think *chunky* is a ridiculous word to describe anything other than a chocolate bar. Secondly, the men that come through the check-out line never give me a second look. Is this because they think I'm a loser for working at the dollar store or because they would never look at a *chunky* woman? I'll probably never know. I do know that the University of Georgia needs to hurry up with my diploma. My self-esteem is waning.

That brings you up to date on my first thirty-two years. I'm a chunky girl who comes from a nice Georgia family. I tend to be an under-achiever and a pie eater. I work at the Dollar General Store. I used to make excuses for that but I don't anymore. I desperately want real love. I'm almost always hungry for sugar. I don't like dissecting rats. Oh, and I live in an apartment with dingy cream-colored carpet and a roommate named Clara. I hold out a lot of hope for tomorrow...'cause the first thirty-two years haven't been much to write home about.

CHAPTER TWO: I Know It's Gonna Get Better (Probably)

CARLIE

September 22

Just got out of my sociology class. Dr. Crusoe said that all of us single guys and gals should be on a mission to find ourselves and not be bogged down with thinkin' about wantin' a woman or a man all the time. All I could think about was how cute that redheaded guy on the front row looked in his faded jeans and plaid flannel shirt. The light blue matched his eyes perfectly. Every time Dr. Crusoe told me to concentrate on finding myself it made me want to eat sugar or kiss a man. I didn't even know which one I wanted more.

September 23

I ate no sugar yesterday. I feel proud and happy. Today is the nineteenth day of my last semester at the University of Georgia. So I'm ten years late. Who's counting? Well, Mom and Dad have probably counted but the point is I got here. I'm writing from the park bench outside the University Commons. All the college kids are playing Frisbee or holding hands with their significant others while walking to class. I hate that term *significant other*. What does that even mean? Let's be real. It's boyfriend or husband. If this is my boyfriend it means that we're not sure if we're in love. We're trying to find out. If this is my husband that means we both are pretty sure. Not that complicated.

September 26

I wish I hadn't told Mom I would go to the college class at church. I felt ridiculous walking into a class full of people who were in kindergarten when I first told Dr. Billings I wouldn't dissect a rat. I felt old, invisible, fat, hungry, tired. It didn't help that my eye liner was crooked and my tan pants felt tight. And wouldn't you know that a fabulous-looking twenty-something man sat down next to me. He never even glanced my direction. I knew the drill. I just turned red and wished I had a Hershey bar.

The teacher had some encouraging things to say about love and singleness and priorities but I rushed out of the room as soon as it was over and sat in the sanctuary with my parents like a fourth grader. Egads! All I needed was some crayons and I would have drawn a picture on the church bulletin.

At lunch, I wanted to say something to my parents but I didn't know how. I wanted to say, "Mom, Dad, I'm a grownup now. I care about my future. I'm really good at my job. I'm friendly when Mr. Porter asks about whether the spray paint we carry is toxic. I look on the label and say, 'Why Mr. Porter, looks like if you follow the directions you'll live to see another day.' I'm good with Mr. Porter...and people like him. I'm always on time. I got an A on my final paper last semester in English 309. I pay my rent two days early every month." But I didn't say it. I didn't say any of it. I knew they still saw me as a fourth grader. A sad and lonely fourth grader. I was lonely, yes. But I was a full-grown woman.

September 30

I lost seven pounds and then I gained five. I think I was celebrating the lost weight by eating a half gallon of ice cream in forty-eight hours. That will only make sense to some people. If you read the pie incident and thought I should be hospitalized you will not be one of those people. I went to Lane Bryant today and bought a pair of jeans and a bejeweled denim jacket. The sales woman said it was *sassy.* I said that sassy was exactly what I was going for. She almost cheered, "Girl, you gonna look like somethin' else when you hit the dance floor in this little number."

I said, "How would it look in the frozen food aisle at Kroger?"

"Oh Hon, don't even be messin' with me. You got it goin' *on* and you know it."

I may have it goin' on but I don't know where it's goin' and I definitely don't know where to take it.

That brings up a tired and over-used question that I have pondered almost every day for the last seven years. Where does a nice girl meet a nice guy? Every morning talk show has a panel to discuss such a question. The panel is usually made up of a bunch of doctored married people who are going to tell me, a *chunky* woman who works at the dollar store, that I should do some kind of exciting cultural extra-curricular thing that makes me seem intelligent. I don't know if telling Mr. Porter that the spray paint won't kill him counts. But if it does count, I'm good. I'm right where I need to be.

I had a big crush on someone last year. But I know now that he wasn't my type. Every time a girl is handily rejected by a man she says, "He wasn't my type." That's code speech for: He didn't like me. I wanted him to like me but he didn't. Jim Flanders liked to flirt and pretend that he hung on my every word. But I realize now that what he really liked was knowing that I liked *him.* It didn't matter that he was never gonna ask me out. He was gonna spend his time making me think he was gonna ask me out just so I would keep volunteering to bring spinach dip to his office. One time he asked my opinion of his tie. "Does this lavender look too girly? I don't want to look like a girly man. You'd never go for someone like that, would you, Carlie?" He knew I would go for him...lavender tie or not. He was yankin' my chain and I've decided I don't like that anymore. Jim is the assistant principal at the primary school and he flirts with every single woman in town. Someday he's gonna flirt with someone who refuses to make spinach dip and who doesn't think the dimple on his right cheek combined with a receding hairline is slightly adorable. I wish I didn't think Jim was slightly adorable. I'm trying not to, every single day.

October 2

Today I did something I hadn't done in a while. I prayed for a man to come into the store. Even if he weren't my future husband, it would still be fun if a man came in the store who paid me some attention, acted interested, maybe bought a corkscrew or a bread machine. God surely cares about things like that, right? And wouldn't ya know...an interesting man *did* come in the store tonight. It was at 8:50 on the dot. I looked at the big clock because we always hope no one comes in after 8:45 so we can close right at 9:00. But I didn't mind. I'd known Mr. Rockford my whole entire life. He was in his late seventies or maybe even early eighties and everyone in town loved him and I'd never heard any weird rumors about him. He'd always carry Mrs. Rockford's purse if she was busy in the store lookin' at wrappin' paper or pickin' out greeting cards. You gotta love a man who loves a woman enough to carry her purse.

"Carlie Ann, I'm sorry I'm so late comin' in. The Mrs. needs some paper towels and two cake mixes. She's got some kind of early mornin' bakin' project planned. First Methodist is having a lunch for the new preacher and they asked her to make two of her famous strawberry cakes. She's got the strawberries, just needs two white cake mixes. She thought she had some in the pantry but then she realized she'd used 'em for Jimmy Moore's eightieth birthday celebration down at the community center. It'll only take me a minute to get 'em."

"No rush, Mr. Rockford. I don't have any big exciting plans for the night. Why, you're the best lookin' man I'll see all day!"

He laughed and he hurried, out of respect for our time. It only took him five minutes to be at the check-out counter with two Duncan Hines cake mixes and a roll of generic paper towels. He was fast for an old guy.

"Carlie Ann, I have a great nephew in Tennessee that you should meet. Mrs. Rockford said the other day, 'Doug needs to meet a good woman, Stanley. That's what he needs.' The way I see it you're a good woman so maybe you'd be willing to meet up with him. Now all the young people seem to be able to do that with the computer, right? Write to him or don't write to him, Carlie. It's all the same to me but it'll sure make Mrs. Rockford happy when I tell her I gave you his card. I've got it here somewhere, let's see, yeah…right here. It has his computer stuff there somewhere. I'll have the Mrs. call him tonight and just let him know he *might* be hearin' from a woman in Georgia who we think a whole lot of. And we do, Carlie. We've always thought a lot of ya. You know that. He's a good man too. Hard worker. Solid. It'd be worth your while to contact him. What could it hurt, right?"

"Well, I just might do that, Mr. Rockford. I just might. Thanks so much."

16

Of course, I knew I wouldn't. Calling a man *solid* was like saying a woman has a great personality. I knew what that meant but I took the card happily from Mr. Rockford's wrinkled hand because he was a wonderful old man who wasn't embarrassed to do errands for his wife or weep during the National Anthem or make conversation with someone who failed out of college. And I respected him for all of that and a lot more. I even acted like I might send Doug a message. Was that a form of lying? I hope not.

October 7

When I was looking for my name tag this afternoon, I saw the business card Mr. Rockford had given me propped up next to that horrible bottle of perfume Mr. Porter gave me for Christmas last year. I hadn't had the heart to throw it out. The perfume that is. I started to throw the business card in the pink trash can by my bed. But then I thought about all the times Mr. Rockford had held Mrs. Rockford's purse and the time he came up to me after the high school band concert and said, "Carlie Ann, I've never heard a clarinet solo that moved me so much." That's exactly what he said. I memorized his words. I thought about the time he and Mrs. Rockford brought a tuna casserole to my grandma after her hip surgery.

Wadding up that business card and throwing it in the trash seemed like wadding up the Rockfords and throwing them in the trash. They deserved better than that. My feelings also explained why I still had a bottle of stinky perfume on my dresser like it was a prized trophy or something. So I sat down and wrote a quick e-mail to Mr. Rockford's great nephew even though he was *solid.* No, I hadn't eaten a whole pie. I was fully lucid. I didn't over think it either. My granny used to say, "Some things you do with your heart, not your head." This was one of those things.

Dear Doug,

I guess the Rockfords told you that they suggested I contact you. They are some of my favorite people in all the world so I decided to follow through. My name is Carlie Ann. I love reading and eating spinach dip. I read Shakespeare in college but it never made me cry and I sometimes think he's ridiculously wordy. I did cry when I read the letters my grandpa sent my grandma from Korea. I'll be a college graduate in less than 3 months but I have no real job prospects. I tell people I work out. But I don't think unpacking large boxes of Hawaiian Punch really counts as a workout in the traditional sense of the word. I work as a cashier and stocker in a boring little wonderful rural store where I know everyone that walks in. I weigh 37 lbs. more than the chart says I should. But I'm done with the chart. At 32, I've decided I'm stunning. I would only date a man who agrees. I pay my rent on time and show up 10 minutes early for everything. I go to church every Sunday but I sometimes skip Wednesday nights. I like old people and I tolerate little kids. Every 6 weeks, I dye my hair the color it was when I was 16. I think it's called Ash Blonde. I've attached a recent picture. If you've dated more than 5 women in your life, I'm not interested. Reply if you want to correspond.

Carlie Ann Davidson

When I pushed *send* it felt scary. Like the time I joined a late-night infomercial dating site three years ago. I should have known the fee was too low. And the fact that their commercials only ran after 1:00 am should have clued me in. For future reference, if I ever join another online dating site it will be one that runs commercials during football games or 20/20 or shows like "The Office." I heard from some real losers. They were like Jim Flanders on emotional steroids. I could tell some of them were liars. I don't know how I knew. I just knew and I'm glad I did. Maybe that's the difference between being twenty-one and being almost thirty. The ability to know that a twenty-seven-year-old man who has a Master's degree and "doesn't care what a woman looks like" is either gay or a liar. I don't want a man who doesn't care what a woman looks like. I want a man who thinks I'm beautiful. A man who can't live without me. A man who wants me in every single way. And I don't care what Dr. Crusoe says either. I found myself…and the woman I found wants to wake up next to a man…a good man. If the good man is good lookin' that would be a plus. But that won't be the case with the Rockfords' great nephew 'cause he's *solid.*

Doug's response came the very next morning. It didn't make my heart flutter or anything. It felt like a nice letter from my grandma. That's not sayin' much. My grandma didn't write things that were very interesting. Mostly boring things like: The cucumbers are comin' in real big now. Pappa fixed the leak in the church basement and everyone is so proud that we can have potluck dinners again. Joe Bob Crawford plans to run for mayor even though he had that bad stroke last year. Things like that. Maybe Doug's response wasn't exactly like that, but it was kind of plain.

October 8

Hi Carlie.

Yes, Aunt Beth called and told me you might send an

e-mail. I'm 28 and I don't read that much. I work as a loan officer at First National Bank in Sharon, Tennessee. I'm mostly in charge of farm and rural loans. I meet a lot of farmers and I assess property value sometimes and stuff like that. I don't wear a tie even though I'm a bank loan officer because my boss said, "Farmers don't like it when someone shows up in a white shirt and a tie." He's smart like that and he's right. I think a lot of people, not just farmers, don't like it when someone shows up in a white shirt and a tie. Maybe it's because funeral directors wear dress clothes. Or maybe it's because some men think that putting on a tie makes them better than someone else. I'm not sure. I usually wear khaki pants and a plaid long-sleeved dress shirt with the sleeves rolled up a little. I'm not sure why I told you that. It's not important. I graduated from college when I was 22 because I was one of those kids who did what my parents asked me to do. They never went to college and they told me I should. I did. I majored in marketing. I'm not good at it though. I mean, the folks who came up with that gecko for the Geico commercials, *they* are brilliant marketers. I'm not very creative and I'm not really interested in marketing anything. I like doing property assessments and loans. And I like not wearing a tie. Write back if you want.

Doug Jameson

October 9 7:32 pm

Doug, you didn't send a picture. I've decided there are a lot of potential reasons for that. Either you have some incredible disfigurement and you want me to first get to know you for you or you are just kind of laid back and didn't think it was important to attach a picture on the first reply. At first, I thought asking for a picture would make you think I'm shallow. But I'm trying to be painfully honest here. I just want to see the person I'm writing to. I don't know if an incredible disfigurement would keep me from writing you back or not. It might. But let's throw caution to the wind and find out, yes?

Oct. 9   8:16 pm

Carlie, the picture is attached. I got the one from the church directory 2 years ago which means it's not that good. This picture looks like I'm running for political office (which I'm not). I will send a more natural-looking picture some other time unless you think I'm disfigured-looking and you choose not to write back. If so, I will know to never send the church directory picture to a woman again.

Oct. 9   9:03 pm

Doug, you're not disfigured at all. You look almost exactly like my 7th grade science teacher, Mr. Harrelson. His hair was curly and brown but not as long as yours. I had a big crush on him but his homework was ridiculous and I'm not good at science. The only thing I'm good at is writing. Writing and telling people where the pork n beans are located. For some reason, a lot of people in our area eat pork n beans. I find that disturbing. Not the beans part but the pork part. You're right. The picture is not natural-looking at all. I think a loan officer who doesn't wear a tie would never make a fist like that and put it under his chin.

21

October 9 9:41 pm

I like pork n beans because I spent my summers staying every day at my grandma's house and she always served hot dogs and pork n beans for lunch. But you're right. The pork is probably a marginal use of the word. But if they were called *tongue and entrails of various animals and beans*, how many people would buy them? Yeah. That observation can be chalked up to my 4-year degree in marketing. Calling them pork n beans was a brilliant idea. I wish I had thought of it.

October 9 9:56 pm

Do you live alone? I live with my roommate, Clara. She is an unusual girl I knew in high school. She teaches kindergarten and sometimes she forgets to turn off the kindergarten voice and I laugh inside but never out loud because it would hurt her feelings. She has a lot of money saved because our rent is really cheap and she's a salaried professional not a pork n beans stocker. I think she's saving and investing money for a rainy day. I'm not saving money at all. Pray it stays sunny.

October 9 10:43 pm

I live alone. I lived with my grandma for a few years after college but she died 2 years ago. I knew I needed to go out on my own anyway. I want to think I would have done it even if Grandma hadn't died. But I probably wouldn't have. I liked having another person in the house plus she needed my help. I've lived in a nice one-bedroom apartment for the last 2 years. It's in the middle of town with very little furniture and nothing but mustard and a jar of homemade pickles in the refrigerator. I'd like to buy a farm. But I'm a lot like Clara. I always feel like there's a rain cloud overhead and I want to be prepared. No, I haven't dated more than 5 women. I've only dated 2 seriously, 3 if you count the girl I went to prom with in the 11th grade. I thought I was in love once. But she said that I wasn't in love. I guess I didn't meet her standards for the way a man acts when he's in love. I'm not like Clara in the fact that I can't speak Kindergarten. I'm just like her because I'm a saver. I won't be checking computer messages 'till mornin'. Good night, Carlie. I hope I hear from you again real soon.

October 10   2: 27 pm

Doug,
Clara doesn't speak Kindergarten all the time. I don't want you to think ill of her. She's nice and super responsible. She'd be real pretty if she thought she was. Someone hurt her sometime. I don't think she has ever been on a real date. And the longer she doesn't go on a real date the harder it will be for her to go on one. It's not like I'm an expert or anything. I was in love my freshman year of college. He acted like he loved me too though he never said it out loud. He joined the military the beginning of my sophomore year and never wrote back. I quit college 6 months later and got the job at Dollar General.

I was completely depressed for a year and drank myself into a stupor on many occasions. I worried my parents senseless. Can you imagine their shame at having to tell everyone that their brilliant

23

daughter was drinking excessively and working at the Dollar General? Well, they really didn't tell anyone. They wouldn't have told anyone. I've dated a few guys at my church. Two years ago, I dated Dan for almost 4 months but it was like going out with my cousin, only worse because my cousin never tried to kiss me while breathing garlic down my neck. Dan needed a breath mint 24 hours a day. There are actually not enough breath mints created in the world in the course of a year to meet Dan's desperate need. Does this mean I'm shallow? If so, guilty as charged. And yes, it was hard to say that I once drank myself into a stupor for a whole year. I was young. I regret that year but I can't get it back. Truth is, I hardly remember it.
Carlie

October 10   3:41 pm

Carlie,

Saying that someone needs a breath mint doesn't mean you're shallow. I don't think his breath was the problem. You would have forgiven that offense and supplied him with Altoids. You just didn't like him. There's nothing you could have done about that. Misty Carlson liked me my senior year of college. But her hair was a total wreck. She had dyed it a lot of different colors and fried it with some kind of curly perm. I wouldn't have cared about her hair if I had liked her.

I drank a lot my last 2 years of college. I think I was trying to prove to my family that I could. They

24

disapproved and it was a way of saying to my parents, "I'm getting this marketing degree. I'm keeping my hair cut short. I'm not cussing in front of women. But I'm not totally compliant. I'll drink as much as I want whenever I want." The truth is I don't like the taste of alcohol and I got tired of the constant hangovers. So one day I stopped drinking. I realized I was only doing it to make my parents crazy. That wasn't a valid reason. I think that's the day I became a grownup. (Yes, I still drink champagne at weddings and red wine when I visit my uncle).

October 10   4:18 pm

Tell me about the girl you once loved. What went wrong?

October 10   6:39 pm

Sandra was a girl I'd known my whole life. Her parents and my parents were great friends. It was one of those awakening moments just like in the movies. When I went away to college she was a freshman in high school. I hardly even noticed her. She was literally a redheaded freckle-faced kid. When I graduated college and came back to work at the bank, she was leaving for Dartmouth. She got this big academic scholarship opportunity. Everyone was talking about her and what an accomplished girl she was. Her picture was in the paper holding up a Dartmouth sweat shirt. She had become this beautiful confident young woman. I remember looking at the picture in the paper and realizing she wasn't a kid anymore. I went by her house one night and told her parents I would take her to Steak n Shake in Jackson to celebrate her bright academic future. I didn't care anything about her academic future.   I think everyone knew that.   But they all loved me.

They'd known me my whole life so her dad let her go even though she was too young to be in a serious relationship.   I knew that.   But it didn't keep me from promising things I shouldn't have.   I said things like, "I'll wait for you."   "I want you to write to me from New Hampshire."   I had never had that feeling in my life.   Not like that.   I bragged about my good job at the bank not realizing how little that would mean to an intelligent 18-year-old.   Can you imagine what she told her roommate at Dartmouth?   "My boyfriend lives with his grandma and works at a bank in my hometown of Sharon, Tennessee."   Yeah.   Nothing could have been more boring.

I did write to her and call her.   We saw each other on college breaks.   But she was right.   I didn't love her the way a man should love a woman.   I think I wanted to pursue her as a prized possession, to tame her, to bring her back home to Sharon.   I was in a competition of sorts.   But I was losing.   I didn't even know who I was competing against.   Eventually, I realized I was competing against her future.   Thankfully, her future won.   She's working on her Ph.D. at a school in California now.   They say she's a brilliant research scientist engaged to a dentist in San Diego.   Or that's what my mom says.   She says it almost every time we sit down to Sunday dinner.

October 10   6:58 pm

Gosh.   It sounds like you let a good one get away. Regrets?

26

October 10   7:40 pm

No. I hate the thought of living in California. I also hate the thought of living in a woman's shadow. And I'm not worried about what that says about me. I stopped trying to win people's approval, remember?

October 10   7:48 pm

Yeah. I get that. It's cold living in someone's shadow. Remember that hokey line from the Bette Midler song? "It must have been cold there in my shadow."

October 10   7:59 pm

Yeah. "Wind Beneath my Wings." The melody is pretty but the words are disturbing. Do we use people to push us upward? Should we celebrate that? I hope not. What about the military man, Carlie? Where is he?"

October 10   8:47 pm

His mother used to always come in the store and tell me about his big accomplishments, "He graduated from this training school and he's now part of so-and-so elite fighting force." or "He flew out of Tel Aviv on a big mission last Saturday night." I mean, there I was trying to find a price check on her Cool Ranch Doritos and she was telling me about his intelligence missions. It was embarrassing. It made me wonder if she thought, "Whew, I'm glad he dumped this hometown loser girl." One day I just told her I'd prefer not to hear about it anymore seeing as how he kind of broke my heart. She doesn't even come into the store on weekends anymore. I think I hurt her feelings. It's been a long time now and the pain has faded for me. Truthfully, she could come in today and say, "Jim's going to meet the President Tuesday morning and he's engaged to a super model" and it would hardly faze me. Maybe that was my becoming-a-grownup moment. I am 32, remember?

After another week of continual e-mail messages, it all came crashing down. I like to think of it as "Relationship D-Day."

October 18 5:31 pm

Carlie, do you want to meet me? I checked my GPS and it's almost 8 hours from my place to yours. But we could meet in Chattanooga. My GPS says that it's about 3 hours from Commerce.

October 18 5:40 pm

We'd have to plan ahead because I work most weekends. I'd have to ask off. Plus, if we put it off a few more weeks, I would fast for 2 weeks straight and then by the time we meet I'll only be 27 lbs. over the ideal chart weight. This has promise.

October 18 5:46 pm

Don't bother with the fast. You could die from that. What about a week from Saturday?

October 18 5:51 pm

I can swing that. Does that mean the e-mail chatting is over until the big meeting?

October 18 6:00 pm

No. But I type pretty slow. You don't even want to know how long it took me to write the story about Sandra. Plus, I'm not a writer so I went over it a lot trying to make sure I didn't make errors. Do you want to talk on the phone?

October 18 6:04 pm

I'm a writer. I don't talk out loud unless you want to know if we carry Liquid Plum'R and in that case I manage to say quietly, "Aisle 9."

October 18 6:09 pm

Okay. I guess I'll keep spending time over-analyzing every paragraph I write. What else do I have to do? This is Sharon, TN. Even the 3-legged dogs are asleep by 8:00.

October 18 6:11 pm

I'm having compassion on you. You can call me at 711 555 0922.

That's when everything changed. I knew he could call me now. I knew he would call me. I was terrified to the point of wanting to eat three frozen burritos, but I knew I'd be meeting him in less than two weeks. Nix the obsessive burrito eating.

About the time I was breaking out in a cold sweat the computer made the ever-familiar "ding."

October 18 6:15 pm

Good. I can't call tonight, Carlie. I told my mom I would come for supper. I'll call tomorrow night around 7:00. Would that work?

October 18 6:18 pm

I'm working until 9:00 tomorrow night. Is 9:15 too late for a bank officer who doesn't wear a tie to talk on the phone?

October 18 6:27 pm

I'll drink Mountain Dew and try to stay awake. I'll call tomorrow night at 9:30. That will give Clara a few minutes to tell you all about her happy chart feelings before I steal you away.

October 18 6:30 pm

LOL. I can't believe I just typed that. I hate the over-use of LOL. I'm not 19.

October 18 6:33 pm

LOL. You're right. You're 32. You told me, remember? I have to go now. I'll call tomorrow night.

CHAPTER THREE: Uh-Oh, This Relationship Is Getting Too Close To Real Life

CARLIE

October 18 10:00 pm

I knew I wouldn't be able to sleep. I didn't want to talk on the phone. I liked the security of typed words. I didn't want to meet either. I liked just looking at the nerdy picture of him with the fist under his chin. He was handsome. Green eyes. Brown curly hair. I could tell he didn't want to pose for the picture but he did it because they told him to do it. Just like the marketing degree. If we never met, I could pretend he was suave and sophisticated. I didn't want to take the chance that he wasn't. I didn't want to wear my tan pants either. They were the dressiest pants I owned but they were too snug around the rear. Why couldn't we just keep *talking* on the computer? Sleep was motivated by two Tylenol PM and an 8:00 class in the morning.

October 19 6:15 am

Computer "ding."

Carlie, Last night's dinner was a setup orchestrated by my mom. This 22-year-old girl who works in her office at the electric company dropped by unexpectedly for dinner at the exact time I pulled in the driveway. I was totally caught off guard. At dinner, Mom just went on and on. "Doug's a college graduate. Doug was always such a good boy. Doug has a great job at the bank. Doug

31

doesn't wear a tie because he doesn't want people to think he's better than them." Embarrassing.

October 19 6:19 am

What about the girl? What was she like?

October 19 6:24 am

She was just a girl, I guess.

October 19 6:28 am

She must have been really good-looking. You said, "She was just a girl" and that's code for "She was a looker." If she hadn't been a looker, you would have said, "She wasn't that impressive."

October 19 6:35 am

You really are 32. You've learned the man code. I'm impressed.

October 19 6:39 am

You're in the presence of a master.

October 19 6:41 am

LOL

October 19 6:44 am

You just did that to bug me. ☺ I need to get ready for class. Talk to you tonight.

October 19   6:47 am

OK. Talk to you tonight.

I sat on the edge of the bed, put my face in a pink paisley
decorative pillow and cried my eyes out. No man on earth
would have understood my tears. It may have been the PMS
but I think it was the sheer sadness. I wanted desperately to
look like the twenty-two-year-old girl from the electric
company in Tennessee. And I didn't even care what she
looked like. I had never even met Doug. Why was I so
messed up? Is this why I drank a year of my life away and
why I still eat excessive sugar? I'm crazy. God, please help
me trust you. I believe. Help my unbelief.

I pulled into my apartment parking lot at 9:10. Twenty
minutes to plan my strategy. What would my opening line be?
Would I try to talk soft and mouse-like or would I try to sound
articulate and intelligent? What if Doug had a duck-like
voice? I knew an old man who worked at the convenience
store out on Highway 7 who literally quacked. It was
ridiculous. If Doug quacked it would be all over. Altoids
don't fix quacking. No, he couldn't be a quacker. He couldn't
work at the bank if he quacked or squeaked. He must sound
good or he couldn't work out professional loans for people. I
cooked up a double dose of hot chocolate, made small talk
with Clara as she cut little pumpkins out of orange
construction paper, and watched the clock.

October 19   9:31 pm

Phone rings. I'll let it ring three times. Don't want to seem
over-eager, y'know?

"Dollar General. How can I help you?" Egads!! I'm the world's biggest idiot. "Oh, I mean, hey, this is Carlie. I'm sorry. That's ridiculous. Occupational hazard, y'know?"

"Hey, no problem, Carlie. This is Doug, I mean, obviously, right?"

"Well, not necessarily, Doug. Several old men were giving me the 'once over' tonight at the store and my number *is* in the book."

"Ha ha. Yeah. Those old men could give me a run for my money. What they lack in looks they make up for in kindness and in their knowledge of women. I don't know much about women."

"I doubt that."

"No. It's true. I never had a sister. I haven't dated that much. My mom drives me crazy. When people say things like, 'You know how women are'…I always wanna say, 'No. I really don't. Tell me.'"

"But you were assertive with Sandra. You told her you wanted her. You pursued her."

"Yeah, I thought she was beautiful and smart and I don't know. It's like she was unattainable. I was twenty-two and I decided I would attain her. But that's not the way relationships work. I know that now. People aren't possessions. They can't be bought and traded."

"Someone's been watchin' Dr. Phil."

"Ha Ha. I should be watchin' but I'm workin'. Somebody's gotta be out makin' those farm loans, Carlie."

"Yeah. I can't tell ya how many times I've gone to bed at night and said, 'Lord, thank you that somewhere in Tennessee someone is making a farm loan.' I sleep better at night knowing that's taken care of.'"

"You should. I mean, if you eat, you should."

"But I'm not eating anymore, remember? We're meeting in a few weeks and I'm on a fast."

"You can't be serious. You haven't done those wacky things, have you?"

"Are you kidding? I could write a book about those wacky things. Doug, didn't you read my first e-mail? I'm not normal. I have issues. Food is just one of my issues. Don't you have any issues?"

"Oh no you don't. You're not putting me in one of those Oprah moments where I'm supposed to start crying and telling you all my deep dark secrets like a teenage girl. Not tonight anyway. I'm not an open person, Carlie. I'm a guy."

"Thanks for establishing that. I forget what guys are like. I work with women and I live with a kindergarten teacher, remember?"

"Forgiven."

"So tell me more about the girl who came to dinner. And why on earth would your mom do that without telling you?"

"Mom called the university to make sure I had enough credit hours to graduate. Mom called my doctor last year to ask what kind of antibiotic I was on when I had the flu. She had read about some kind of antibiotic that affects fertility. She literally said, 'Dr. Smith, I need this information. I wanna have grandkids someday.' She asked me if I thought 'Stephen' was a good name for her first grandchild. She's not big on boundaries, Carlie. I put up boundaries and she crosses those boundaries. That's why I could never ever live with her. I haven't lived with her since I was eighteen and went away to college. It just wouldn't work."

"Yeah, but she must have thought this girl was a good match for you. She wouldn't have tried to set you up unless she believed it was a good match."

"I'm not questioning her motives. I'm questioning her methods."

"So was the girl a good match for you?"

"She smacked her gum and wore too much make-up. When I asked her what her interests were she said, 'shopping.' She laughed and said, 'Yeah. That's my final answer.' She wouldn't eat dessert because she said she doesn't eat sugar. What kind of woman never eats sugar?"

"You're right. The gum and shopping was one thing. But the sugar makes her suspect. There's something I want to ask but I don't know how to ask in a way that doesn't make me look bad."

"Are you kidding? You told me you might not write back if I was disfigured. You said you were a drunk for a whole year. You confessed that you're broke. Now you're acting scared to ask me something? I doubt it. Ask away."

"Right. But those things were just confessions about my life, things in the past. I'm talkin' about the here and now. Okay. How tall are you, Doug?"

"Wait. You're saying you went through that whole ordeal just to ask me how tall I am?"

"Yes. It's kind of a big deal."

"Really. Why is it such a big deal? Do you have some kind of 'height standard'? I mean, when people walk into Dollar General do you look over at that massive height ruler on the door to see how tall they are and think 'Yeah, I'd go out with him….or no, he's too short?' Carlie, that's a height ruler for criminals…not for deciding whether you should date a guy. That height chart is so that when someone runs out of the store with a case of pork n beans under his arm you can say to the officer, 'He was about 5'10 according to the big ruler on the door. And of course he was skinny….cause you know a fat guy could have never gotten away with a whole case of pork n beans.'"

"Go ahead and laugh. You're not answering. You must be under 5'8."

"No. I'm not under 5'8. I'm just wondering why you care so much."

"Look Doug, there's something I didn't tell you. I'm not one of those cute little short pudgy women. I'm freakishly tall. There. I said it."

"How tall is freakishly tall?"

"Why does it matter, Doug? You said it yourself. We shouldn't use that as a standard, right?"

"Okay. This is why I don't understand women. Right here. This right here is why I haven't been very successful at dating. Women are masters at turning my own words against me. I'm not good at keeping up. So I'll cut to the chase. I'm 5'11. Does that meet your height standard?"

"Not really...'cause that means you're really 5'9. Men lie about height, Doug. I mean, even really good men lie about height. It's like women with weight. Most men who would never lie about anything...I mean, men who would never cheat on their taxes or their wives or lie about their education or keep the extra change mistakenly given to them by a cashier...even *those* men add at least two inches to their height. I bet you're 5'9. Maybe 5'9 ½ 'cause you seem to be a straight shooter."

"Look, I'm not 5'9. But what if I were 5'9? It's no big deal. Some very nice men are 5'9. Being 5'9 doesn't make someone an ax murderer, right?"

"The problem is I'm taller than 5'9. I'm 5'11."

"So....you're really 6'1? Carlie, you could have just told me you're 6'1. It's no big deal."

"Ha Ha. A loan officer who sidelines as a comedian. I'm not 6'1. I'm 5'11. The doctor's office measured me two years ago and I know I haven't grown. I'm 5'11. But still, 5'11 is freakishly tall for a woman, don't you think?"

"I don't think I've ever spent a moment of my life trying to decide what is freakishly tall for a woman. I'll have to think about it and get back with you."

"Okay. Tell me this. How tall are the people in your family? I mean, stop and think about it for a minute."

"My dad was probably 5'11 as we were about eye to eye. My mom is 5'4. My grandma was about 5'4 probably. My grandpa wasn't as tall as me, probably 5'9. I don't have brothers or sisters. Is that good enough?"

"See, this is what I'm talkin' about, Doug. Your family is normal. I'm 5'11. My dad is 6'6. My brothers are 6'4 and 6'7. My mom is 5'10. We look like a pasty white tribe of giants everywhere we go. People actually stare. Trust me. Men don't always like tall women. Remember that thing you said about not wanting to be in a woman's shadow. That could be taken literally here."

"Models are tall women, Carlie."

"Right. But here's the crucial difference. They don't have big behinds. Not every man could be attracted to a tall woman with a big behind."

"Okay. I don't know for certain…but I have a feeling that if my grandma were here and she were giving me advice about this phone call …which I would most certainly take…she would say, 'Doug, I think it's nice that you're going to call this young lady on the phone. Whatever you do, Doug, do *not* get into a conversation about the size of her behind.' Yes. I am almost one hundred percent positive that Grandma would advise me to take this phone conversation in a different direction."

"Yeah. Your grandma is right. It's getting late anyway. Thanks for calling, Doug. Do you still want to meet in Chattanooga? I mean, you know now that I'm a little neurotic and that may not be what you're looking for."

"I don't know what I'm looking for, Carlie. But how will meeting a friend in Chattanooga be a bad thing?"

"Yeah. You're right. Well, guess it's time to call it a night. G'night, Doug."

"Good night, Carlie."

After hanging up the phone, I grabbed the same damp paisley pillow from the morning and had the second big cry of the day. Top three crying reasons: My genetics had made me freakishly tall. My pie eating had given me a big behind. Doug said he was meeting *a friend* in Chattanooga. He had made me cry twice in one day. And I couldn't wait to talk to him again.

October 20   5:00 pm

Not one computer message from Doug today. That's okay. I think I scared him away. I am pretty scary looking today. Unmotivated. No make-up. Hair in a pony tail. The redheaded guy in sociology made a stupid comment in class today about man's innate need to sexually conquer as many women as he can. His blue eyes don't look as good now and the jeans do nothin' for him. What an idiot! What woman would run up to him after class and say, "Yes, let me be the next one conquered! I'm moved by your sense of nobility and romance." I should have been in college in the 1950's. Guys are wimps now. Romance is all but dead.

October 20   10:00 pm

Computer "ding"

Carlie, I'm just now gettin' to my computer. The bank did a big foreclosure today and it was really messy and because I'm from here, I know everybody. It's bad to foreclose on a friend. But we have a job to do. Kind of like when a small town policeman has to arrest his cousin because he has marijuana in his trunk. Conflicted. I didn't call 'cause you may be in bed and I don't want to be one of those needy people who disturbs people when they're sleeping. I'm tired and I probably won't check the computer till mornin'. I hope you had a good day. How did you do on your political science test?

October 20   10:23 pm

Doug, I'm sorry about the foreclosure. My aunt and uncle lost their farm a few years ago. Yeah. Real sad and messy. And yeah, they hated the bank guys. Plus, the bank guys wore white shirts and ties when they came to take possession. Not a good move. But you're right. It's not your fault. You have to follow the law. Clara is still up. You can call if you want. I mean, I'll be up for a while but I know you're tired so don't feel obligated and I understand if you don't feel like calling. I don't want to sound needy either. Besides, you said you weren't going to check the computer till mornin'. I probably made a C on the political science test. I definitely could have studied more. The story of my life. I'm sorry about your day, Carlie

Phone rings.

41

"Hey!"

"Carlie, thanks for letting me call so late."

"No problem, Doug. I'm sorry about your day. That sounds really hard."

"Yeah, the day was a total loss. This family, I mean, I've known them my whole life. I was a teenager when they got married. I was at the wedding with my parents. My uncle even did the ceremony. Their kids were standing out front today and they would look at me and just…I don't know…like they were sayin' to themselves, 'We'll never grow up to be a bad man like that bad man.'"

"You did what you had to do, Doug. You have a job. You did your job. You should take a Tylenol and sleep well. When a judge sentences someone to thirty years in prison, he can feel sad. That's normal. But he still had to do what he did. They didn't pay. You had to take it back. The fact that you felt lousy about it just means you're a real person."

"Thanks. My personhood was definitely in question today. I'm tired and I haven't eaten anything all day and I'm still not hungry."

"Okay now, Doug. This is where you and I differ. If I had had a day from Hades, I'd be hittin' the ice cream carton right about now. But it wouldn't solve the problem. Drink a big glass of water, eat a peanut butter sandwich, take two aspirin, and call me in the mornin'. You do have peanut butter, don't you?"

"Yes, I have peanut butter. You're a pretty decent on-call doctor…and with late night hours. That's a plus. Good night, Carlie."

"G'night, Doug."

He needed me. He was tired and sad so he called me. I like that.

October 21   6:45 am

"Hello."

"You told me to call."

"Doug, it's a figure of speech, 'take two aspirin and call me in the morning.' It was a joke. I haven't even had coffee yet. But believe it or not, I'm glad to hear your voice."

"Thanks. I just called to say that I'm not one of those needy guys who's always feeling unsure of himself. I know who I am, Carlie. I'm a man and I'm capable of doing difficult things. It's just that yesterday, well, it was different. I mean, it was just hard to watch another man's dreams go up in smoke. It got to me. That's all."

"Hey, I totally get that. And I wasn't feeling like you were being overly needy. Doug, let me clarify something. Overly needy men knock on a woman's door at 1:00 am and start crying in a drunken stupor. Overly needy men ask to borrow money when they know it's a woman's payday. I've been there. I know. Feeling sad about someone in your hometown losing their family farm is not being overly needy. It's being the Christian man you are. Now…go to work and do a good job and try not to think about yesterday. Did you sleep well?"

"I did. I ate a peanut butter sandwich, drank a big glass of water, and took two aspirin."

"Wow. I don't know who gave you that advice, but whoever they are….they're brilliant."

"I'm starting to think that. Have a good day, Carlie. Bye."

"Bye."

The day flew by. I don't even remember what I did. I went to class. I went to work. But mostly, I thought about his voice. About the way his voice sounded when he said, "I'm a man, Carlie." And I thought, "Yeah. I'm startin' to believe you may be right." There were a lot of boys in my college classes. But in a small town in West Tennessee there was someone who was wearing khaki pants and a plaid dress shirt with the sleeves rolled up slightly. He was a man. Was he a man who could be attracted to a tall woman with a large round behind? The verdict was still out on that one.

October 21   7:30 pm

Computer "ding."

I know you're working until 9:00. I just wanted to see how your day went. I won't be home till late so we probably can't talk tonight. Mom has some things she needs me to do at the house. I need to put up some shelving in the shed 'cause this summer she canned like 1000 jars of green beans and pickles and every other kind of thing. She's a canned food hoarder, I believe. But there's not a reality show for that specific type of hoarding so I'm at a loss for what to do with her. My dad died last year and it's been hard on her in so many ways. He did everything for her. I think he liked giving her everything she wanted. And she knew not to want more than he could give. Yeah. That was what made it work. They understood each other.

Anyway, I don't think it's going to be another setup evening. I told her I was going to wear faded overalls seeing as how I was working in the shed. I also told her I would take a Sharpie and black out one of my front teeth and embarrass her if she did that again. My mom is the type that if she thought I would wear faded overalls and blacken one of my teeth, she would never ask a woman to dinner. She cares desperately about appearances. Threatening her with the Sharpie pen gives me some leverage now. I hope no one said anything stupid in your sociology class today.

October 21   10:15 pm

I ended up working late because we got behind on stocking. It was busy up front tonight. No run on pork n beans but evidently school projects are due because an inordinate number of frazzled parents were looking for poster board, markers, glue in a tube. The little girls all wanted glitter glue. I remember school projects and loving glitter glue. I'm sorry your dad died. How old was he? My parents are in their mid-60's. I hope all your shelving went in perfectly. Your mother sounds a bit like mine. Good intentions. Just misdirected at times. It sounds like you're a good son. Good night. I hope you didn't foreclose on anyone today.

October 21   11:30 pm

Computer "ding."

The shelving went in fine. No problem. But mom started crying at about 9:30, how she missed Dad and how he

45

loved to do stuff she needed done, how a young person with a full-time job shouldn't have to come put her shelving in at night, how sad she was that she woke up alone every morning. We sat and drank coffee and I just let her talk. Now I'm highly caffeinated and I can't sleep. Dad was 59. He was in perfect health or at least we thought he was. He died of a heart attack. Mom didn't even get to say good- bye. No, I didn't foreclose on anyone today. Enjoy the fact that both your parents are alive. I miss my dad every day. He kept my mom (and her intentions) grounded.

October 22   7:00 am

Doug, I'm sorry about your mom. It must have been a shock for your dad to go so young. I'm off to class. I hope you eventually got to sleep. It's only 8 days till we meet in Chattanooga. I will not eat today. ☺ Actually, I probably will. If you want to call, I'm not working tonight.

October 22   7:30 pm

Phone rings.

"Hello."

"Hey Carlie, this is Doug. How was your day?"

"It was pretty glamorous, Doug. Out here in rural Georgia there are a lot of things to distract a beautiful young single gal like me."

"Oh yeah, same here. A small town in West Tennessee is the hot spot for all forms of exciting night life. I can't believe I

46

took a break from all the disco dancing downtown to give you a call. I'm pretty merciful like that."

"Yeah. You really seem like the disco dancing type. You gotta watch those loan officer khaki pants/plaid dress shirt kinda guys. Let's see. Here's what's goin' on in our downtown right now. I can tell you without even being there. Mr. Peterson is probably sweeping the sidewalk in front of Pizza Palace. George Davis is saying, 'Peterson, I gotta cut down on my pizza consumption. Not good on my waistline, don'tcha know. I'll never get me a woman if I don't trim down some.' Mr. Peterson then says, 'George, I know you'll be in here tomorrow night by 6:30. I've got ya hooked. No woman is gonna look at ya anyway, ya old buzzard.' They both laugh. Mrs. Madison is probably locking up the Downtown Florist right across from Pizza Palace. She's acting all nervous while she turns the key on the front door. She'll then hide the bank bag in her hundred-year-old carpet bag purse like she thinks some small town criminal is gonna jump from the bushes and knock her over the head for $97 in cash and a $34 check from The Rotary Club."

"You live in Sharon, Tennessee, Carlie!"

"I guess small southern towns have a lot in common. So why *did* you go back to Sharon? You graduated from college. You could have tried living somewhere else."

"If I wanted to sound impressive, I'd say that I went back because my grandma needed me. Or that I went back because a good job at the bank came open and it was a good career opportunity. Both of those are true and they seem like pretty noble reasons, right? But I don't know. There's somethin' else. I'm a hometown boy. I didn't wanna be. But I am. When I first went to college I thought I'd be one of those ones who would get a job in Nashville or Atlanta. You know, the

47

kind of guy you read about in your hometown newspaper but never see anymore. People in our town say things like, 'Yeah, ol' Jake's made quite a name for himself down at that law firm in Memphis. We'll not see the likes of him in Sharon 'cept on holidays.' Yeah. I thought that would be me. But it wasn't."

"I get that. That's part of growing up. Understanding who you really are and accepting it."

"What about you, Carlie? Do you dream of going to New York City or Miami and *finding yourself?*"

"Sometimes. But stocking gallon jugs of Hawaiian Punch at the local Dollar General Store for ten years hasn't been the fastest track to the glamour life in Miami. Hard to believe, isn't it?"

"Shocking."

"Actually, you may not understand this but I don't feel like a loser, Doug. I mean, my parents probably thought I was a loser until I went back to college. My brothers may have felt that way. They may still feel that way. I don't know. But I don't. I'm not a loser, just a late bloomer. It took me a while to come into my own, gain some confidence, learn who I am, make a plan."

"What is the plan?"

"I had a feeling you would ask. Truthfully, it changes a lot. But overall, well, I'm getting this English degree and I'd like to write for newspapers maybe. But newspapers are struggling. I'd love to write a novel. But the world is full of aspiring novelists. I wrote a book once. A book that no one wanted. I wouldn't mind working for a magazine or even a company writing brochures. I'm open. I'd work for Hallmark if they'd offer me a job writing sappy cards. That wouldn't be a bad gig."

"So, if none of that lands in your lap next year, will you still work at the dollar store?"

"I don't know. Are you embarrassed to be meeting a friend in Chattanooga who works at the dollar store? I mean, would the folks in Sharon give you a hard time about that?"

"I'm my own man, remember?"

"Oh yeah. I keep forgetting. So no problems then with meeting next Saturday?"

"No problem. But I'm gonna be gone for the next week. No phone and no internet. It's an annual camping trip thing I do with some old friends. We've done it for years. We'll take a week off and drive up to Reelfoot Lake, fish every day, and sleep in a rusty old camper my dad used to store in the backyard. We'll talk about old times and about our jobs. They're good guys."

"Sounds fun. So these are guys you've known your whole life?"

"Yeah, mostly. I met Carl in college, but the rest of them, yeah, the rest of 'em I've probably known since kindergarten."

"That's a lot of history."

"Yeah, I guess it is. I'll be back Friday night. I'll see you Saturday at Cracker Barrel. 12:00. I'm sorry we won't be able to talk before then. I'm gonna miss talkin' to ya. If you run into a problem with the plan, leave a message on my computer. I'll check that before I leave on Saturday. I'm lookin' forward to meetin' you, Carlie. I really am. Have a good week, okay?"

"Well, yeah. And you too. I mean, be careful and don't get bit by a fish or anything. I'll see you Saturday. Bye."

"Bye."

Shoot. Why did I say something so stupid? Don't get bit by a fish. How ridiculous. He's 5'9. What's a fish gonna do to him that's gonna cause him any real danger? I am an idiot.

Clara: "So, it's gettin' kinda serious with that guy in Tennessee, yes? I mean, you seem to be wearing your big happy face all the time now, friend."

"I'm pretty darn happy, Clara. But until we actually meet, I can't know if anything could come of it. I mean, he's just a friend."

What was I saying? I'm such a good southern liar. Doug wasn't just a friend. I had lots of friends but I didn't think about them several times a day. I didn't wait by the phone for them to call. The week passed ever so slowly. I hardly even looked at the computer. The phone rang a few times. Mom asking why I was leaving town. Sam asking if he could borrow my bread machine. (Hello! You have an MBA, Sam! I'm thinkin' you might be able to swing buying a bread machine. Such a baby brother.) But of course, I just said, "Sure, Sam! Come get it and do you or Melissa need any recipes?"

My neighbor, Rachel, called twice, asking for advice concerning her horrible boyfriend. I don't know why she would ask me for advice other than the fact that I've managed to maintain a decent quality of life for seven years without a horrible boyfriend. No boyfriend at all, actually. Not yet.

CHAPTER FOUR: Face To Face...Egads!

CARLIE

October 30
On the way to Cracker Barrel, Chattanooga, Tennessee

I'm a mess. I don't know what to say. Should I hug him when we meet? I mean, isn't that what a *friend* would do? Wouldn't a friend hug another friend? Yes. We should hug a greeting. Plus, I'd like to get a feel of what it would be like to hug him for real. I am wearing my sassy jeans outfit from Lane Bryant with a bright pink shirt. The sales lady said that when I wore that outfit I had it goin' *on*. And she said it with enthusiasm. I hope she wasn't on commission.

October 30   11:53 am

I have to get out of the car. Checked my hair three times. Re-applied cool watermelon lip gloss twice. I cannot stay in the car. I must exit the vehicle. I want to just throw up in the purple pansies and drive home. But this is not an option. Is that him? Wait a minute. It *is* him. I'm gonna watch him stand by the rocking chairs for a minute. Gosh, he is darn cute and he looks more like 6 feet than 5'11. He's wearing jeans instead of khakis. Yeah. That's good. It's Saturday. We're runnin' a casual operation here. Okay. That's it. Too good lookin'. I'm driving away and pretending that I have to go to my best friend's grandma's funeral this afternoon and I just got word by cell phone while I was on my way to Chattanooga and "Oh, how I hated to miss meeting you, Doug. Let's do it again sometime soon, shall we?" No. I'm getting out of the car. Lord, help me walk. I cannot walk. Lord, help me speak.

"Doug! Hey, you made it. Great to see you! I almost didn't recognize you without your fist under your chin." He has a great laugh. Big hug. He smells unbelievably good. Strong hands too.

"Yeah, Carlie, good to meet you. Did you have any trouble with the directions or the GPS?" She's a lot prettier than the picture. She's right. She's as tall as I am and yes, she has a really big butt. But it suits her perfectly. It's kind of erotic actually. She's confident and she smells like vanilla. Hug seemed almost passionate.

"No. Everything went like clockwork." I want to run my fingers through his curls.

"Hey, me too. Well, let's go in and get seated." Her hair is beautiful and I hope she takes her denim jacket off.

Doug opened the door for me and we moved to the front to get our names on the waiting list. He was a take-charge man without being rude. He was 5'11, at least. I was sorry I ever doubted him and regretted bringing it up at all. It was warm by the fire where we were seated and I wanted to take off my denim jacket, but I felt self-conscious. No. The be-jeweled jacket stays on, for now.

"Carlie, what do you like here? I'm in for the breakfast menu."

"Absolutely, I've never met a biscuit I couldn't learn to love."

"You're funny. I guess people tell you that all the time."

"Not really. But thanks. I have a question for you, Doug."

"We're already to the questions? Did you write them down on a piece of paper?"

"No, this is an easy one. Why did you do it? Why did you answer my e-mail? I mean, truthfully, you're twenty-eight, a college graduate, gainfully employed, good lookin'. It doesn't seem like you're a criminal, though I can't be for sure. Why did you wanna write to a girl who lives eight hours away?"

"You get right to the point, don't you? I haven't had much luck with the girls from home. The ones over twenty-five are married. The ones under twenty-five seem like seventeen-year-olds, even if they're not. That's like the girl the other night. She was twenty-two but she seemed like a teenager. Her world is pretty small. Her experiences are pretty limited. Plus, I trust Uncle Stanley and Aunt Beth. They said you were worth getting to know."

"So you end up meeting a thirty-two-year-old woman from a small southern town who works at the dollar store? Lucky you."

"I thought you said you weren't defined by your job. You asked why I wrote back. Several things. You were courageous enough to say that Shakespeare didn't move you, that he was wordy. Girls I know may not like Shakespeare but they would say it's because they don't understand him...that maybe he's better than them or smarter than them. They wouldn't have the confidence to say he might not be all that. Most people would be afraid to criticize Shakespeare. You mentioned the letters between your grandparents and the fact that you go to church. Plus, you said you had decided that you're stunning. Confidence. I haven't met a confident girl in quite a while. I don't know. And you seemed painfully honest, like you were done with all the silliness of dating. Almost like you were daring me to respond after you told the truth about your life and its messiness. I'm not good at dating. You seemed like you weren't afraid of it. And then, there was...well, the picture. The picture made a big difference...of course."

He looked down as he said that last part. Was he tryin' to say he thought I was good lookin'? Yeah. That's what he was tryin' to say. And the best part...he doesn't work on commission.

"Why aren't you good at dating?"

"I don't know. Not much practice. I think the system's a little faulty. Plus, I never know where to go. I think a lot of girls would think my life is pretty boring in Sharon."

"Is it boring?"

"No. It's quiet. Quiet doesn't mean boring to me."

"What do you like to do? I mean, what would you be doing on an average Saturday?"

"Mowing my mom's yard. Going to the movies. Sittin' on the porch. Sometimes I read the free magazine that comes from the electric co-op or drive through the country. I have some friends that I go fishin' with. I told you it's quiet. I'm not writing a novel or staying up all night. I go to bed at 10:00 most nights. And speaking of questions, why did you not want to meet a man who's dated more than five women?"

"I'm suspect, I guess. Like some men are always lookin' for someone better around the next corner. I don't want a man who's always lookin', someone who's motivated by the chase and unhappy when he gets to the finish line. That would be scary."

"But what if the women broke up with him? What if he wasn't lookin' around the corner but he just got with the wrong women and they dumped him? How can you fault a man for that?"

"Good point. But a man who's been dumped by five women would probably be having a crisis of confidence, wouldn't he? This may sound bad but I can't spend my life propping a man up."

"You mean like telling someone he's not a bad man just because he foreclosed on a family farm?"

"No. That's not propping a man up, Doug. You have a life. You're not asking me to tell you that your life's valuable. You already know that it is."

Interrupted by the waitress' high-pitched voice, "What can I get you two today?"

"Two cups of coffee and water and we'll both take the Sunrise Sampler with biscuits. Carlie, you want grits or hash browns?"

"Grits."

He was smiling, "Yeah, she's from Georgia. We'll both take the grits."

I had dreamed of this moment my whole life. In thirty-two years no man had ever really ordered for me. Dan always said things like, "I don't know. I can't decide. Let Carlie go first." or "Carlie, do you know what's good here? I'm a little afraid of the shell fish." Doug didn't seem afraid of the biscuits or the grits…or me.

56

"What bugs you, Doug? I mean, what really chaps your hide?"

"A friend from college used to come spend weekends with me. He'd say things like, 'What's there to do in this one-horse town? Why did you let yourself get stuck here? Get a life, Doug. This is depressing.' Eventually, I realized he thought he was better than Sharon, Tennessee, and better than me because I chose to live there. I hate that. Even if you're the President or a movie star, you're not better than a place...or a person. Haughtiness makes a person seem insecure. And that's what he was, insecure. What bugs you?"

"Okay. I hate it when romantic movies always begin with two people hating each other. In the beginning of the movie, if there's this girl who's a hippie left wing radical and a guy who's a straight-laced right winger in a suit and they're at this protest rally screaming at each other...you know...you just know that they'll be in love within two weeks. But I don't think that's how love usually works. I'm not saying it could never be like that, but no, it wouldn't be like that very often. Most people who disgust me on first meeting...still disgust me today. And I've never fallen in love with someone whose core values were so completely different from mine."

Two hours passed as though it were ten minutes. In that two hours I had memorized everything about his appearance. The green chamois shirt was the exact color of his eyes. I wondered if someone at the store had picked it out for him. He didn't seem like the kind who knew about clothes. New brown leather shoes double-tied with round shoe strings. Had he bought new shoes for today? Or did he just need new shoes? Dark socks which were perfect. His hands were man's hands, a little hairy but not like Bill Whitman's back. (Every summer Bill swam at the municipal pool in Commerce and it was something that should have been on YouTube.) Clear skin. One little mole on his left cheek. A little bit of chest hair showing. White teeth but not perfectly straight. Never had braces. Bushy eye brows. No man jewelry. I like that. A black diver's watch.

When he stood to go to the restroom I noticed that his faded Levi's fit perfectly. He may have been fifteen pounds over the weight chart max and he was perfectly proportioned. Great posture. I was clearly out of my league. Doug finally looked at his watch at 2:10 which made me cringe inside. I feared he would say that it was time to call this lunch date over. He had done his time and he was ready to return home…and that maybe he'd decided that reading the electric co-op magazine on Saturday afternoon was more interesting than watching a chunky girl eat grits in Chattanooga. But what happened next took me completely off guard. God was clearly on the side of the chunky girl.

"Carlie, do you have to get right back?"

"Well, no, not really."

"Good! Then spend the night with me." His face immediately turned the brightest red I had ever seen on a human being. "Uh, no, I don't mean spend the night with *me*. I don't want you to spend the night with me, Carlie. I really don't."

"Oh you don't, huh? So you haven't even thought about it? Gosh, my female ego is shattered beyond repair. The lady at the store said that I really looked like I had it goin' *on* in this outfit. Now I realize she lied to get a commission. This moment feels like when I went to the prom with my cousin."

By this time, he was laughing and laying his head on the table. He knew I was just making fun of him to ease the pain of his verbal misstep.

"Look, Carlie, let me try again. What I meant to say is that I'm staying with my cousin and her husband here in Chattanooga tonight. They moved here two years ago and I told them I was gonna be in town and they asked me to spend the night. They have lots of room and they really wouldn't mind. How 'bout it?"

"I didn't even bring clothes or anything."

"We could go shopping. I hear women love to go shopping."

Oh my gosh! This is the best and worst day of my life. A good lookin' man wants to spend more time with me but we'd have to go clothes shopping. What if I try on something that looks like the tan dress pants or even worse? Someone please kill me and make it look like an accident.

"Well, see, Doug, with you bein' the kind that doesn't know much about women, I think you'd be shocked at what it would be like to actually go clothes shopping with a woman. We tend to be picky and ridiculous."

"That's precisely why I need to go. I'm trying to learn more about women, remember?"

"Yeah, but don't you think you need to start slow. Talking on the phone with a woman is like elementary school. Meeting for lunch today was like high school. But going clothes shopping? Going clothes shopping would be like getting your Ph.D. Are you sure you're ready for that?"

"I'm feelin' brave."

"Well, alrighty then. I guess I could take you up on your offer. My name is Carlie and I'll be your instructor today in 'Shopping with a Woman 101.' Fasten your seat belt, Mr. Jameson. This could be a bumpy ride."

"I'll ask about the nearest mall when I pay the bill."

I pretended to be looking around the gift shop while Doug paid the bill. But I wasn't interested in smelling candles or listening to the stuffed singing turkey. Trying not to be obvious, I watched his every move. The way he pulled his worn leather billfold out of his back pocket and organized the bills. The way he treated the person at the cash register with kindness. Friendly not flirty. I had this overwhelming desire to walk up behind him and wrap my arms around him pretending that we were a real couple. Maybe the cash register lady would even think we were married. She'd probably think, "She must be a really great girl because this is a really nice guy…and a looker to boot."

"Carlie, we're all set. There's a mall just about a mile from here."

"Let me call Clara and tell her I won't be home 'till tomorrow. Wow, I don't remember the last time I did something on the spur of the moment like this."

"Me either."

"Let me get some things out of my car and I'll call her and then meet you at your car."

"That's fine. I'm in this blue F-150."

I nodded my head but I wanted to say out loud, "Of course you are, Doug. You're in the truck because you're a truck man. You live in a small town. Your mom cans green beans. You don't wear a tie. You're taking me clothes shopping at a mall even though my big behind is hard to fit. This is a nightmare. I hope I never wake up."

His truck was immaculately clean. I'm convinced that he bought new shoes and cleaned his truck because he was meeting the Georgia girl in Chattanooga today. I must be special or he's kind of desperate.

"So Carlie, is there any particular store you like to shop at? I'm not much of a shopper myself. I order most of my clothes from JC Penney online."

"I was wonderin' about that. You look very nice and yet you don't seem much like a shopper. Confession time. Do you actually pick out your own clothes or does your mother or a woman who works at the bank tell you what to buy?"

"I have a system. A man system."

"A man system? Of course, a man system. Well, do tell, Doug. I thought I was gonna educate you on shopping with a woman but I'm gettin' ready to hear about the man system for shopping. I'm all ears."

"Okay. I don't mind doing laundry so I don't need a lot of clothes. I have a washer and dryer right there in the apartment. So I figure I need five pairs of work pants and five work shirts. I need a few pair of jeans and some t-shirts, casual shirts, and maybe a jacket or something. So, I found these pants I like from JC Penney. Every fall I order five pairs of 'em, two tan, two navy, and one brown or gray or something. I buy five shirts that go with the pants. I get two pair of jeans. I do it all online. I never have to even enter a store. That is the man system and I'm glad to have been able to enlighten you on this."

"So how did you know that this green shirt would match your eyes?"

"I don't. I just order the colors I like. I like green, brown, blue, but not bright colors or pastels. I went shopping with my cousin one time and she tried to tell me I wasn't very enlightened."

"How were you not enlightened?"

"My cousin said, 'Doug, stop being afraid to wear pink. Lots of men are wearing pink, lavender, yellow and colors like that now. You should be secure enough in your own masculine identity to give them a try.' So I said to her, 'Why can't I be secure enough in my own masculine identity to say that I don't want to wear pink, lavender, and yellow?'"

"Touché."

I like him. He's beyond likeable. Smart and funny. The women of Sharon have tried to sweep him off his feet. It's a given. Probably even the girls from neighboring towns. I bet a lot of farmers' daughters have seen him coming toward the house with a loan application and have gone running to call their girlfriends, "That cute guy from the bank is coming to talk to Daddy about the loan for the Simpson place!" They've tried to snare him but they've been unsuccessful. Why? Hmm. Something is definitely amiss here.

"Okay. This is it. The mission begins. Carlie, do you wanna just start walking or do you wanna plan a shopping strategy?"

"Doug, I have a feeling your apartment is immaculate. All the glasses are organized by height in the kitchen cabinet, and there is not one thing out of place on your bathroom sink right now."

"Wow. You *are* good. How did you know?"

"The fact that you even mentioned developing a shopping 'strategy'...well, it was a dead give-away. I'm more of a free spirit kind of person. I've never even developed a strategy for my life much less a strategy for an afternoon at the mall. But don't worry, Doug. I like the way you think. You're organized. This could be a plus."

"Well, I guess there's nothing left to say. You know everything about me. I'm a neat freak who won't wear pastels. I like blackberry jam, black coffee, and ordering clothes online. You can go back to Commerce now. You're all done."

He laughed. His laughter was music. Like a really comforting ballad from a favorite radio station in high school. I wanted to grab a hair brush and sing at the top of my lungs! I wanted to hold his hand and believe he'd sing with me.

"Let's just start walking and see if something hits us, shall we? I guess I need to ask what we'll be doing tomorrow. Will we be meeting with any local dignitaries for lunch? Do I need country club wear? Will we be going to any kind of balls or galas that require a long sequined dress? Information is the beginning of shopping power."

"Yes, the long sequined dress is a must. In our family, we always wear formal wear for Sunday breakfast. Where's the nearest formal wear store?"

"If I buy a sequined dress, you'll have to buy a tux."

"Done."

We both laughed when we turned the corner and saw a formal wear store.

"Doug, God has spoken. We must go in. You have to put your practical online shopping tendencies on the shelf and live a little."

"Do I look scared? I'm not scared."

As we wandered through the store, we both laughed at things we thought were ridiculous. We agreed that the classic black tux was tolerable but the black and white plaid sport coat was ridiculous. Finally he said it. The unthinkable.

"Carlie, try something on. Go ahead. Live a little."

Oh no. I'm dead. Someone call my mom and tell her to start planning my funeral. Ask Cousin Isabel to sing "Amazing Grace" accapella. I love that song. Louise, my best friend from high school, should quote the twenty-third Psalm.

"Doug, I doubt there's anything in here that I would look good in. I'm not much of a sequined gown person, y'know?"

"I disagree. Not everything in here is for some anorexic teenager on the way to the prom. What about that blue dress right there? It's real pretty."

"This is ridiculous. I have absolutely no place to wear that and I doubt they'd even have my size."

Call Mom and remind her that I want Pastor Jim to come from Atlanta to do my eulogy 'cause I've always loved him and he baptized me when I was eleven. Be sure to give Grandma medication as she'll miss me terribly, especially my banana bread.

"Go ahead, Carlie."

The sales lady found a size sixteen and agreed with Doug that I should try it on. (I whispered into her ear to bring an eighteen too...just in case. In case the biscuit and jelly had already gone to my thighs. I tended to operate a super fast highway in that regard.)

"Okay, Doug. I'm ready for the try-on. Which tux are you wearing?"

He smiled and chuckled. A woman who stood up to Shakespeare would not take "no" for an answer. He never even protested. We decided on a classic black and the sales lady found his size with almost no effort. She agreed to bring him back to the women's area when he was all ready.

I liked the fact that the blue dress wasn't one of those horrible show-everything-God-gave-you dresses that people wear to the Oscars and then get made fun of because they were coming out of it on stage. It was form fitting but it had a natural girdle of sorts to squeeze in my everything-God-gave-me and probably make me look thinner.

I stuffed myself into the blue dress. Literally. I took all the extra Carlie that was found in various places and stuffed it into the girdled area of the dress. When I finally turned around to look in the mirror, I was shocked. Utterly shocked. I looked good. Better than good. Thank you, God. Cancel the call to Mom about my funeral. Cousin Isabel can save her vocal chords for now. The three-quarter length sleeves fit perfectly and the fitted sequined top was just right. Unbelievably, someone had been on my side in New York City and had made just enough room for my enormous behind in a tapered understated skirt.

He used a loud clear voice I hadn't heard before, "Carlie, I'm out here in the monkey suit now but there's no rush at all. And if the dress isn't working, don't worry about it. This was all kind of a silly idea anyway, right?"

I held my breath and just opened the door. I knew that if I thought about it, I would never do it. I walked out with a confident smile and said, "Well, I guess we're ready for the debutante ball, Doug."

And there he was. The tux fit him perfectly. He looked like James Bond only friendlier and less pretentious. More approachable. When I walked out of the dressing room he stopped adjusting the sleeves on his white dress shirt and looked up. His olive green eyes were staring straight at me, especially certain parts of me. He took a deep breath. That was a look I hadn't seen on a man's face ever. The look I believed only existed in movies. And yet this wasn't like the movies. It was better because I wasn't afraid to eat jelly on my biscuits in front of him. He knew I stocked shelves for a living. He was a real person. A man.

"Gosh, Carlie. I'm speechless. I mean, uh, you look beautiful. Stunning really."

"Thanks, Doug. You look pretty great too. We're gonna look fabulous at breakfast in the morning!"

"Yeah, I guess these aren't very practical, are they?"

The sales lady swooped in for the sale, "You guys look perfect! You should buy 'em. Have a big night out on the town. Do Chattanooga up right! Live a little!! Give me a big commission."

Okay. She really didn't say that last part. I'm just smart that way. I mean, I cracked the fact that Doug was a neat freak, right? Trust me. The woman was working on commission.

I pulled us back down to reality, "Thanks, but I think we're gonna have to go for something a little more casual."

I saw Doug's sadness when I went back in the dressing room. That made me happy.

We left the store with no formal wear but we were both smiling.

"Doug, can you believe that dress was $475?"

"Are you serious? Wow, I had no idea. But you did look pretty unbelievable in it. You gave it life, Carlie."

I liked the way he said my name. And he said it a lot. "Carlie, would you like grits or hashbrowns?" "Carlie, would you like to start walking or develop a strategy?" "Carlie, you look beautiful." "You gave it life, Carlie."

We went on to other stores. We looked at shoes and I confessed that my feet were enormous. I told him Daddy always said, "God was building something beautiful and he needed a strong foundation." He said my daddy was right. He smiled when he said it. I knew he really meant it. I bought a few things. But I kept remembering those words, "You gave it life, Carlie." No. I didn't give life to the blue dress. If I had tried it on three months ago it would have looked completely different. It was Doug, the way he looked at me, the way he laughed out loud when I teased him, his hairy hands, perfect posture, crooked teeth, curly hair, his kindness, the masculine way he opened the door for me, the e-mails, the phone calls. Doug Jameson had given me life, not an expensive blue dress in Chattanooga.

We settled in at a tiny table in the back corner of Starbucks and told each other our life stories. He had been bullied in eighth grade. I was a foot taller than everyone. Then there were the bad-date stories. His senior prom date left the prom with two of her girlfriends and drank uncontrollably in the parking lot. By the time he found her, she was almost passed out. He had to literally carry her to her front door.

"Oh my Gosh, what did you say to her dad?"

"I said the only thing I could think of, 'Karen drank a little too much and that's why we're home early.'"

"He must have wanted to *kill* you."

"Oh yeah. And I was just seventeen so I didn't know how to tell him what really happened. He thought I had let his little girl down. But the truth is…she had let me down."

"Well, it's been eleven years since the tragic prom date. What would you say you've learned since then?"

"If you're on a date, always keep your eye on 'em. And smell for alcohol. I've already sniffed you up and down several times, Carlie, especially when we got separated at JC Penney. Things happen, y'know. I don't know what you have in your purse or who you could have met in the parking lot." He was funny without having to be funny all the time. A rare find.

Someone hand me another macchiato. I don't want this moment to end.

"Carlie, it's 5:30 and I told my cousin we'd be there for supper at 6:00. Did you get everything you needed?"

"Yeah, I'm good to go."

I had bought a pair of black dress pants and a pink sweater at Lane Bryant, some pajamas and unmentionables (that's what my granny always called them) at Penney's, make-up and deodorant at Walgreen's. Doug had offered to pay every time with some sweet excuse like, "Look, this whole inconvenience was caused by me, can't I pick up the tab?" Or "I hate for you to have to buy things you already have, why don't I just pick this up?" But I refused. I assured him I could use every purchase and that it was no problem. I'm not sure I was truthful. Anytime I spend money it's a problem.

"Okay. I have a question. I noticed you haven't called to tell your cousin that I'm comin'. Don't you think you should let her know?"

"Uh, well, she knows you're comin'. I mean, that you *could* be comin'."

"Doug Jameson, you did that thing, didn't you? You told her that if things went well, you'd invite me to stay the night. But if I looked like your Uncle Charlie, you'd just escort me to my car after a one-hour lunch? I'm surprised you didn't ask her to call your cell phone at 1:00 and explain that there had been a grave family emergency."

He was smiling like a sixth grader who'd been caught splashing water in the school bathroom. "Look, it seemed like a good plan at the time."

"Oh, I understand. I can't say I blame ya. I mean, after all, we're talkin' about a man whose drinking glasses are organized according to height, a man whose toothpaste tube is perfectly creased, a man who won't wear pink. It's no wonder you couldn't take the risk, Doug. I'll take it as a compliment that I got the invitation and just leave it at that."

He pretended he was embarrassed. I pretended I was offended. But we both knew the truth. We were happy. Deliriously happy.

Dave and Shannon lived only fifteen minutes from the mall. It was an older middle-class suburban neighborhood that reminded me of where people always live on TV sitcoms. Not too wealthy. Not too poor. A neighborhood with kids on bikes and pansies out front and a few cats and dogs runnin' across the street. A few houses needed new roofs. A few needed paint. But if the neighborhood could talk it would say, "People like living here. They stay warm and dry and they look out for each other."

On the fifteen-minute trip, Doug gave me the run down on Dave and Shannon. Shannon is Aunt Clarice's daughter. Aunt Clarice is his mother's sister who lives in Palm Springs, California, and has a dark tan, talks very loudly, and plays way too much bingo. Dave and Shannon lived in California too but moved to Chattanooga when he got a job as pastor of Grace Community Church. Married three years. No kids. Shannon sells life insurance part time. I was prepared. I wondered what they knew about me.

We rang the doorbell and then Doug spoke loudly, "It's just us!"

Dave opened the door and hugged Doug. It was one of those hugs that said, "We're fraternity brothers and our team just won the big game." Lots of slapping and hitting on the arm and physical touch. I put out my hand and he shook it briskly and said, "Carlie, it's so great to meet you. Doug has told us a lot about you. We can't wait to get to know you."

"It's great to meet you too, Dave." Dave looked like an all-American football player who sidelined as a movie star. Blonde hair, blue eyes, big friendly smile. But he wasn't pretentious. He opened the door in his sock feet. His big toe was sticking out of a large hole in his right sock. And he seemed okay with that.

"Shannon, they're here! She's trying to get the rolls in the oven. She'll be here in a sec. You're lookin' good, Doug. Bank business must be good…that…or somethin' else is goin' well." Dave winked at me and smiled and I knew that Doug had told them about the e-mails and the phone calls. They were in the know.

Shannon almost ran into the living room and gave me a hug as though she'd never even considered shaking my hand, "Oh Carlie, I'm so happy! I'm glad you could come! We're just so tickled to meet you. Doug thinks you're awesome but you already know that, I'm sure."

"Oh, I think he's pretty great too."

Shannon looked almost exactly like Jeanie Parker, the head cheerleader in my high school (Go Bulldogs). A Jennifer Lopez look-a-like, she was perfect. But it was like Shannon never got the memo telling her how perfect she was. She seemed happy being one of us regular mortals.

"Okay, everyone, dinner will be out in a few minutes. Tell us all about what you guys have done today. I know you were meeting at Cracker Barrel at noon. I'm guessing it was really scary when you first met each other. Oh Carlie, were you scared to death? I would have been about to pass out!"

"It was pretty unnerving. I guess confession is good for the soul. I was in my car waiting when I saw Doug walk up to the rocking chairs. I sat there for at least five minutes trying to get up the courage to get out of the car."

Dave chimed in, "Look, Carlie, if I saw Doug for the first time...it would take me a while to get up the courage to get out of the car too! I might have just driven back to Georgia."

Doug smiled and said, "She's here, isn't she?"

"Dinner's ready, guys. Carlie, come on in and I'll show you to your place."

The table was set beautifully but not over-the-top-I'm-better-than-you ridiculous. The salad was crisp. The lasagna tasted like the lasagna from that little Italian place in Athens, and the company was beyond enjoyable. Never a moment of uncomfortable silence. Dave kept us all in stitches.

"Carlie, there are things Doug hasn't told you. But that's why it's good you came here so that you don't have to be in the dark any longer. Okay, where to start? Well, he hates dumb girls. This is one of his rules. He has rules just like that rule book that came out for girls a few years back. It seems like a lot of people have tried to fix him up with dumb girls and the minute the girl says, 'Like, I was so totally goin' to the tanning bed today but I couldn't remember where the tanning salon was located and I was like, Oh my gosh, I'm like totally gonna be totally too white to show my face in public' well,

Doug checks out then and starts checkin' football scores on his I-phone. Let's see, what else? Oh yeah, did you know about him being a neat freak? Yeah, you need to know that. I'm talkin' shoes lined up perfectly in the floor of his closet. I'm talkin' silverware drawer without a crumb in it."

"Hey! You're not so bright, Dave. She figured that one out all by herself today...without me even tellin' her...somethin' about me askin' if she wanted to develop a shopping plan. From that statement she completely had me pegged. I mean, told me what my kitchen cabinets were like, the whole nine yards."

"Okay, she seems to be unusually perceptive. We can check 'not dumb' off of Doug's check list. Let's go on to another one..."

"Dave, take a break, Honey. It's time for cookies and coffee. Let's go to the living room. Carlie, he's not usually this bad. He just loves Doug and Doug's such a sweet guy, he makes a pretty easy target."

"Oh, I'm not worried. Besides, I need to know about these rules, don't I?" I laughed along with the rest of them but I really did want to know about Doug's standards. There would be time later. I had a feeling there was a lot that Shannon could tell me, things she wasn't letting go of right now.

After three rounds of Pictionary (Dave and Shannon were unbeatable) and hours of conversation, time had crept up on all of us. Dave finally said it out loud, "It's after 11:00. We better hit the hay. Big day tomorrow. Carlie, again, we're just so proud to have you here. You're definitely okay in my book...not that Doug cares anything about my opinion." Doug patted him on the back again in that fraternal way.

73

Their relationship was sweet, but in a masculine way. I wasn't sure I had ever seen anything like it.

Dave was fun but Shannon kept everyone feeling loved and cared for. They were perfect for each other. "Carlie, let me show you to your room. There's a bathroom right down the hall with fresh towels. Please don't hesitate to let me know if you need *anything* at all. Just knock on our door. I'll have muffins and coffee ready at 8:00, but breakfast is come-and-go so sleep as long as you want. Dave usually leaves for church real early, but the rest of us can leave at 9:30. Is there anything you need? Anything at all?"

"Shannon, really, thank you...I mean, it's just been wonderful meeting you and Dave. The dinner was delicious. The room looks great. I can't tell you how much I appreciate it."

"Well, a friend of Doug's is a friend of ours. Or...uh...I guess you're probably more than a friend and in that case, you're *really* a friend of ours, Carlie. Good night, sleep tight!"

As I stepped into the room with the light blue carpet, Doug called my name, "Carlie, I got all your bags out of the truck and I'll set 'em on the rocking chair right here." He walked into the room with such confidence. He didn't hesitate at all or seem uncomfortable. But I knew he wouldn't stay long. I knew that much about his character. I would have to speak quickly.

"Doug, it's been a great day. Thank you. I don't remember when I've laughed so much. It's good for the soul."

"Thanks for coming, Carlie. I've had fun too. You...well...you make everything...better."

Standing in that room looking at him eye to eye, I desperately wanted to reach out and put my arms around him. I wanted to feel the green chamois shirt up next to me again. I wanted to tell him that I needed a man like him, that I wanted a man who would carry my bags in from the car and set them on the rocking chair, that I wouldn't be bothered by his shoes being lined up perfectly in the closet. But of course, I said none of that.

"Sleep well, Doug. See you in the morning." He walked out of the room but turned just as he got to the door.

"Yeah, you too. And for the record, I'm glad Uncle Stanley gave you my card. I owe him one."

And at that moment he looked at me exactly the way he did when I wore the blue dress. His eyes were consuming me. I smiled and tried to look straight at him but felt a sudden onslaught of shyness. I looked down and simply said, "Good night." I knew I would replay that moment at least a thousand times in my mind.

The room was simple and meticulously clean (runs in the family, maybe?). I walked down to the bathroom, washed my face, and then quickly snuck back to my room before anyone saw me without make-up. I would get up bright and early and shower and be completely dressed before 8:00. Doug and I had not known each other long enough to have the no-make-up meeting yet. I knew I wouldn't be able to sleep. The bed was comfy and the light blue sheets smelled like gardenias but a girl just can't sleep in these circumstances. I knew he was right next door.

If this had been a movie, he would have knocked on my door after everyone went to sleep. When I opened the door, he would have kissed me passionately. He would have stopped kissing me only long enough to say, "Carlie, I want you. I need you." But I knew for absolute certain that Doug Jameson wasn't going to knock on my door. He wasn't going to kiss me passionately. He wasn't going to tell me that he wanted me. Not tonight anyway. That knowledge made me happy inside.

October 30   11:50 pm   DOUG

I wonder if she's sleeping. I wish she didn't live in Georgia. Today went well. She laughed when I told my prom story. She seemed impressed with my job. She's beautiful. I can't sleep.

CHAPTER FIVE: When Tragedy Strikes

CARLIE

October 31

My cell phone alarm went off at 6:00 am. I jumped out of bed like I was going to a fire. Happy to be alive. Happy to be in Chattanooga. Happy that Doug Jameson was sleeping peacefully next door. I tiptoed to the bathroom and showered quickly. I then put my pajamas back on and tiptoed back to the room with the light blue carpet. Applying moisturizer and make-up became priority one. As I looked into the mirror, I thanked God for the way Doug saw me, the way he looked at me. God had rendered a miracle. I was grateful.

At 8:00 I was completely ready. Black dress pants, pink sweater, hair and make-up done. I wondered if Doug would give me that look again. I wondered what it would be like to sit with him in a regular kitchen and drink coffee and eat muffins. I couldn't wait to find out.

When I entered the kitchen Shannon was wearing a bright purple terrycloth robe and pulling blueberry muffins from the oven. But something wasn't right. When she turned to face me, I saw the tears. Her eyes were puffy. She looked like she had been hit by a bus.

"Shannon, what's wrong? Is everything okay?"

Tears flowed freely, "Oh Carlie, no! Everything is not okay. It's Aunt Susan, Doug's Mom. Doug's not here." She looked at the clock on the oven, "He's probably back home by now. I'm so sorry, Carlie. I'm truly sorry! It all happened so fast!"

"What happened, Shannon? What do you mean Doug's back home? What happened to his mom?"

Shannon pointed to the chairs and said, "I think we need coffee, Carlie."

"Agreed."

She sat two cups of coffee on the table. She got up from the table to retrieve a container of vanilla creamer from the fridge. Even in grief, she was hosting me.

"Okay. What we know right now is kinda sketchy. It was all so crazy when we got the call. At about 1:00 this morning, a friend of Aunt Susan's called trying to find Doug. If I understand the story right, Aunt Susan was supposed to be at Charlene's birthday party Saturday night. Charlene is the Rockfords' daughter. Anyway, Aunt Susan was supposed to bring potato salad and sweet tea and she acted like she was happy about it, really lookin' forward to the party. When she didn't show up at the party, Aunt Charlotte (her sister) tried to call the house but she didn't answer. Thankfully, at 10:30 Aunt Charlotte and Uncle Bart went over to the house. The lights were all on but Aunt Susan wouldn't answer the door. Uncle Bart knew where the spare key was. When they found her, she was all dressed for the party but passed out on the bed. She took too much medication. The doctor gave her pills to help her sleep but she took the whole bottle. They called 911 but when they arrived...oh Carlie, she was already gone!"

Shannon began sobbing again as I handed her a Kleenex from the counter. I hugged her real tight and started weeping myself. Doug's mom was dead? That couldn't be. He was just over there putting shelving in the shed. She just fixed him up a few weeks ago with the girl from the electric company.

78

I'd never even gotten a chance to meet her. And poor Doug. His grandparents were gone. And now both his mom and dad were dead. No brothers and sisters. He must feel completely alone.

"Shannon, I'm in shock! I mean, I want to do something to help but I'm not sure what to do. When did he leave? Was he okay to drive?"

"Of course, when the phone rang at that hour, I knew there was trouble. There's an older lady in our church who's been terribly ill and I thought it was bad news about Norma. But when they asked for Doug, I couldn't imagine what had happened. He started crying uncontrollably when he got the news. He kept saying, 'It must have been an accidental overdose.' But Carlie, it doesn't look like it could have been an accident, I mean not what we know right now. Dave hugged him and prayed for him. All of us were in shock. Aunt Susan has never had any emotional problems, none that we knew of. Dave insisted that Doug not drive back to Sharon alone. But, of course, Doug said, 'Dave, you have a sermon to give this mornin' and you need to give it. I'm okay to drive. Aunt Charlotte will meet me at the house. Please don't worry. Take good care of Carlie and tell her that I'm sorry I had to leave.'"

"He could have knocked on the door. I wouldn't have minded."

"We tried to tell him that. We said, 'Maybe Carlie could be a help to you, Doug. Don't be afraid to tell her.' But he was completely torn up and said that it was best for you to sleep. Plus, he wanted to get on the road. He left here around 2:30."

"I'm...I mean, I don't even know what to say, Shannon. Doug said she was missing his dad, but I never got any indication that...well, things were..."

"Oh no. None of us knew. Doug said he had no clue she was in any real danger. He kept saying, 'Why didn't she come to me? Why didn't she call me? I could have helped.' I think she just had a bad night. She and Uncle James always loved going to family gatherings. I think this birthday party for Charlene just reminded her how much she missed him, how much she hated being alone. When she was supposed to leave, it just got to her and she snapped. I don't think she planned it. I don't think she even thought through all the pain it would cause. She missed Uncle James. She wanted to be with him. She lost her emotional balance and stopped thinking straight. Oh, Carlie, we feel for Doug. She was all he had left in the way of immediate family. Truth is, she would have never done anything to hurt him."

"I know. I want to help but I'm not sure how. Are you and Dave going up for the funeral?"

"We're leaving right after lunch. Dave will announce today that he'll be gone a few days. Doug will need us right now. He and Dave have always had a special bond. They've only known each other five years but they're a lot alike. Neither of them had siblings and I think they just decided to be like brothers. And they are. We think the world of him, Carlie. You know that."

"Yeah, I love the way you all seem to genuinely like each other. And yes...I think the world of him too...even though I don't know him very well. I need to go home today, Shannon. But I wanna go to the funeral. I'll have to talk to my professors and the people at work and I'll need you to keep me posted about the arrangements."

"Oh, we can do that. It may be a few days before the funeral because I'm sure there'll be an autopsy...uh, under the circumstances. Please feel free to stay for church and lunch. We've so enjoyed meeting you and we'd love for you to stay a while longer."

"I can definitely do that. Plus, I've always wanted to hear a sermon by someone who can draw a triceratops with such incredible detail."

"We need your humor right now, Carlie. Maybe your visit had a greater purpose than you even understood. Dave left for church at 7:30 and I'm sorry but I need to pack our things for the trip. Feel free to have muffins and coffee and if there's anything else you need, I'll be in our room. Again...I'm glad you're here, Carlie."

Church was exactly like I pictured it. About 150 people in an ordinary looking building. Some wore jeans. Others wore dress clothes. Many friendly people introduced themselves to me and it was complicated to explain why I was there, how I knew Dave and Shannon, how I knew them without really knowing them.

Shannon had a rare people gift. When someone introduced themselves to me, she would put her arm around me, jump in and say, "Oh, Marlene, it's kind of a sad story. My favorite cousin, Doug, was here to have some special time with Carlie. She's from Commerce, Georgia. But we got news this morning that his mother died. So he had to return home and Carlie was thankfully able to stay with us this morning." She gave me another big squeeze on the arm.

After meeting Dave and Shannon, I had envisioned the way it would be at church. The dress would be casual. The people kind. But my vision didn't turn out exactly right. I had visualized Doug standing next to me while we sang. I would feel like holding his hand but I wouldn't.

Dave surprised me with his absolute ability up front. His message about God's never-ending love seemed especially appropriate. I wish Doug had been there. I couldn't fathom what was going through his mind.

CHAPTER SIX: Living Through Drama...I Mean, Trauma

DOUG

October 31   7:30 am

God, please tell me Aunt Charlotte isn't at the house yet. I'm too tired for all the family drama. And I think that Ben-Gay smell would make me throw up right now. Oh no, there's the ever familiar '96 Crown Vic...and Uncle Bart's old truck is in back...and Charlene's mini-van...and Chester's Ford Focus...and Billie Sue's getting a coconut cream pie from the back of the Trail Blazer. Looks like Jim Smith from the hardware store and Jessica, the twenty-two-year-old girl from the electric company, are standing outside smokin'. I need an escape route. Oh no. Too late.

"Oh Doug!!!   Doug!!   Bart, Charlene, Chester, Everybody, Doug's here!!!"

I managed to get out of the truck and make one step before the big assault. Hugs, kisses, tears, Kleenex, nose blowing, and words coming at me like bullets from an automatic weapon. An emotional ambush of sorts.   I couldn't even tell you who said what. "Oh Doug, Sweet Doug, we're so sorry!" "Susan was such a gem. She was a gem, wasn't she, Chester?" "A great lady." "Oh Doug, you must be just torn up. Are you torn up?" "Of course, he's torn up, Charlene." "Why on earth did she do this to you, Honey?" "I'm so sorry. She must have just lost her mind." "You look awful, dear. Just awful. Here, have some pie."

Finally Aunt Charlotte suggested everyone give me space to breathe, "Let's all go inside and give Doug a chance to rest before we have to go to Groeden's." Groeden's is the funeral home that everyone in my family and most people in our town use. I didn't know which was worse, eating Billie Sue's rubbery coconut pie at 7:30 in the morning or going to the funeral home to pick out a casket with Mr. Groeden, the man who remembers me as the boy who brought his daughter home drunk after the prom. But of course, the worst thing was that my mom was gone. Dead of her own choosing. This was a day from hell and it could only get worse. Aunt Charlotte removed her old wire-rim glasses and wiped her eyes with the tail of her apron. As she led the troops into the house, her slip was showing out the back of her yellow too-tight knit dress. Some things never change.

Jessica was acting strange. While everyone else cried and blew their noses, she just stood against the kitchen wall. I had only met her one time when Mom had pulled that ridiculous set-up and I couldn't figure out why she was even here. "Um, Doug, your mom...well, she was a great lady. She really was. And she was crazy about you, really she was. I don't know why she...well, why she wasn't feeling well."

"Thanks, Jessica. Yeah, it was a blow. And yeah, she was a great lady." I wanted to just go in the bathroom, lock the door, throw up, and then fall asleep on the freshly-washed navy blue bathroom rug. But about that time Aunt Charlotte and Uncle Bart came up behind me and patted me on the shoulder, "Doug, you ready to go see her, Honey?"

Go see her? What are you talkin' about, Aunt Charlotte? There's no going to *see* her anymore. Didn't you get the news? She's gone, Aunt Charlotte! She's outta here. She ditched me, tossed me aside, forgot about the whole I-want-grandkids thing and went straight for eternity. She's *dead,*

Aunt Charlotte. All that's left is a cold corpse, a dead body. But I would never say that to such a nice old lady even if her slip was showing and she smelled like Ben-Gay.

"Yeah, Aunt Charlotte, we can go now. But could you do me a favor? Could you ask everyone to give me the afternoon here by myself? I want to go through the house alone. If everyone wants to come back at supper time, that's fine. But I need the afternoon...and maybe I'll even try to sleep some."

"Oh absolutely, dear! NOW LISTEN UP EVERYONE, we all need to go home until 5:30. If you want to be with Doug and family and friends, you can come back at 5:30. Spread the word please. Doug needs to rest and process everything that's happened, the poor dear. Let's give him some space. He's suffered a drama y'know." I wanted to say, "That's *trauma*, Aunt Charlotte." But on second thought, yeah, drama works too.

The morning at Groeden's was a blur which is what everyone always says. The red carpet smelled almost moldy. Too much rain. When someone asked me a question, I answered without even thinking. "Yeah, that gray casket's fine." "Yes, Bro. Dan will do the service. Can you call Sandy Caldwell about singing 'Great is Thy Faithfulness'?" "If they do the autopsy Monday or Tuesday, we could have visitation Wednesday night and the funeral Thursday morning." "Aunt Charlotte, would you like to say a few words? And is Aunt Clarice coming from California?"

I must have looked horribly tired because in the middle of it all, Aunt Charlotte promised me she would do the rest of the funeral schedule exactly the way Mom would have wanted. She instructed me to go home, eat, and take a nap.

I pulled my truck into Mom's driveway at 12:09 and just sat there. It was windy and the front porch swing was making an eerie sound as it swayed. The white farm house was old, built in 1917. But it had been meticulously cared for. No peeling paint. No missing shingles. She wouldn't have stood for it. Leaves had fallen on the sidewalk. Mom would have gotten the broom and said, "What messiness on the walk! Just give me a moment and let's get this solved." She had painted the swing and all the chairs just a few weeks ago. I remember her big dilemma about it too. "Doug, I've thought of trimming the front porch and the swing in a real color. Maybe mossy green or a lemon yellow. People in the city are doing red now. Can you believe it? That seems so...I don't know, showy maybe. I guess I'll just do white again. There's nothing cleaner than a crisp white. Everyone loves a crisp white." Yeah. Mom would be the one worried about what seemed cleaner. And unfortunately, she had passed on her obsession to me. Even the yard had been picked clean of any natural untamed life. If it were in Susan Jameson's yard, it would be conventional and all lined up in a row. We mustn't let things grow wild and free. What about people, Mom? Can they be wild and free? Too late to ask.

When I walked in the house, everyone had cleared out. But there was already a pile of food on the kitchen table. I knew there would be. I had seen Mom rush over to the bereaved home on many occasions with potato salad and a chocolate cake or a crockpot full of mini meatballs. None of the food called my name. I grabbed a pimento cheese sandwich just to make the growl go away. And then I did something I had never done. Ever.

I walked into the living room and sat on Mom's favorite cream-colored couch and ate the sandwich. When I was done, I rubbed my hands on the arms of the couch. For some horrible reason, I was trying to hurt her. But it didn't matter.

86

She was gone. I started crying into a tan throw pillow and eventually fell asleep on the couch. It was probably the first time human feet had ever really rested on that couch. And lightning didn't even strike.

I woke to the sound of loud whispers. Louder than some people's regular voices. "Sh! Doug's asleep in the living room. Don't go in there and please whisper!"

I stood up, rubbed my face a little, and tried to find my balance. The grandfather clock in the corner said it was 6:20. Everyone must be here by now. Before I walked into the kitchen, I did a quick overview of voices. Uncle Bart, Aunt Charlotte, Chester and Ida, Jim Smith, Jessica (I couldn't figure this one out), Charlene, Uncle Stanley, Aunt Beth, Ralph (Uncle Stanley and Aunt Beth's son), Brother Dan, and yes, Dave and Shannon. Thank you, God.

"Dave! Hey, ya think I was gonna sleep all night?"

"We weren't worried. How's it goin', friend?"

"Well, not too great, as you can imagine."

Uncle Stanley and Aunt Beth approached slowly. I knew Uncle Stanley's gray wool jacket would smell of moth balls and lemon drops. Aunt Beth was wearing an old navy blue suit with a huge sunflower pin on the lapel. She was at least a foot shorter than Uncle Stanley and her hair was pulled tight in a gray bun. I had never seen it any other way. Ever. Comforting. I reached out to hug them. Yes, there's that smell. I'm just like Mom. She would have noticed the smell. But unlike Mom, I had the good graces to remain quiet. Mom would have scrunched her nose up and said something like, "Uncle Stanley, haven't worn this coat in a while, eh?" I knew better. They had both gotten a little more fragile since

87

the last time I'd seen them. I wished they lived closer, especially now.

"Doug Honey, well, we're just torn up. Torn up. We just got into town. Ralph drove us in. I hated for Stanley to drive under the stress. Plus, it's a long way for us old folks. Ralph's a good boy. We'll all stay with Charlene a few days. How're you doin', Sweetie?"

"Thanks for comin', Aunt Beth. Really. You and Uncle Stanley are special. You were special to Mom. You know that. I'm not doin' too well right now. But it'll get better."

Aunt Beth started crying. I knew that it was because I told her she was special to Mom. She was. She always tolerated Mom's obsessions better than anyone else. She loved her even when she was difficult or critical of other family members. Aunt Beth would say, "Now Susan, we can't control what other people do. Maybe it's best we not even try." God knows she was right.

"Well of course, the shock alone would be hard to deal with, Honey. Bless you, Doug. Bless you. Your mama was a fine Christian woman and don't ever forget that. Perfect? No. But she loved all of us, Doug. You can take that to the bank."

Uncle Stanley felt uncomfortable with all the emotional talk especially considering the circumstances. He just stared at the tan linoleum for a while and then poured three glasses of lemonade. Finally, he said with a grin and a pat on the back, "Well, the talk around Commerce is that Carlie Ann Davidson has a boyfriend up in Tennessee. I wouldn't know. But that's the talk."

I was happy to be talking about a more pleasant subject. "You've got good taste, Uncle Stanley. She's somethin' else."

88

"She is, Doug. She's like an undiscovered treasure. I've always known there was more there than the people in Commerce had uncovered. Go slow. Play your cards right. This one's worth workin' for."

"Right now I don't think I have the strength to work for her, Uncle Stanley. I'm tired and pretty useless."

"You're not useless, Boy. You're a fine man. Every man gets knocked down sometimes. We can't always explain it. But don't turn away from her, Doug. That'd be a mistake. Especially now." He held Aunt Beth's arm and led her to a chair. "I'll get ya a sandwich and some meatballs, Beth. You wait right here."

Wearing a tight-fitting black dress that was more than just distracting, Jessica approached me with a smile. "Doug, did you rest well? I hope so. You need your rest. I brought some chicken soup. It's in that crockpot on the counter if you'd like to try some. It's my grandma's recipe and it's really good. I hear that Oprah Winfrey has a good soup recipe but I've never made it. I've always wanted to be at her show. Again, I just want you to know that I'm here for you if you ever need anything." She put her arm around my shoulder in a way that seemed like more than friendly consolation. Jessica is not a bad lookin' girl but she smells of smoke and I get the feeling she's lookin' for a ticket out of her current situation. How in the world did she con Mom into arranging that setup?

Shannon had been working with Charlene to display the food on the now-extended dining room table. Someone brought in a huge cornucopia from City Florist and sat it in the middle of the perfectly polished table. Dave helped Shannon make some decaf coffee with the coffee maker Chester brought from the church. Finally she approached me with a hug, "I'm so sorry, Doug. Really, there are just no words. Hard to believe that just last night we were all sittin' around the table laughing. Now we're here in your mom's house making coffee and talking about a funeral."

"Yeah. I can't even remember where I am half the time. Like I'm watchin' a movie of someone else's life. Thanks for taking such good care of Carlie, Shannon. I mean, I guess you told her and everything."

"I did and Doug, she was sad for you. Really sad. She went to church with us and had sandwiches at the house before she headed back to Commerce. Dave and I really like her. She's her own unique kind of girl. She wanted me to give you this." Shannon pulled an ivory-colored envelope from her purse. "Doug" had been written in cursive on the outside. I had never seen Carlie's handwriting. It was that extra loopy real pretty handwriting that girls often had and boys rarely did. She was pretty. What would it be like if she were here standing with me in the kitchen right now? Would she be bringing me coffee, rubbing my back with her hand? Meeting all my crazy relatives? Would she tell Billie Sue that her pie was delicious and then find a way to dispose of it in a napkin? Yeah, she would. What would it be like if she were here after everyone went home? What if she took all her clothes off in the guest room and laid down beside me on the double bed? The room would smell of vanilla, just like her. She would kiss me and love me with no reservations. I decided that would be heaven on earth. Truth is, being with a woman like Carlie would make everything easier.

But I knew that scenario would mean that she was my wife. A wife who had never even met my mom, had never eaten her pot roast for Sunday dinner, had never heard my mom talk about the pansies she wanted to plant in the window boxes and the fact that she was afraid of an early frost. Carlie would be a wife who would never hear the words, "James and I were always so proud of Doug. Good grades, good manners, and a fine son." I sat in the green recliner, put my head in my hands, and cried. Why did Mom do it? How in the hell could she leave me here to deal with all this? God, please make everyone go home.

Aunt Charlotte came to put her hand on my shoulder, "Doug Honey, go ahead and cry. We don't mind."

"Aunt Charlotte, it's after 8:00. Could you ask everyone to go home? Don't get me wrong. I love the family, but I have to go to my apartment and I need to work on some things. I asked Dave and Shannon to stay here. But I need some time away from the crowd."

"Oh absolutely. OKAY EVERYONE, go home now! It's time to go home! You can come back tomorrow! Doug, when can they come back tomorrow?"

"Uh, I dunno. How 'bout 10:00?"

"Okay. No one comes back 'till 10:00 tomorrow. Chester, this means you. If you and Ida would like to take some food home, there are paper plates on the counter. But leave poor Doug alone until 10:00 in the morning. No exceptions. And Jim, get those God-awful cigarette butts off the front porch as you leave. Susan would have had a cow over that. Charlene, can you help me put the potato salad and other cold items back in the fridg? Rest of you, OUT!"

The great thing about giving Aunt Charlotte a job was the knowledge that she would be thorough. God knows no one would be left wondering what she really meant. Oh no. She had the gift of clarity.

Unlocking the door of my apartment felt normal. This is where I live. It's where I had my own memories. I could sleep in my own bed and take a shower in my own bathroom. I laid out on the brown bedspread and reached into my pocket to pull out the cream-colored envelope. The room looked bare. Had my obsessive cleanliness actually created a cold space where the life had been choked out of every corner? I'd never even thought about it before now, before her. I'd wanted to read the note from Carlie all evening. But as Aunt Charlotte so aptly said, "I've been through a drama."

Even the envelope smelled of vanilla and it made me want her. I wanted her right beside me.

Dear Doug,

I'm sorry. People always look for really special or creative words to say during times like this, but I find the words "I'm sorry" are what I really want to say. So I will not try to find something more brilliant.

I wish I could be there with you at this moment. I am sending a long embrace. I'm getting things in order here so that I might come to the funeral. I know you are tired, but if you ever need to talk, you have my number. Don't be afraid to use it. Shannon said they didn't find a note. I'm sure she wasn't thinking clearly. If she had been

92

thinking clearly, she would have never left you, Doug. She wouldn't have. She loved you deeply. What little I knew of her makes me assured of that. What I know of you makes me realize how very proud she must have been. Any woman would be proud to have a son like you. You gave your parents joy.

I read a poem once by Neil Gaiman
"You mourn, for it is proper to mourn,
 But your grief serves you;
You do not become a slave to grief.
You bid the dead farewell, and you continue."

I always wanted to add the words. "You bid the dead farewell, and you continue...because death is not the end." This is what we believe, yes?

I will see you soon.
Love, Carlie

I dialed the phone without thinking. God, please let her be home.

"Hello."

"Uh, Carlie, it's me. Is this a bad time? Is it too late?"

"Oh Doug, I'm so glad you called. I didn't want to disturb you while you're with all the family and friends…but I was so hoping you'd call."

"It's been a pretty bad day and I'm not sure a peanut butter sandwich and some Tylenol will fix this one."

"Yeah, you may have to graduate to two tacos and a pint of Ben and Jerry's this time."

"I've been eating Mrs. Ida's pimento cheese sandwiches since I've been here. Will that count?"

"It will if you've had banana pudding or red velvet cake or some other sugar-filled evil with the sandwiches."

"Two chocolate chip cookies and a lemon square."

"You're good. Shannon called me on her cell phone at about 6:00 and said you were asleep on the couch. I felt so sad for you. I wanted to be there. Have a lot of people been at the house?"

"I wish you were here too. Yeah, a lot of people have been in and out at Mom's house. And I appreciate it. I mean, I know they're just trying to help. Who wouldn't want to help a poor orphan boy, right?"

"Doug, I'm sorry. Your mom loved you. She did. You know that. It was a moment of craziness. You have to find a way to forgive her."

"I guess. Let's talk about something else."

"I talked to my boss this afternoon and I have Wednesday, Thursday and Friday night off. I'll have to talk to my professors tomorrow and let them know I'll be out Thursday and Friday. Shouldn't be a problem. I'll leave Wednesday after my 1:00 class. I should be there by 9:00 or 9:30. I'll have to come home Friday after lunch 'cause I work Saturday morning. Shannon already has a place for me to stay there. Michelle's house, I believe."

"Carlie, you don't wanna stay with Michelle and Buster. Shannon doesn't realize how much she's let the house go since the twins came along. It's craziness over there. Trust me. I love Michelle. She's a wonderful woman but between four kids, three Labradoodles, and a cat who has a urinary tract infection, you wouldn't survive."

"I'm tougher than you think."

"Look, Dave and Shannon are staying at the house. There's plenty of room for you there. I'm staying at my apartment and just going over during the day."

"But what about when Shannon's mom comes in from California tomorrow?"

"Aunt Clarice can stay in Mom's room. Dave and Shannon can stay in the guest room. And you can stay in my old room. It still looks like it did in high school. It may not be the prettiest but at least you won't be attacked by Labradoodles in the middle of the night."

"Yeah, but what about all those letters from old girlfriends? Am I allowed to read those?"

"Absolutely. When I was in fourth grade Sally Colton sent me a letter on pink paper saying, 'I like you. Do you like me?

95

Check yes or no.' I think I still have it in a drawer somewhere. So yeah, knock yourself out. You can even dig through my old closet if you'd like."

"I can hardly wait."

"Speaking of letters, thanks for taking the time to write the note. It meant a lot to me. You're gifted with words. Even the envelope smells like you, like vanilla or whatever that is."

"Thanks. Doug, it's getting late and you need to rest. I'll be there Wednesday night. Try to get some sleep. Again, I'm truly sorry. Call anytime."

"I'm sure the next few days will be busy around here. I'm sorry our time in Chattanooga was cut short. I've been thinkin' about you though. Even today, in all the grief, I've still thought about you."

"Same here."

"I wish you could have met my mom, Carlie. She would have liked you. She would have driven you absolutely crazy, but at the end of the day she would have realized you were special and she would have done anything for you."

"I have no doubt that's true. I know this. She raised a boy into a really good man."

"Thanks. Carlie, keep praying for me. I have a big journey ahead. I'll be counting the hours till you get here."

"Me too. See you soon. Bye."

"Bye."

The moment I heard the click, I was lonely again. Lonely, but extremely hopeful. Even hearing her voice made me feel...I don't know, like the way I felt when I saw Sandra holding up that Dartmouth sweatshirt in the Daily Messenger years ago. Except this time it wasn't just a sexual feeling. I mean, it definitely was sexual. It was predominantly sexual. But it was other things too, like the fact that she can quote poetry, that she makes me feel good about my job, that she thinks of me as a man, not some pitiful little boy. She's funny and smart, and Shannon and Dave like her. She goes to church and knows God but she's not all cold and better than everyone else, like she wouldn't spend the rest of her life holding things over my head or holding up a bar knowing I would never be able to reach it. She's horribly flawed and sometimes sinful...and all of that has made her a forgiving person. She's a lot like Dave, except I've never wanted to see Dave naked.

CHAPTER SEVEN: To A Funeral We Must Go

CARLIE

November 3

I don't even know what clothes to take. Isn't it terrible that a woman is trying to find funeral clothes that make her behind look smaller and her top half look more appealing? Yeah. I'm pretty sure most people don't get ready for a funeral by saying, "Wow, my behind will look great in this!"

I only have one viable option. I'll bring the black dress and the teal jacket. Appropriate. Today I'll wear the new black dress pants and the peachy-colored jacket I wore to Jeanie Parker's wedding. I'm glad I decided to skip my 1:00 class and hit the road at 11:00 so I can be there during visitation. The American Revolution will have to be discussed without me today. Somehow I can live with that.

November 3   7:19 pm

I thought I'd never find a parking spot. She must have known everyone in town. After taking the block several times, I finally parked my car in front of "Sammy's Sandwich Emporium." I hoped Sammy didn't get mad. Trust me, Sammy, I was desperate. I don't believe I've ever even heard of a sandwich emporium. Looks like they also sell old comic books, children's toys, dog beds, and used clothing. I could get a Reuben and chips for $4.99 and a winter coat for an additional $11.99. Gotta love a business that can multi-task. Small town livin' at its best.

The line was out the door of the funeral home and circling around the sidewalk. I decided to stand there patiently rather than say something stupid like, "Excuse me, I'm Doug Jameson's new girlfriend from Commerce, Georgia. Can you clear a path for me?"

An older man with a shiny bald head, dressed in a faded pinstripe suit and carrying a cane, had gotten in line right before I walked up. "Beautiful night, isn't it? Glad to see a little warm spell come in today. How'd you know Mrs. Susan?"

"I really didn't. I know her son, Doug."

"Oh, now that Doug is shore a fine fella. Yes ma'am. Sad that he lost his daddy last year and now his mama."

"Yeah, it sure is."

"I'm Samuel Jones, but everyone in town calls me Chester. I'm married to Ida and Ida is kin to all them Jamesons somehow. Don't really know how. Are you from 'round these parts?"

"No sir. I live in Commerce, Georgia."

"Commerce…Commerce. Isn't that where Stanley and Beth Rockford live?"

"Yes sir, it is. That's how I got to know Doug, through the Rockfords."

"Wait a minute!! You're that gal they fixed him up with! Why, yes! The boys down at the coffee shop was sayin' jest

the other mornin' that ol' Stanley Rockford done found a
woman for Doug Jameson down in northern Georgia. A
Georgia peach, yeah, that's what they was sayin'. Bill
Peterman said he'd heard from Charlene that you was a big
tall woman and they was right…big and purdy. Real purdy."

"Well, thank you."

"A guest from outta town shouldn't have to wait in this gall
darn receiving line. Here, let's take you on in to where the
family is."

"That's not necessary, Mr. Chester. Really, I'm fine. I can
just wait with everyone else."

"Nonsense. Jolene, make room up there at the door!! This
here's that big purdy woman from Georgia who's tryin' to be
Doug's new girlfriend. Ain't no reason for her to get stuck out
here with the rest of us town folk."

Jolene was quick with a reply, "Then bring 'er on up, Chester.
We'll squeeze her through!"

Chester led me through the crowd as though he were my
personal bodyguard. And if someone had tried to attack me, I
think he coulda done some serious damage with that cane too.
Finally, he turned into a room where I could see just a corner
of a gray casket way up front. The crowd was maddening.

"Here, let's see if we can go up in this side door up front.
Follow me."

I followed obediently until we turned the corner and the casket
was right there. I saw Shannon and Dave in the front of the
receiving line. I knew the woman in the white suit was Aunt
Clarice because her hair was bright blonde but her skin was

darker than an African American's and her finger nails were painted a bright red. Then I saw Doug. Dark suit, light blue shirt, burgundy tie. His curly hair was wet with sweat. His face looked tired as though he were merely going through the motions. An older woman reached up to hug him and I could hear her say, "Your mama was a fine lady."

About that time Chester made his pronouncement, "Hey Doug! Your woman's here from Georgia. Don't worry. I took good care of 'er!"

Doug put his arm around the older woman and gave it a squeeze, then excused himself from the line. He locked eyes on mine, smiled really big, and walked at a fast clip. Not saying a word, he wrapped his arms around me and held on for a long time. His hands were rubbing my back and I even put my right hand on the back of his hair which I thought I would never do in public. It was so warm and crowded in the small room and he held me so close that I could smell his deodorant. Some kind of Irish happy place smell. Sheer bliss. Finally a young man from the back of the line said, "Well, what have we here? Looks like Doug's woman from Georgia!"

Doug ignored the comment completely. He finally let go and then just stared at me. "Carlie, I thought you wouldn't be here till after 9:00. I'm so happy to see you. But, I have to stand in this line for thirty more minutes. Visitation runs 'till 8:00 and from the looks of the line, more like 8:30."

"Don't worry about it. I wouldn't have even come in this way except Chester insisted. You don't have to babysit me. You should do what you need to do. I'll be glad to just wait in a chair over there."

"Would you stand in line with me, Carlie? I mean, are you too tired from your trip? If so, just say the word."

What? I never even expected this. The line was for relatives.

"Doug, I'm not too tired. But are you sure you wanna do this?"

"I'm sure. I'm tired of all the crying and the hugging and the 'Oh Doug, I'm so sorry' and 'You must be dreadfully sad.' They all mean well. They're wonderful people. But I'm weary of grieving right now. Introducing you will give me a pleasant distraction. Besides, every person looking at us right now knows who you are. The ones who don't know are asking the person in front of them at this very moment. Trust me. Within about forty-five seconds, they'll all know who you are, where you're from, your mother's maiden name, and who you voted for in the last national election."

He laughed a little, put his arm around my back and led me to where Dave and Shannon were standing. They introduced me to Aunt Clarice who yelled very loudly that she had a great aunt who was probably 5'11 but she still managed to get married and have children, so I shouldn't worry. The four of us smiled. Then Doug and I took our place in the line. I thought Chester was a character. But he was not alone.

"Mrs. Mabel, this is Carlie Ann Davidson from Georgia."

"Carlie, I have one question. How'd you snag this ol' rascal? The gals around here have been trying to get their hooks into him for years. Marcie Jenkins at the drug store did everything short of camping out in his front yard last year. She colored her hair, lost ten pounds, and made him a fruit cake for Christmas. He was unmovable. My husband, Jim, said, 'Doug must think he's better than the girls 'round here.'"

"Well, I'm sure it's not that, Mrs. Mabel. I'm just a small town girl myself. And we haven't known each other that long so I probably haven't snagged him yet. So, tell Marcie Jenkins she still has a shot...but I wouldn't recommend that she camp in his yard. Might try a more subtle approach."

Doug winked at me like he wanted to say, "You're funny and adorable...and Marcie Jenkins doesn't have a chance."

It was a pleasure to meet the members of his community one by one. They loved him. They respected him deeply. Now I saw clearly why he never moved to Nashville or Atlanta. It wouldn't be the same.

After meeting people for almost thirty minutes a beautiful young woman with dark hair and a green skin-tight knit dress came through the line and grabbed Doug around the neck. "Oh Doug, you know how sorry I am! I loved your mother. Your mother loved me too. I think that's why she invited me to the house that night. She was tired of you being so lonely!"

"Yeah, she was a good lady. Jessica, this is Carlie Ann Davidson. She's from Georgia." He put his arm around my back and pulled me to his side as if to say, "This is my woman." When Dr. Crusoe said we shouldn't tangle our lives with relationships, he was wrong.

I put out my hand, "It's so nice to meet you, Jessica."

"You too. Did Doug tell you we were on a date recently? It's really kind of a funny story. His sweet mom...may she rest in peace... invited me to the house for dinner and didn't tell him. But we had a great time. Oh, the laughs we had that night, didn't we, Doug? Yeah, ol' Doug here's a good guy. He never even mentioned he had a girlfriend that night. I guess he forgot to tell his mom too 'cause she thought he was like totally available."

"Yeah, he's a good guy alright." I was proud of my self-control and maturity. I was the bigger person. Literally and figuratively.

Doug spoke firmly, "I was still tryin' to win Carlie's heart at that point, Jessica. I wasn't sure I had much of a chance." He looked right at me, brought me in even closer and said, "I'm feelin' a little better about my chances lately though." He smiled broadly. Crooked teeth? What crooked teeth? His mouth was perfect.

Jessica looked disappointed but wasn't flying the white flag just yet. "Well, Doug, you know I'm always here for you. Anytime you need anything at all, you just call me. I'll be right over." Her long red fingernails patted his arm. "Carlie, how long does it take you to drive here? A few hours?"

"It's more like seven hours."

"Seven hours? Well Doug, bless your heart! I guess there'll be some lonely nights at your place, huh? You know you can always come down to the Wildwood in Jackson and have a drink with the gang. You know James Carter, works down at Co-Op. I think he graduated the year before you. He and Blake Donaldson go there all the time! Ranae and I go there almost every weekend. I get tired of watching the grass grow around here. There's always somethin' happenin' down in Jackson."

I kept thinking Jessica would eventually take a breath. Clearly, she had the lung capacity of a Navy Seal. "Last week they had a Dolly Parton look-a-like contest and $1 drafts. Do you know Jane Lawson? Well, she works at the electric company at the front window. The blonde with the well...anyway, she won the contest! Can you believe it? Two hundred fifty dollars cash and two free beers a week for a whole year! Ranae and I got blonde wigs and tried our luck but we didn't even place. But, several guys *did* ask for my number, so I guess Dolly Parton isn't everybody's type, right Doug? When things get back to normal, we'll have to get you out enjoyin' some night life!"

I wanted to say, "Yeah. You and Marcie Jenkins might wanna work together on that project. And even if you make a killer fruit cake, you haven't got a chance!" But I was proud of my smiling silence during Jessica's beer-laced monologue. Now I totally knew what Doug meant. She was a pretty girl, real pretty. But her demeanor was...I don't know, kind of flaky and immature. She was a talker, not a conversationalist. Her endless talking could get old. But she did bring up an interesting question. What was Doug's type?

"I'm not much on night life, but thanks anyway, Jessica." He immediately turned away from her and greeted his fourth grade teacher who swore up and down that she'd waited in line for more than an hour even though her sciatica was flaring up...and that his mom made the best deviled eggs in the county.

Doug had pushed Jessica away. She pushed herself on him and he pushed back. He was being kind but he was clearly not interested. Thank you, Doug. She wants you more than a bear wants honey but I'll not feel threatened by that. It is what it is. I'm almost sure I heard my grandma's voice, "Stand tall, Carlie. You're not selling anything."

Eventually the funeral home cleared out of everyone but close family. The funeral director pulled Doug aside to talk about tomorrow's plan. I was glad that Dave and Shannon invited me to have a seat on the front row where Shannon had taken off her shoes. They both looked like they'd been hit by a bus. A large bus.

Dave spoke first. "Wow! That was intense. I've never seen so many people in my life."

"How long have ya'll been standing there?"

"Carlie, can you believe the visitation was supposed to start at 5:00 and there was already a line around the sidewalk at 4:45? We've stood there off and on for more than three hours. I know Doug is exhausted."

"It means so much to him for you two to be here. You guys bring him a lotta comfort."

Dave smiled. "He's a great guy, Carlie. Really. I love to joke about his quirks, but he's solid and I'd trust him with my life."

"I get that. I haven't known him that long, but that's definitely my first impression. That he's not a user or a player. He seems genuine and, well, there's something incredibly attractive about that."

Shannon smiled from ear to ear. "He likes you, Carlie. Dave and I remember the first time he called to tell us about your e-mails and phone calls. I hadn't heard him talk like that in, well...forever. He hadn't been that happy in a long time. When we saw you two together, it was obvious that it was mutual. But this thing with his mom's death, it won't be easy."

"I know. I'm worried about him. Sad for him. That's why I'm glad he has you and Dave and the rest of the family."

Dave piped up, "Well, I suggest Shannon and I take our comfort home for the evening. How 'bout it, Shannon? Ready to soak your feet a while?"

"Sounds good. I shoulda never worn these stupid heels! Carlie, we'll visit some tomorrow afternoon if Doug agrees to share you. You're staying till Friday afternoon, right?"

"Yeah. I guess Doug will bring me to the house later. So, leave the light on for me and the door unlocked too unless you think there's gonna be a lot of crime and mayhem in the neighborhood tonight."

"Yeah. Mabel's ol' Blue might drag a dead squirrel into the yard. That's about as murderous as it's gonna get out there on Sandy Hill Road. We'll see ya later, Carlie." I knew they'd both hug me before they left. It's who they are.

Doug's face looked stressed as he talked to the funeral director and made notes on his I-phone. It must be hard being the only kid. All of it rested squarely on his shoulders. He looked like a man who was up to the challenge. He had taken off his suit coat and rolled up the sleeves on his blue oxford shirt. He needed love, yes. But he didn't need propping up. He was capable. A few relatives were still gathered around the casket and I realized I had not really looked at Doug's mom. I stood and walked up quietly. A chubby older woman whose slip was hanging out the back of her black skirt whispered in my ear, "I know you're Carlie, the girl from Georgia. Everybody's been talkin bout ya. I'm Doug's Aunt Charlotte and I jest want ya to know that she was a lot purdier than this when she was alive. Everybody knows that. She was one of those women who never had a hair out of place. Never went out without make-up. A real classy lady, my sister." She began to sob quietly.

I put my arm around her shoulder. "Mrs. Charlotte, I know she was a wonderful woman. She raised a fine son. And Doug, Doug is blessed with a sweet family to support him right now. I know he appreciates all of you. You've done so much for him the last few days."

In a failed attempt at whispering, Aunt Charlotte spoke into my ear, "I like you, Carlie from Georgia. And I don't care what Mrs. Mabel and Jolene said...I don't think you're too tall for him."

I hugged her and said quietly, "Thanks, neither do I."

Doug approached us and said, "Let's call it a night. Chester, there's some fried chicken in the break room. I've already got tons of food at the house. Ya think you could take that home with you?"

Chester and Mrs. Ida looked like they'd won the lottery.

"Charlene, Sandy Caldwell says her truck is still in the shop. Can you pick her up in time to rehearse the song before everyone gets here?"

"No problem."

"I want all of you to know, well, I couldn't have made it these last few days without..." He started wiping his eyes with a Kleenex. "I'll see all of ya in the mornin'." I could feel the tears running down my own face. In that moment, I saw a man who had lost both his parents in tragic circumstances. Heart-breaking.

Aunt Charlotte and Uncle Bart re-arranged chairs on their way out. Chester and Ida grabbed the box of chicken and a funeral employee let them take a two-liter of Dr. Pepper and a half-eaten box of graham crackers. Charlene told her two young boys to pick up toys. "I don't want some old person trippin' over Darth Vader tomorrow mornin'. That'd be scandalous." Bro. Dan put his arm around Doug and said, "She was always so proud of you, Doug. And with good reason. Don't ever doubt that for a moment."

I walked toward the door but noticed that Doug was standing in front of the casket alone. So I quietly slipped up behind him. "I don't know what you need right now. Should I walk outside and give you some time alone? Or should I stay with you? I'm fine either way. Just tell me."

He turned around, eyes red and filled with tears. Without saying a word, he held out his arms and I willingly embraced him. We didn't speak. He pulled me in so close I thought I would stop breathing. I rubbed his back and laid my head on his shoulder. His hair was wet with sweat. His left arm was around my waist and his right hand was gently touching my hair. When his face touched my right cheek, I felt his tears mix with my own. It was the most intimate I had ever been with a man. Ever. Sure, I kissed Dan a few times despite the garlic breath. Jim Jackson and I kissed my whole freshman year of college. He even groped me on several occasions. Last year I kissed Bill Henley, an old high school friend and my parents' insurance agent, at the New Year's Eve party and a few times after that. But I'd never had this. This was something completely different. He finally let go and put his arm around my shoulder and slowly led me to the door. "I'll miss her, Carlie."

"I know."

"Let's get a limeade."

"Absolutely."

Doug said I could leave my car at Sammy's for the night. He loaded my suitcase and hang-up clothes into his truck and drove to the local Sonic. One of his high school classmates recognized the truck and walked over to share condolences. Billy Caldwell was twenty-eight years old, same as Doug, but he looked forty. Hard livin'.

"I'm real sorry about your mom, Doug. Real sorry. They was good people, your mom and dad. I worked the farm out there a few summers when I was down and out and they was always good to me. Real good. Can't believe they're both gone."

"Thank you, Billy. Thank you. What are you doin' these days?"

"Nothin' worth talkin' 'bout, Doug. Nothin' worth talkin' 'bout. But hey, who's the purdy lady?"

"This is Carlie Ann Davidson. She's from Georgia. Carlie, this is my good friend, Billy. We've known each other our whole lives."

"Nice to meet you, Carlie. Is she a relative or your girlfriend?"

Yeah. Now there's a question. Thanks for asking that one, Billy Caldwell, and maybe you don't really look forty after all. Come to think of it, you don't look a day over twenty-five.

"She's my girlfriend."

"Yeah, well congratulations, Doug. You deserve a nice lady like your mama. Your mama, she could make some cornbread like I ain't never had in my life. Good people, yeah, good people."

"Thank you, Billy. We've always thought a lot of you too."

Billy spoke softly, "See ya, Buddy" and he walked back to an old green Lincoln Town Car that was covered with Bondo. It had seen better days, just like Billy.

I liked the gentle way Doug treated Billy. The way he said, "This is my good friend, Billy." A lot of people in Sharon would have been embarrassed to say that Billy Caldwell was their good friend. But Doug…Doug was gracious like that. He was different. And I was Doug's girlfriend. I liked that even better.

When we pulled into his mom's driveway later, everything looked exactly as he had described. An old white farmhouse in immaculate condition. Beautiful. I could have drawn a picture of it. We sat in the truck and drank the limeades. He loosened his tie. We laughed about the obsessive cleaning tendencies he inherited from his mom. I confessed the dried up toothpaste in my bathroom sink. We talked about the autopsy results. Drug overdose, pure and simple. He asked about my parents. I made fun of my over-achieving brothers. The truck clock read 12:18.

"Carlie, it's getting late and it's been a long day. I'll show you to your room. I'll come by in the morning at 9:30. Sleep as long as you can. But let me warn you, if Aunt Clarice gets up before you it's all over. She thinks she's talking but it's more like screaming. You'll hear about her bathroom habits, the bitter coffee, and whether or not her neighbor will remember to feed Fluffy three times a day and give him his blood pressure meds."

"I've been warned."

Doug came around and opened the truck door. He took my hand as though I needed help. I didn't. I think he knew that. We quietly opened the kitchen door and he pointed toward the hall. He walked into the first door on the right, turned on the light, and whispered, "Gosh, this brings back so many memories. Shannon changed the sheets today so you should be good to go. The bathroom is right next door."

The room was flawless. It looked like a boy's room, yes. But it was immaculate. Red and blue plaid bedspread. Bright blue walls. Baseball trophies everywhere. "You never told me about your illustrious baseball career."

Smiling, "Yeah, I could have been a pro, but I wanted to do bank loans."

"No tellin' how many great pro athletes we've lost to the rural banking business."

We both laughed but tried to be quiet.

"I better go. Rest well, Carlie. I'll see you in the morning. Thanks again for coming all this way." He hugged me one more time. We both lingered and he touched my hair again.

I touched the back of his head and said, "I'm so glad I came." I knew he wanted to kiss me. He knew I wanted to kiss him. But I knew he wouldn't. It's like when I knew that Jim Jackson would try to grope me after he'd had too many drinks at the Chi-O house. I knew Doug Jameson wouldn't kiss me while we were surrounded by his baseball trophies in his parents' house. I would have bet all the money I had ($167.29) that he wouldn't. Sadly, I would have won.

November 4

Doug was right. I woke to the sound of Aunt Clarice. "Shannon, where's the sugar bowl? Somebody's done something with the sugar bowl!"

The clock by the bed said 7:09. I was happy Aunt Clarice woke me up. I hated to be in a rush in the morning. The sun was coming through the window and shining right at a plaque that read, "Doug Jameson, Academic All-Star Student of the year, Sharon Middle School. 1995." He was an all-star alright. He had the trophies to prove it.

I walked toward the coffee pot and saw all three of the other house guests at the table drinking coffee and eating monkey bread. "Good Morning, Everyone."

Shannon spoke with a cringe, "Oh Carlie, I hope we didn't wake you!" She looked apologetic as if to say, "I know my screaming mother woke the dead, but I'll just say 'we' as though I was part of the sinister plan."

"Oh no. I wanted to get up. I hate to rush around in the mornings. Did all of you sleep well?"

This was Aunt Clarice's golden opportunity. "I slept horribly. God knows how my sister got a moment's rest on that horrible hard bed. Like sleepin' on a flat rock. Plus, there were dogs barkin' and an owl hootin'. I got a Charley Horse in my right leg at about 2:30. Couldn't even get to my dang pain pills 'cause I was in so much pain."

"I'm so sorry, Mrs. Clarice."

Dave was too positive to play Aunt Clarice's negative game. "Looks like it's gonna be a beautiful day. It's supposed to be

113

sunny and high sixties this mornin'. That always makes a funeral a little bit easier."

"Yeah. Will she be buried near here?"

Aunt Clarice was quick on the draw, "She'll be buried out at the cemetery behind Klondike Methodist Church where all James' people are buried. It's about five miles from the funeral home, kinda out in the country. All our people are buried out at Cottage Grove Community Cemetery. I don't know where Doug has a plot. Probably over at Klondike."

"Probably so. I'm gonna hop in the shower if no one needs this downstairs bathroom." I didn't particularly love talkin' about Doug's burial plot, especially at this time of the mornin', and when I still hadn't even kissed him.

By 9:20 I was dressed and sitting at the kitchen table, watching for him. It reminded me of that scene in a movie where the girl is lookin' out the window longingly, waiting for the man to ride up on a white horse or a navy blue F-150. Aunt Clarice was on the phone explaining loudly why Fluffy's food had to be cut with a plastic knife which kinda killed the movie atmosphere. Dave and Shannon were still getting ready.

He pulled in the drive at 9:28, stopping to check his hair in the rearview mirror before he got out of the truck. I knew he didn't care what Chester or Dave or Aunt Clarice thought about his hair. That moment was for me. He wore a solid dark suit, white shirt, gray striped tie. He looked rested and handsome and his hair seemed particularly curly. Had he put something on it? I could almost smell that Irish delicious smell on his body. The kitchen door kinda stuck and made a screeching sound when he opened it. I stood up and said a simple, "Good morning." Doug stared for a moment. As my high school cousin would say, "He was checkin' me out."

"Good morning, Carlie. You look beautiful. Really beautiful." He reached out to hug me and I was right about the smell. Delicious. Better than the smell of a cinnamon roll. I touched his hair again and hoped he didn't mind.

"Doug, would you like a cup of coffee or anything from this bountiful spread? There are even some deviled eggs in the refrigerator."

"Wow, the deviled eggs are tempting but seeing as how it's 9:30, I better not hit 'em too early in the day."

Some people would think it inappropriate to try to make Doug laugh on the day of his mother's funeral. But I knew it was a gift to him. The sadness and tears would come soon enough. There had to be moments of joy and happiness or he wouldn't survive.

"So, how does all this work today, Doug?"

"Visitation will be from 10 to 11. Funeral will be at 11. Then to the cemetery for burial. The ladies of the church are making lunch for us in the church basement. Then it's over."

"I'm sorry. I know none of this will be easy."

"Thanks. If you're ready, let's go. Are Dave and Shannon comin' now?"

"They said to tell you they'll be there by 10."

"Okay."

We pulled into the funeral home at 9:45 and the parking lot was already full. He sighed.

"Doug, this community... they really love you. I mean, they loved your mom and dad, but they're here today for you. You've captured their hearts....well, you and your mom's deviled eggs."

He laughed out loud. "Yeah, if it weren't for those dad blame eggs, visitation could have been done in thirty minutes."

He came around and opened the truck door on my side and just stood there for a moment looking at me. I laid my hand on his shoulder and said, "Let me help you. Tell me what I need to do."

"Just stay with me today."

"Doug, it's not that I mind but I'm not sure 'a friend from Georgia' should really be on the front row with the relatives. We haven't known each other that long. I mean, this is just our second date. And no offense, but we're at your mom's funeral.

"Yeah, I'm a real romantic, aren't I? Technically though, this is our fifth date. Don't cross me on this, Carlie. I've given it a lot of thought. I took you to Cracker Barrel for fried eggs and biscuits for the first date. Then there was that late afternoon latte at Starbucks which counts as number two. Third date we ate lasagna and Dave told you I was a neat freak...which you already knew...and about how I never let my food touch. Fourth date you stood with me in a funeral line while Aunt Clarice yelled about your height and Aunt Charlotte blew her nose into Uncle Bart's shirt sleeve. Okay. The real question is not, 'Will you stay with me?' The real question is, 'Why are you still here?'"

116

"Good point, Doug. Come to think of it, unless my car was stolen last night in front of Sammy's Sandwich Emporium, I should make a run for it."

He reached out and grabbed me by both arms. "Just try."

"Don't underestimate me. I'm faster than you think." I leaned into him and he helped me out of the truck and held me for a minute.

While his arms were still wrapped around me he whispered, "You're right, Carlie. We hardly know each other. But I want to know you better. Does that count for anything?"

"Good enough."

We walked into the back entrance of the funeral home. The funeral director was there looking very sympathetic. I wondered if he ever got tired of looking sympathetic, if he were ever standing there thinking about football scores or burritos from Taco Bell. I'm sure he was.

The room was already three-fourths full. Doug stood by the casket for a moment and wiped his eyes. I felt cautious about showing any physical affection as half the town was staring at us. I just stood next to him quietly. An older woman wearing a purple double knit suit and carrying a red handbag approached him and held his hand while they both stared at his mom's lifeless body.

"Doug, your mama told me somethin' one time down at the electric company. I came in to pay my bill and we were jest chit chattin'. I asked about how you were doin', whether you liked your job at the bank. She said, 'Karen, Doug's doing so well at the bank. He's good with people, y'know. God gave us a gift with that one. James and I always said that we didn't deserve him.'" The lady in purple kissed his cheek. It was sweet.

Doug started crying in a way I hadn't seen yet, deeper, in more pain. There was finality to all of it today. I began to cry too and took a seat on the front row. Eventually the woman walked back to her seat and he sat down next to me. Most of the people in the room had already gone through visitation last night so he might get a bit of a break this morning. His eyes were still red and he just stared down at the red carpet. He gently picked up my right hand and held it with both of his. This wasn't exactly how I had pictured it. The first time Doug held my hand we were looking at his mama's dead body.

THE FUNERAL

I liked Brother Dan. He didn't speak in *preacher talk*. He spoke like Dave, in real conversational style. He talked about God's love and about how Susan always brought lasagna to church potlucks and how much everyone loved her. He introduced Aunt Charlotte who told about the time she and Susan nearly fell out of the back of Uncle Charlie's chicken truck. And how chicken poo got all over Susan's hair and how she declared at that moment that she would never ever live on a farm…and how five years later she fell in love with James and spent the rest of her life on one. That's when Aunt Charlotte started crying and took her seat. Then came the shock. Brother Dan smiled at Doug and said, "Susan's beloved son, Doug, will now share a few words." I had no idea. Doug stood quickly, straightened the back of his suit coat, and approached the front but didn't stand behind the podium. With no notes in hand, and without one sound coming from the over-crowded room, he looked as though he were comfortable being there.

"Thank you, Brother Dan, and all the rest of you too. I don't know what I would have done the last few days if it hadn't been for all of you, your kind words, your presence here at the funeral home, and the food? Gosh, the food has just been overwhelming. I'm incredibly blessed to live in this community. I've always known that, but I know it even more today. I loved my mom. I'm sure you all know that. She wasn't perfect, but she cared deeply. She never gave up on me. She took good care of me and Dad. She took good care of a lot of you too. I never doubted that she loved me, never for one moment. And that's a gift. I owe her a debt of gratitude. I've always appreciated people who tell the truth and I've no reason to skirt around the truth today. In a moment of incredible weakness, Mama took her own life Saturday night. I can't explain it. I wasn't prepared for it. I tried to think it was anything but what it was. There's a lot of power and freedom in telling the truth. So the last few days I've had to ponder what all that means. Is taking a life a sin? It is. Any of you who've read the Bible know that. It's not that complicated. But if you have read the Bible you also know there's hope and comfort for my mom and for me. I'm thankful for the grace and mercy of God that comes through Christ. I hope I've always been thankful for it. But today I especially am. Because of such a gift, this life is not the end. Thank you all for coming."

That's the moment I fell in love with Doug Jameson. A few days after he put up shelving in his mom's shed and made coffee in her kitchen, she selfishly took her own life. She wouldn't be at his wedding or ever know his children. She left him. It was wrong. But he forgave her. He forgave her because he understood human weakness and sin. He forgave her because he had been forgiven. I fell in love with Doug Jameson on our fifth date at his mama's funeral. And I'd never even kissed him.

119

Absolute silence filled the funeral room. No one was looking through her purse for gum. No old men were coughing into a monogrammed hanky. Charlene's kids were even quiet. Doug sat down beside me and grabbed my hand again. When Sandy Caldwell started singing "Great is Thy Faithfulness" there wasn't a dry eye in the house. Brother Dan closed in prayer. The funeral director closed the lid on the casket. It was over.

The pall bearers carried the casket up the aisle slowly. Aunt Clarice and Aunt Charlotte stepped out next. Then Uncle Bart and Dave and Shannon. Doug put his arm around my waist and we joined them. But halfway up the aisle Doug was startled, the way a person reacts when a deer jumps in front of the car. I looked to the left and that's when I saw her. Sandra. I knew it was her. The beautiful red hair. Sophisticated tan suit. Expensive shoes. Big confident smile. Tell me the San Diego dentist is here somewhere. Lord, please provide a dentist. I don't think I had ever prayed that prayer before.

CHAPTER EIGHT: Along Comes Sandra

CARLIE

As we rode to the cemetery, I determined I wasn't going to mention the Sandra sighting. After all, he said she was engaged to a dentist, that he didn't love her the way a man should, that he didn't want to live in California, and that he definitely didn't want to live in a woman's shadow.

"Doug, what you said in there… it was beautiful. It was spoken so simply and with such truthfulness. I don't know how you did it but it was the most moving part of the service."

"Thanks. I told Brother Dan I wanted to say a few words. I just wanted to clear the air, try to put some perspective on it all. I believe everything I said in there. I mean, about forgiveness and the power of the truth."

"I know. I don't think anyone in that room had doubts about your sincerity." Oh, and I love you. I love you, Doug Jameson. The way I see it a man who can forgive all that…can forgive a woman for leaving globs of toothpaste in the sink. I'm yours and I want to marry you and sleep with you and cook breakfast for you and love you for the rest of my life. No, of course I didn't say any of that last part. I talked about the fact that the weather was perfect, that Aunt Charlotte's story was touching, that I wished I had known his mom and dad.

The cemetery service was short. Yes, of course, I checked the crowd for Sandra. She was near the back with an older couple. I bet they're her parents. No young good-lookin' dentist in sight. I dreaded what would come when the final "Amen" had been spoken.

Brother Dan said loudly, "Everyone is invited to come to the church basement for a meal. The women have worked real hard on this and we all appreciate it."

Jim Smith from the hardware store patted Doug on the back and lit a Marlboro cigarette. Jessica came forward and explained to both of us that the huge spray of orange gladiolas was from the folks at the Electric Company. Only she gave a lot more detail than I'm giving. Then came Sandra. Doug could see her coming and I couldn't tell what was running through his mind. I didn't wanna know. Of course, she hugged him but not in a tacky Jessica-like way. No. She hugged him like someone who knew him well. Like someone who had known him all his life.

"Carlie, I'd like you to meet Sandra Miller. Sandra, this is Carlie Davidson. She lives in Commerce, Georgia."

"Nice to meet you, Sandra." Gosh, she is ridiculously pretty and sophisticated to boot. She's not at all skinny though. He must like curves. Her teeth are perfectly straight. Clearly, her parents sprung for the braces.

"Nice to meet you too, Carlie. Doug, I'm so sorry about your mom. She was a great lady. She was always so supportive. She'll be missed in this community. My parents are broken up by it all. But Dad's not feelin' too well so Mom took him back to the house. I'm sorry we weren't able to be at visitation last night."

"Oh, I'm sorry about your dad. I'd heard he was having some heart trouble."

"Yeah, he's goin' to Vanderbilt this week. It's been a hard thing but we all feel pretty hopeful."

"So how is it that our most famous California resident has returned to her humble hometown? I bet it's been a year since I've seen you."

"Can you believe I finally finished the program? It felt like it took forever. But I got the Ph.D. in August so that's Dr. Miller to you, Doug Jameson." She wasn't saying it in a proud or haughty way. She was funny and I liked her. I mean, I would have liked her if her teeth weren't perfect, and if she weren't looking at Doug like she wanted to marry him.

"Finally? Sandra, you're twenty-five. I don't think you're running behind on life's fine-tuned schedule, at least not yet. Oh, and Mom had said you were engaged, a dentist in San Diego?"

"Not anymore. That went south." She looked down at the ground and bit her lip as though she were embarrassed. "The plan was for me to graduate in August, get a job, get married in December and live happily ever after, right? Last month he decided he'd live the happily-ever-after part with a gal who recently got her wisdom teeth removed. I crashed. I'm talkin' emotional break-down. But I'm okay now. Mom and Dad suggested I come back home for a while. Get grounded. Do the job search from here. I've been here a week and it's workin' out so far. There are definitely some prospects on the horizon."

Uh-oh. Perhaps I shouldn't have fallen in love a few minutes ago. Now that the dentist has bitten the dust, I fear that Doug Jameson is a prospect on her horizon. Gosh, Sandra, stand in line behind Jessica and Marcie. What is it about this guy? No wonder his parents didn't pay for braces. Clearly unnecessary.

"I hope you'll join us for lunch back at the church, Sandra."

"Sure. I told Mom to just take Dad home and I would get a ride with someone."

"Oh, you can ride with Dave and Shannon. You remember my cousin, Shannon?"

Okay. If I weren't in love before, I definitely am now. Ten points for Doug Jameson for not inviting his pretty redheaded former girlfriend to ride in the truck with us on our fifth date coming home from the cemetery where his mom was just buried. Try saying that five times fast.

"Uh, yeah, I remember Shannon."

"She and Dave are right over here. Shannon! Can Sandra ride with you guys to the church?"

"Sure! We'll meet her at the car."

"Sandra, looks like your Nissan Altima awaits."

I could see the disappointment all over her face. I felt for her. I had been there many times. Like all those times Jim Flanders was goin' on and on about whether I liked his tie. But the handwriting was on the wall. Jim Flanders wasn't interested in me. Doug had just written something like that on Sandra's wall or at least I thought he did. I couldn't be sure.

He opened the truck door for me and held my hand while I slid onto the flawlessly clean gray upholstery.

When he got into the truck he just put his hands on the wheel, took a deep breath and said, "Whew! It's been quite a day."

"It all went well, Doug. I mean, I know it was terrible and sad and tragic. But the whole funeral and burial, it was beautiful. I can't think of how it could have been any more meaningful."

"Yeah. Brother Dan did a great job. But I'm glad it's all over."

He started the truck and backed out of the grassy area where we were parked.

And at that moment I made a decision. I wasn't going to be like some needy little puppy who'd been dropped on the side of the road, crying out for love and protection. I wasn't going to say something like, "Sandra sure is pretty. What was it like to see her standing there?" or "Doug, should I be worried about the fact that Sandra's living in Sharon again?" I wasn't going to say, "That's too bad about Sandra getting her heart broken by the dentist in San Diego." No. I was gonna leave it alone. I was gonna be Carlie Ann Davidson and let it all fall where it was destined to fall. The hardest part? The hardest part was not looking into his eyes and saying, "Doug, pick me."

Only about forty people came to the church basement for the meal. I knew it would be that way. Just relatives and close family friends. Most people left the cemetery and went home for lunch or went through the drive-thru at Dairy Barn. That's kind of the unwritten rule in small southern towns. The after-funeral meal was always when people took off their shoes or their ties. It was the time when out-of-town relatives could re-connect and children could run around unsupervised while old people told stories about hog killin' or walkin' to school in the snow. Doug introduced me to his great Uncle Charlie who looked to be about one hundred. Seated in a metal chair, he was wearing a tan leisure suit and combing his hair with a comb that said "Vote Dan Smith for School Board." I had a feeling Dan Smith hadn't run for school board in several decades.

"Uncle Charlie, this is Carlie Ann. She's from Georgia."

"Georgia? I spent some time at Fort Benning, but that was long 'fore you was born. So you like our Doug here, do ya?"

"I do like him, Sir."

"Yeah, I reckon you could do worse. Reckon so."

Doug spoke up, "Uncle Charlie, just stay right here and Carlie and I will get you a plate."

"No need. Charlotte's done gettin' me fixed up. Promised me some of Mabel's pecan pie if Chester ain't got to it first." We all smiled as if to say, "Chester's not all that bad."

Doug and I walked toward the buffet table which was overloaded with everything that had ever been on the cover of a church cookbook. There wasn't a can of cream soup left on a grocery store shelf within ten miles. Broccoli casserole. Chicken spaghetti. Tater tot casserole. Hash brown casserole. Every kind of vegetable which could be cooked to death and then combined with a stick of butter and a can of soup was present and accounted for. Doug handed me a Chinet plate and said, "Dig in, Carlie."

I wasn't hungry. A shocking revelation for someone who could eat a whole lemon meringue pie and still walk straight. My stomach was in knots. I kept glancing over toward Sandra who was now talking to Dave and Shannon and Doug's fourth grade teacher. I wondered what Dave and Shannon thought. In the car, had Sandra asked about me? Had she said, "Doug's girlfriend sure seems nice." or "How long has Doug been

126

dating the tall girl from Georgia?" Did Dave and Shannon think Sandra was funny and smart and perfect for him? In Pictionary, could Sandra Miller have drawn a triceratops that wouldn't have made Doug yell out, "chocolate chip cookie!"? Yeah. She could have. God and everybody in the room knew that Sandra Miller wasn't going to take second place. Her triceratops would have been perfect. Just like her.

"Doug, believe it or not, I'm not that hungry. I guess it was that blueberry muffin I had for breakfast. Pretty rich."

"But it's almost 1:00, Carlie. There are some plain ham sandwiches over there. Does that sound good?"

"Yeah. That's great."

I put the ham sandwich on my plate along with some coleslaw and a cluster of grapes. Doug loaded his plate with all the cheesy casseroles, two yeast rolls, a piece of chocolate cake, and a lemon square. He didn't seem nervous at all. I guess he wasn't worried about Sandra's keen ability to draw a triceratops. He took off his suit coat and when he did I wanted to hug him right there in front of everybody. But of course, I didn't. He took off his tie, unbuttoned his shirt, and got comfortable. I wanted to watch him do that every night. Not the tie part because savvy rural bankers don't wear ties. Everybody knows that.

We sat at a long table across from Aunt Charlotte and Uncle Bart. It didn't seem like Doug was looking for Sandra. I mean, he didn't glance around the room nervously. He didn't seem distracted by her presence. He was determined to tell me the origin of everything on his plate. "Mabel always makes the tater tot casserole. Mrs. Ida brought this broccoli casserole. That coleslaw is homemade by Jim Smith's mother and she's ninety-four. She still works at the hardware store three days a week.   Imogene Simmons makes these homemade rolls that would make you slap your grandma."

I was listening and smiling but I was hurting a little bit inside. He had kissed Sandra Miller. Lots and lots of times he had kissed her. He may have done a lot more than that. How would I know? When he saw her picture in the newspaper years ago it had made him want her. I knew what *want her* meant. He was a man. She was a woman. He told her he would wait for her. He told her that he loved her. And now she was standing next to a sign that said, "Jesus loves fifth graders" and he hardly seemed to notice.

Dave and Shannon went through the line with Sandra. I knew they would. It spoke more of their kindness and character than it did of Sandra. She was there alone and they would take it upon themselves to host her, make her feel comfortable, love her. When they approached our table, I wondered how it was all gonna go down. I was right across from Uncle Bart. Doug was across from Aunt Charlotte but no one was sitting on the other side of him. Dave quickly sat down next to Doug. I took it as a personal favor. Shannon sat next to Dave. Sandra sat across from them right next to Aunt Charlotte. Here we all were. Uncle Bart and Aunt Charlotte had been married forty-two years. Dave and Shannon had been married three years. Doug and Sandra thought they were in love once. They kissed a lot and made big plans at the Steak n Shake in Jackson. And me? I was on a fifth date with someone I hardly knew. Someone I loved.

Charlotte grabbed Sandra's hand and spoke loudly, "It's so good to see you, Child. You're as purdy as you ever were. And it was good to see yer Daddy out too. I hear he's doin' a little better these days."

"Yeah, we hope so. Did ya hear, Mrs. Charlotte? I'm back in town now. I got my schooling done and I'm looking for a job. Most of my job hunting can be done on the internet and through some of my colleagues back in California."

"Well, bless yer heart! Welcome back to Sharon, Baby. I know yer Mama and Daddy is proud as punch! And I bet yer a big help to yer Mama right now. It's a big job takin' care of somebody that feels poorly. Yes, it is."

"I'm glad to be back. When I left, I guess I was young and impulsive and I thought I had the world by the tail. I'm older now and things have changed. Maybe I appreciate Sharon a little more…and the people here especially." She looked right at Doug when she said it.

Sometimes a thirty-two-year-old woman just knows things. I knew Doug's coffee cups were perfectly organized in his kitchen cabinet and I knew what Sandra Miller's comment meant. It wasn't really the town of Sharon that she appreciated. It wasn't the fact that there's only one policeman in town and he hangs out at the barber shop talkin' about high school football. She didn't appreciate the fact that Jim Miller's mom could still make delicious coleslaw and keep the books down at the hardware store even though she was ninety-four. She wasn't excited about the new convenience store opening up out on the bypass and the fact that they were gonna sell take-out pizza. No. Sandra Miller appreciated the town of Sharon because there was a kind, solid, good lookin' banker here who had once loved her. Time had passed and she hoped he could love her again.

I stopped eating. I tried to smile. But it was the same smile that movie stars plaster on their faces when they don't win the Oscar. The TV camera focuses in on them and they smile real big as if to say, "It was a privilege just to be nominated. I'm glad Meryl Streep won for the millionth time in a row. I'm happy for her. Really I am."

I think Shannon knew I felt like I'd been beaten out of an Oscar by Meryl Streep. She looked behind Dave's head, caught my eye, and smiled as if to say, "It's okay, Carlie. God is in control."

Lunch seemed to take forever. People were hugging Doug and patting him on the back. Others were getting re-acquainted with Sandra. How did she like living in a small town again? How was her daddy? What did it feel like to be Dr. Miller? I was pleasant and tried to make small talk when called upon. But I was busy pondering. I remembered that afternoon I almost threw Doug's business card in the trash...but I didn't. I remembered Mr. Rockford's kind words as he checked out two vanilla cake mixes and a roll of paper towels. I remembered my grandma saying that someday a man would sweep me off my feet and I shouldn't settle for less than the best. All those experiences had led to this moment. So, why did I want to go to a corner and cry? Because I'm a girl. It made me think of that time when Julia Roberts looked at Hugh Grant in "Notting Hill" and said, "I'm just a girl...standing in front of a boy...asking him to love her." Yeah. Not an easy moment. Ask Julia Roberts. She was crying when she said it.

Doug touched my arm and it brought me back to reality. "Carlie, I think they're getting ready to start cleaning up. You wanna get out of here and go for a drive?"

"That sounds great."

I stood and hugged Dave and Shannon good-bye. Shannon whispered in my ear, "We'll talk later at the house. Have fun with Doug, Carlie. Don't be afraid." Shannon was the sister I had always begged my mom and dad to have.

I tried to sound friendly and wonderful. "Sandra, it was a pleasure to meet you. And congrats on the Ph.D. I know that wasn't easy and it sounds like you have a bright future ahead of you."

"Thanks, Carlie. You too. I don't think I even asked about your job. Are you in banking too? Is that how you guys met?"

"No. It's kind of a funny story. You may know his great aunt and uncle, Stanley and Beth Rockford. They were here today. They know me from back home in Commerce and they gave me his business card and suggested I contact him. I did. He wrote back and I don't know…I guess we just clicked."

"I can see why. Doug is a great guy. One in a million. I'm sure you know that by now. Enjoy your time here in the metroplex of Sharon. Will you be staying a while?"

"Just till tomorrow afternoon."

"Well, it was good to meet you, Carlie. Doug, I guess we'll be seeing each other around town. Or as Grandma used to say, 'See you at the dollar store!' Carlie, all the folks around here joke about how they spend most of their time and money at a little place called Dollar General Store. Small town livin' at its best, y'know."

Doug looked at me and smiled, "Yeah, I'll definitely see you at the dollar store, Sandra. I've taken a great interest in that place lately. Thanks for comin' to the funeral and give your parents my best. Mom always thought a lot of you and your mom and dad. You know that."

"Well, she was a great lady. She'll be missed, Doug."

I think Doug could sense that my demeanor had changed since this morning when he walked into the farmhouse. He helped me into the truck and asked, "Carlie, are you feelin' okay? I know it's been kind of a stressful and tiring day."

"Doug, look at you. You're like the nicest person on the planet. Your mom died. Today was her funeral and her burial and you're worried about *me* having a stressful day. You're the one who has been under stress."

"Actually, I feel pretty good right now. Kind of like the calm after the storm. Have you ever been to Reelfoot Lake?"

"I haven't. Are you seriously thinkin' about drivin' to the lake?"

"On a day like this? Absolutely. Are you okay in those clothes or would you rather go to the house and change?"

"I'm fine. These shoes are comfortable…uh…unless you're talkin' about goin' mud boggin' or somethin'."

"I hardly ever take a girl mud boggin' on the sixth date."

"Oh, is our fifth date already over?"

"Yeah, it was kind of a stressful situation, don't ya think? Maybe it's best that we move on to the sixth date." I knew what Doug meant by *stressful situation*. The whole town had come out to hug him because his mom had taken her own life. He had spoken at the funeral, cried a lot, visited with every person he knew, grieved the death of his last parent. That's what he meant. And I felt bad for him. Who wouldn't? Why was it stressful for me? Only one reason. Because in the middle of my falling-in-love moment Sandra Miller had shown up without her dentist.

The weather was perfection. Sunny and 68 degrees. Cool enough for a jacket but not so cold that we wanted to go inside. We walked around parts of the massive lake and Doug explained about the famous eagles' nests that were everywhere. We stopped on a deck that went out on the water.

"When I was a boy my dad brought me here and we went on an eagle tour. That's where the park folks take you around and show you where the nests are and where the eagles can be spotted. We rode on a boat later. I was mesmerized. I still love being here. It's killin' me not to throw a line in the water."

"Well, don't let me be the death of you. If you have anything in the truck, fish away."

"No, I'm good. Does your family like to fish? Would your dad or mom like a place like this?"

"My dad took us fishin' a few times. Mom wouldn't have gone for it though. She's a little too *clean* for fishin'. She's kinda prim and proper."

"Are you prim and proper?"

"I already told you there's toothpaste in my bathroom sink. So, if you mean hyper-clean and organized, no. But I do like having company and cooking for people. I like hospitality and decorating and making people feel at home. But Mom...well, Mom cares whether people think she's...I don't know...whether she's acceptable. I know I'm acceptable. I know I'm acceptable for the very reasons you talked about today at the funeral. I want to be more focused on others. I'm not the center of the universe and I wouldn't want to be."

"Good philosophy."

He took my hand and we walked around the other side of the lake. I felt comfortable next to him. That's saying a lot. I feel kind of clumsy around men sometimes. They feel clumsy around me sometimes too. It's like they don't know what to do with a woman who's as tall as they are. Doug had no such insecurities.

"Doug, do you wanna talk about your parents? I mean, would that help?"

"Truthfully, right now, I wanna just forget the last few days. I wanna pretend it's the way it should be. I wanna just sit on that bench over there with a beautiful woman and enjoy watching the water."

"Gosh, that sounds great. I mean, I wanna help you out and all, but where would I find a beautiful woman on such late notice? It looks like we're the only ones around." I pretended to be searching the park and then I started laughing quietly. He smiled and grabbed me by the arm and held me, just like in the movies. Only this time it was a hundred times better. It was real. Doug Jameson was wearing a white dress shirt and smelling like sweaty Irish bliss when he looked into my eyes, put his hands on the back of my head and kissed me for the first time. It was our sixth date. And it wasn't at a funeral. It was at a beautiful park surrounded by eagles' nests. And everyone knows eagles mate for life.

We sat on the bench at Reelfoot until dusk. Talking. Kissing. Sometimes just sitting quietly hand in hand.

At one point, Doug turned away from me and stared out toward the lake. He placed both hands on his knees the way a basketball coach does when the game is tied and his star player is taking the last free throw shot with only seconds left on the clock. "Carlie, there's a question I've been meaning to ask."

"Ask away."

"When Uncle Stanley gave you my card at the dollar store that day, well, you must have been suspect, right? I mean, it must have sounded like I was pretty desperate. Why did you write to me?"

"That's a great question. And yeah, it did kind of make you seem like a loser." I hoped my smile would make that information easier for him to process. "Truth is, I didn't plan on writing to you, Doug. I didn't. I was nice to Mr. Rockford and I told him I appreciated him for thinking of me. But yeah, my plan was to just throw the card in the trash. "

"I can't blame ya. I probably would have felt the same way. People around here have tried to fix me up with their cousins or their old college roommates for years. I've gotten pretty suspicious. A guy at the bank came right up to me once and said, 'Doug, my cousin is comin' to town this weekend and you've just gotta meet her and hey man, she could be the one. She was crowned Corn Queen of Northeast Arkansas in 2009. She's a lawyer, graduated with honors from Memphis State and she raises German Shepherds on the side.' I'm serious, Carlie. He said that. Out loud. I don't know... like I'd been waiting all my life for someone who raised German Shepherds. All the information started running together. Too complicated. Plus, I never really had the goal of marrying a corn queen dog breeding attorney. At least I didn't think I did."

135

"Are you kidding? You should totally change your priorities, Doug. I mean, all the corn on the cob you could eat for life? Free legal services and a puppy to boot? That would be like strikin' it rich!"

"Wow, you're right. Come to think of it, I should have gone out with Shelly Simpson's cousin who was the Grand Marshall of the Pickle Parade in Dyersburg. She's a notary public, an opera singer, and a referee for kids' basketball games. Plus, I coulda gotten some free pickles outta that deal and there's just nothin' like a bread n butter pickle on a grilled hamburger." Doug smiled and put his arm around me again. But I could tell he was still waiting for my answer.

"Okay. So Mr. Rockford gave me your card and I just put it in my pocket. A few days later I saw where I had propped it up on my dresser at home. And well…no, you'll think it's silly."

"I won't."

"When I decided to write that note, I wasn't thinkin' about you at all, Doug. I could have never known that you'd be this great guy and that things would turn out like this. Truthfully, I was thinkin' about the Rockfords. Especially Mr. Rockford."

Doug started laughing. "You have a crush on Uncle Stanley? No offense, but that's weird, Carlie."

"Ha ha. Here's the deal. I've known Mr. Rockford my whole life." Doug brushed a strand of hair away from my forehead and stared into my eyes while I spoke. "People in Commerce, they trust him, Doug. They do. He's worthy of that trust and he's kind and hard working and I don't know…solid. I've watched the way he treats Mrs. Rockford, like they're on a date and he's hoping she'll like him and want to go out with him again. And she does. She does like him. She loves him. Even after all these years, she still looks at him like she won the prize or something. And he looks at her, well, like she's the only woman in the room... or in the world for that matter. So, that's why I wrote to you that day, Doug. Out of respect for the two of them. Maybe deep down I believed they knew something about life that I didn't. Something I wanted to know."

Doug turned his head slightly to look out at the lake. Once again he took the nervous coach position with his fingers tapping lightly on his knees. I could tell he was thinking something he couldn't say out loud. So was I. For at least two minutes we sat in silence on the bench but it wasn't uncomfortable silence. No. It was sweet silence.

He kissed me gently before he spoke. "That's a beautiful story, but we have a problem, Carlie."

"Oh no. What's our problem?"

"There are too many fish still swimmin' around in that lake."

"Gosh, Doug, that's shameful. You could have caught a whole mess of 'em if you hadn't been wasting all afternoon with me."

"It wasn't a wasted afternoon. Thank you, Carlie. Thank you for making today more bearable. Thank you for being here with me. Thank you for sending that e-mail. But as much as I'm enjoying the quiet, we better get back to the chaos. I need to make an appearance at the house. Aunt Clarice is flying out early tomorrow and she asked if I'd be back before she went to bed. I promised I would, but I have an even more important deadline. She takes her teeth out at around 9:00, says they start to make her gums swell. Yeah, I think we both wanna hit the road now, don't you?"

We both laughed. Doug wanted to kiss me and sit with me on a bench at Reelfoot Lake. Yes. But he also knew that we weren't the center of the universe. We had to operate in the real world, a world that involved other people and responsibilities. I liked that. Not just a childish fling. Adulthood.

As we approached the Sharon city limits, Doug said in a serious tone, "Carlie, I wish you didn't have to go back tomorrow. I wish you could stay."

"Me too."

I had a feeling the old farmhouse would have several cars in the driveway. I was right.

"Okay. Time to take inventory. Looks like Dave and Shannon, Chester, Aunt Charlotte and Uncle Bart, Uncle Stanley and Aunt Beth, Ralph and Charlene. That's it. Good. I was thinkin' there might even be more folks. This won't be too bad."

When he opened my door, he reached for my hand and I started walking toward the house. But he pulled me back to the truck.

"Carlie, this'll be our last moment of privacy before all the family craziness begins. I just wanna thank you again for coming all this way, for being with me through the visitation, the funeral, for being kind to my crazy relatives, and for not yelling at Aunt Clarice when she was…well, being Aunt Clarice."

"Are you kidding? Doug, this has been an amazing time. I mean, I'm horribly sad about the circumstances, but your family…well, they're wonderful. Dave and Shannon are like my new best friends. I'm keeping them even if you never wanna see me again. Your aunts and uncles and friends are funny and enjoyable and real. 'Salt of the earth' my grandma would say."

"They're pretty salty sometimes. I'll agree with ya there." He held me close and I could feel him breathing.

Porch light flickered on. "Doug! Carlie! Hey Everyone, they're back! Honey, come on in. We've got food fixed if you're hungry!" Adulthood had arrived and hit us squarely between the eyes.

"Thanks, Aunt Charlotte! We'll be there in a minute!"

He grabbed my hands and said quietly, "When can we see each other again? I'll come to Commerce or do whatever I need to do to make it work."

"I will too. It hurts me to think of leaving tomorrow. We can talk about a plan in the morning."

"Okay. I'll be by around 8:30 and we can spend the morning together. I have to get a bunch of paper work started at the lawyer's office and the accountant's place tomorrow afternoon 'cause I'm planning to go back to work on Monday."

"I need to leave by noon anyway."

"I'm gonna miss you, Carlie."

"I'm gonna miss you too. But we still have tomorrow morning, right? Oh and Doug, we better get in the house. It's a quarter 'till 9."

He held my hand securely as we walked into the house. Something had changed. I was no longer *that girl from Georgia.* I was Doug Jameson's girlfriend. Doug Jameson was my boyfriend. Marvelous.

The scene in the farmhouse was priceless though not exactly Norman Rockwell-ish. Mr. Rockford had his arm around Mrs. Rockford and they were sitting so close to each other on the cream-colored couch that my old band director would have separated them for *public displays of affection.* They both sipped iced tea. Chester was eating a chicken leg at the dining room table and telling Ralph about the time he put a snake in Mrs. Simpson's school drawer and how she chased him out of the school house with a coal shovel.

Despite the chatter, Uncle Bart had fallen asleep in the green recliner with a "Sports Afield" magazine lying on his chest. Charlene and Aunt Charlotte were working in the kitchen and explaining to Doug how he could eat for a week if he'd use freezer bags appropriately. Doug smiled even though I knew he had no plans for using freezer bags 'cause the food had sat out all day. A man whose coffee mugs are organized according to height doesn't eat food that has been sitting out all day. I knew that. They'd known him his whole life and hadn't yet figured it out. I could hear Dave and Shannon talking in the little alcove just off the laundry room. Doug and I walked in to find them seated at the little card table.

Doug was smiling from ear to ear and still holding my hand when he asked, "What's the game tonight?"

Dave piped up, "Texas Hold 'Em."

Dave and Shannon were looking at their cards but another set of cards was lying face down on the table. I heard the bathroom door open but wasn't prepared for what came next.

"Hey Guys! Trust me. I'm not stalking you. Dave and Shannon asked me to come over for a while. I didn't have anything to do so I took them up on their offer, but really I was getting ready to leave. I mean, it's almost nine. I need to get home." Sandra was no longer in the sophisticated tan suit with her hair pulled back. She was in jeans and a white peasant top. With her hair down, she looked even more beautiful than at the funeral.

"What do you mean you're getting ready to leave?! We're in the middle of a heated game here, Dr. Miller. Besides, we're your ride home, remember? Stop being a wimpy card player and give us your best shot." At that moment I wished Dave weren't so competitive.

"Okay. But I'm just staying through one more hand." Sandra took her seat at the table and picked up her cards even though she was clearly uncomfortable. Not really. Who am I kidding? She wasn't uncomfortable at all. She could have gone home a long time ago. She wasn't playing cards. She was waiting for Doug Jameson to come home from the lake where he'd been kissing his Georgia girlfriend.

Shannon looked at me as if to say, Hey, we invited her because we're friendly and wonderful but we didn't really expect her to come. That's what country people do a lot. When someone is comin' out of church we say, "You better go home with us." Then they say something like, "No, I better get back to the house and feed the cows." Clearly, Sandra had forgotten about feeding the cows.

Doug spoke calmly, "Well, we'll leave you guys to your game. Is Aunt Clarice still up?"

Dave smiled real big and motioned toward his mouth. "I think she's in the upstairs bathroom, Doug." Uh-oh. Too late. But that's when we heard Aunt Clarice coming down the stairs.

"Has Doug come back yet? Doug promised he'd come see me before bed. It's getting late!"

"We're in here, Aunt Clarice!"

"Well, look at you two! You've been gone all afternoon and here I am leaving early in the morning on a big dreadful plane that will probably be filled with people wearing flip flops and listening to those ridiculous little music machines. Doug, Honey, I don't know when I'll be back. Come see me in California sometime, won't you?"

"I'd love to go to California, Aunt Clarice. I don't get a lot of time off from work. But that would be a great trip."

Sandra jumped in, "Where do you live in California?"

"Palm Springs, Darlin'. It's lovely. Sunny and beautiful year round."

"I've lived the last few years in the San Diego area. Yeah, it is beautiful."

"Well, Sandra, why on earth would you want to live here then? Go back with me. Go back before you turn into a country bumpkin, Sweetheart."

Other people (normal people) would have said something like "No offense." or "Of course, not that any of you are country bumpkins." But Aunt Clarice would have never put an exception clause on anything she yelled at the top of her lungs.

"Well, Mrs. Clarice, I've had my time in California. Now I'm lookin' to settle in around here or as near as I can get."

"What kinda work do you do, Hon?"

"I'm a doctor of Bio-Ethics and I'm looking for something in research or development."

"Well, aren't you the smart one? Our Doug here graduated Valedictorian and graduated come somethin' or other from the University of Tennessee."

"Yes Ma'am. I realize that. I've known Doug all my life."

"Doug probably should have gone on to more schooling but he was a hometown boy and took this little job at the local bank. I guess you're stuck there now, Sweetheart. But no matter. You should just be happy to have a job at all. Shannon's brother's been outta work for eleven years now and no job in sight. Thank God his wife is a fourth grade teacher or they'd be on the street. He says he's working on some kind of video game invention. Doug, Honey, when Jeb becomes rich and famous as a video game inventor, you can tell everyone that he's your brilliant cousin. Yes sirree."

"Yes Ma'am." Doug's smile was so insincere that I had to look at the floor to keep from laughing.

"Well, it's time I take the teeth out and hit that hard ol' bed. Dave, you know we need to leave by six in the morning. I hate to feel rushed in an airport. Last time one of those horrible security people said that the underwire in my brassiere was makin' the big machine beep. Embarrassing and ridiculous! I mean, look at me. Do I look like I'm gonna blow up a plane? I mean, seriously! Plus, they confiscated all my Avon hand crème, a new bottle of White Rain hairspray, and a Diet Sprite that cost me $2.50. What's this world comin' to?"

Trying desperately not to laugh out loud, Doug reached out to hug Aunt Clarice. "I love you, Aunt Clarice. Come back when you can."

I wanted to be as friendly as possible so I extended my hand and said, "Mrs. Clarice, it's certainly been a pleasure to meet you."

"You too, Dear."

I was glad the airport story had worn her down so she didn't have the energy to say, "You don't seem like Doug's type but seein' as how he settled for that job at the bank he's not one to hold the bar too high lately." Thank you, God, for small favors. Aunt Clarice walked loudly up the stairs. I felt like a woman standing outside a trailer park after a tornado. Aunt Clarice blew through, did her damage...and then she was gone. Did I think a woman like her could blow up a 747? Are you kidding? Absolutely.

"We'll leave you to your card playin'. Carlie and I need to visit with the folks in the living room a while."

But by the time we got to the living room, Uncle Bart had risen from the green recliner and was yellin', "Charlotte, get yer things and let's get to the house." The Rockfords had gathered their coats and Charlene was outside loading a plant from the funeral home into the back of the van. We all agreed it would look good on her front porch and that Doug already had too many flowers to deal with. Ralph and Chester had already gone; Chester had asked for the lemon meringue pie and the chicken spaghetti and Doug was happy to oblige.

Soon the house was void of life except for Sandra, Dave, Shannon, Doug, and me. But Shannon was my advocate and she was on the move. "Look Dave, I don't know about Sandra but I'm ready to call it quits. You beat us. Fair and square. Take your victory lap and let's call it a night." He joyfully agreed and we all stood in the kitchen for a few minutes while he poured a Diet Coke and outlined his winning strategy. Sandra put on her Kelly green jacket which looked adorable and matched her eyes the way Doug's green chamois shirt had matched his eyes at Cracker Barrel that day. The good-byes were pleasantly brief. Sandra expressed sympathy again. Dave and Shannon said they'd be back in about twenty minutes. And then they were gone.

The minute the tail lights faded in the distance, Doug kissed me on the cheek and whispered, "We better be quiet. We wouldn't want to raise Aunt Clarice from the dead."

We both laughed as quietly as we could. "Doug, I know it's been a long day. If you need to go home and rest, I understand."

"Rest? Are you kidding? I have twenty minutes alone with you. This may not happen for a while. Besides, I think there's something you wanna say that you're not saying."

"You're right. I'm mad that you let Chester take the lemon meringue pie. Where are your priorities?"

"Hey, let's go over to his house and I'll arm wrestle him for it."

"Are you kidding? You wouldn't have a chance. When it comes to pie, that old man is motivated. Trust me. It takes one to know one."

"Carlie, I don't think you have a problem with the pie or lack thereof. I said today at the funeral that I value truth. And I do. But I don't read signals very well. Is something wrong?"

A tear came to my eye though I did everything humanly possible to make it stop. But there was no going back. Soon they started flowing like a slow trickle from a leaky faucet.

Doug hugged me and whispered in my ear, "What's wrong? What could possibly be wrong? Are you having second thoughts? Do you wish you hadn't come?"

"No, Doug. I guess...I mean...we haven't even said anything about...well, about her."

"Sandra?"

"Yes. Sandra."

"Yeah, I can definitely see why that would rattle you. I mean I made that big deal about how I thought I was in love with her and all. I understand why that would be a problem for you. If Jim Jackson came walkin' in the door right now wearing his Army uniform and acting all friendly with you, that would bother me. But how would it be for you? I mean, if Jim walked through that door right now and hugged you and said, 'It's great to see you, Carlie. I've been thinkin' about you a lot. Even when I was on those exciting espionage assignments in Tel Aviv, you were on my mind.' What would you do, Carlie? Would you say, 'Forget this stupid rural banker from Sharon, Tennessee. I'm going for Jim Jackson because I dated him for a whole year and we have this big history together.'?"

"No. Not a chance. But that's because Jim Jackson's not half the man you are, Doug. He was a selfish, stubborn, difficult person. Sandra's not any of those things. Or at least she doesn't seem to be."

"Look, I could tell you some things about Sandra that would make you rethink your evaluation. But there's no need to go into that. There's one thing that makes it impossible for anything to happen between me and Dr. Miller."

"What's that?"

"She's not you."

Forget the slow trickle. I put my face in my hands and cried uncontrollably. I had jumped off a high cliff without even checking for a parachute. I was desperately in love and there was no goin' back. A part of my life was now in the hands of another. I had given him power. The power to bring me joy. And the power to bring me pain. The exhilaration of flying through the air was mixed with fear. If the parachute didn't open, the crash landing would be life-changing.

"Doug, I don't know what to say. Thank you."

He reached over and kissed me and held me close as though he were protecting me from something. And he had. He'd protected me from my own insecurity. He had been the first man willing to do that.

"Let's change the subject. We've only got nine minutes left before Dave and Shannon get back. When can I come to Commerce?"

"Tomorrow."

"Hmm. Terribly tempting, but not gonna work. What's my second option?"

"It's like a seven-hour drive. Would you be able to leave early on a Friday afternoon sometime? Do you ever take a few hours off?"

"Yeah, it's not a problem to leave at 1:00 now and then. I work a lot of extra hours in a typical week. What are you doing this Friday at 8:00?"

"Shoot, not gonna work. Clara and I had planned to clean out the kitchen cabinets this Friday night. I love to just organize all the glasses and the plates and put down new shelf paper. Oh, wait! That's perfect timing. I mean, you could give us all kinds of pointers. We could even use little color-coded labels and sticky notes and maybe even one of those little labeling machines! Wow! This is your lucky day, Doug!"

"Go ahead. Make fun of a man for appreciating order. I'm not gonna help with your kitchen cabinets. I'm going straight to the bathroom and get that glob of Colgate out of the sink."

"If you drive all the way to Commerce, Georgia, to see me... I promise there'll be no toothpaste in the sink."

"I believe you."

CHAPTER NINE: Floating Through The Air

CARLIE

Sadness came with the sudden glare of headlights. I loved Dave and Shannon. But the timing was painful.

Even walking up the sidewalk, Dave had us in stitches. "I know you two were missin' us somethin' awful. Well, we hurried back as fast as we could. I wanted to speed through town tryin' to get here, but Shannon reminded me that the barber shop was closed and that I better obey the law. I bet ya'll have been in there working on that freezer bag project. Yeah, I can always look at a man and tell when he's been working with Ziploc bags. You look guilty, Doug."

"We saved some of the freezer bag project for you, Dave. Seein' as how you'll have a little time in the mornin' before Aunt Clarice gets her teeth in, we thought you might need somethin' to do."

I loved Dave and Shannon. Doug did too. There was just something extremely comforting about them. We all sat at the dining room table and talked until 10:30. When they excused themselves, Shannon hugged me good night and whispered, "I'll meet you in here for coffee at 7:00. It'll just be the two of us." I was overjoyed.

Doug stayed until 11. His eyelids were getting heavy when he finally resolved, "It's been a long day. Are we still on for 8:30 or do you need more time to sleep?"

"8:30 is perfect."

We stood on the porch for ten minutes longer. Every time he started to leave, he'd change his mind. I wanted him to stay forever. When he finally got into the truck and pulled away, it was physically painful. Jim Jackson? Are you kidding? Jim Jackson could never hold a candle to you, Doug.

I set the alarm for 6:00 so I would be fully dressed by 7:00. I couldn't wait to talk to Shannon alone. How did she and Dave meet? What had Sandra asked about me? What did she think about our chances?

November 5   7:02 am

I already had the coffee made and was sitting at the table wearing jeans and a bright blue sweater. Hair and make-up done. Ready for the day. Shannon had been up a maximum of three minutes as she came down the stairs in red plaid pajama pants and a gray sweat shirt that said, "UT Chattanooga."

"Carlie, you're making me look bad. What on earth motivated you to get up so early and look so good at this time of the day? Wait a minute! Don't answer that. I know the answer." Her smile was beautiful even though she hadn't brushed her teeth. I'm sure Dave thinks he's the luckiest man on earth because he gets to watch her pour coffee every morning.

"I'm in love with him, Shannon."

"I know."

"There's nothin' I can do about it. People can say what they want about taking time, getting to know each other, slowing down. But I'm thirty-two years old and I've been on dates and I've had relationships but I've never been in love. It's not just

150

a physical thing. He's a man of faith, character, and integrity. I like the way he treats other people, not just me. Last night when he pulled out of the driveway I was in physical pain. I wanted so badly for him to stay."

"I remember, Carlie. I remember." Shannon beamed when she said it.

"I didn't expect the whole Sandra deal. I mean, Doug had told me about their relationship, how she lived in California and was engaged and all. Then I looked up at the funeral and she was just sitting there, being perfect and caring and beautiful."

"As you can imagine, she had a lot to say about Doug in the car yesterday. She came back to win his heart, Carlie. You know that. Her heart got broken and it caused her to look at the past differently. She said he was the only man who had ever really treated her like a person, with respect, like a friend. She asked if I thought you guys were serious. I said I really didn't know."

A tear came to the corner of my eye. "He says he's not interested in her. But how can that be? I mean, look at the girl. There's nothing she can't do. And she's friendly and beautiful and educated and she wears expensive shoes."

"Oh my gosh, Carlie, you're right! Ever since Doug was a little boy he always talked about how he wanted to grow up and marry a woman who wears expensive shoes! Why didn't I think of this before?"

"Very funny, Shannon. But when Doug and Sandra elope next week and come back to town and have beautiful babies and Sandra becomes a famous research scientist and Doug becomes the president of the bank…well, well, you'll feel bad for takin' this lightly. You'll know I was right to be worried."

"Look, Carlie. You're beautiful. I've seen the way he looks at you. Dave even said it and he's a guy. He said he's never seen Doug act this way. He's enamored with you. Trust me. Trust him, Carlie. Doug may be a lot of things but he's not a user. He won't tell you something that's not true."

Shannon spent the next hour building me up. She made me feel that God was on my side. I wasn't sure God took sides in matters of the heart. And if He did, why would He take my side? Maybe because He knew that Dr. Miller would meet another dentist someday but I would never meet another Doug.

At 8:26 Doug pulled in the drive. He was perfectly punctual and he did that check-hair-in-the-rearview-mirror again which made me smile. He was wearing a tan plaid shirt and jeans and his hair was still damp. Handsome. I stood at the kitchen door. I didn't care if I seemed over-eager.

"Mornin' Girls!" He reached out and gave me the now familiar hug. "Carlie, you look stunning! That blue is just wow...I'm speechless. Shannon...you look like...well, like it's mornin'!"

"Laugh it up, Cuz! I've been sittin' here for the last hour tryin' to convince Carlie why she should make a run for it. I was just gonna tell her about the time you took the ladder and left me on top of Uncle Charlie's barn with no way down. But it's no use. No matter what I say it's like I'm not gettin' through to her." She laughed and excused herself saying she wanted to get cleaned up before Dave got back from the airport.

I poured Doug some coffee and the minute I heard the bathroom door close, he came up behind me and asked, "Did you sleep well?"

"I did. No. That's a lie. I hardly slept at all."

He laughed. "Me either. I thought I would go home and be asleep within five minutes. But I don't know. I didn't fall asleep till after 1:30. Thinkin', I guess."

"Me too."

The morning flew by. We walked through the back property and found some ripe apples on the tree behind the barn. We drank tea and ate peanut butter sandwiches on the front porch swing. But the clock was a cruel enemy.

"Doug, it's almost 1:00. I really do have to go. I'm workin' in the mornin' and I have a British Literature test on Monday."

He pulled the blanket around my shoulders while he gently rocked the porch swing. "Maybe I could help you study."

"Let's see. How much British Literature does the average marketing major usually take? Two, three semesters?"

"Ha Ha. Are you saying that I'm illiterate when it comes to the finer nuances of British Literature? Oh, Carlie, Carlie, Carlie, you underestimate my vast academic abilities. Go ahead, quiz me."

"Okay. What do the poems 'The Doubt of Future Woes' and 'On Monsieur's Departure' teach us about Queen Elizabeth?"

"Uh, that's easy. That she always carries a purse even though she never pays for anything."

"Now I totally see why you graduated 'come somethin' or other' from UT."

"Be inspired, Carlie. Be inspired."

"I am." And with that I reached over to gently touch his curls one last time. He put his arm around me and I could hardly hold back the tears.

"Doug, I have to go. I'm sorry that Dave and Shannon had to go back to Chattanooga. I hate to leave you here alone. This can't be easy. It's been a tough week."

"Don't worry. I'm not gonna stay here. I've got the appointments with the lawyer and the accountant this afternoon. Then I'm goin' back to my apartment. I'm not ready to be here by myself yet. I don't wanna go through Mom's stuff. I've got some time before I have to do that. Charlene's invited me for dinner tonight. Uncle Stanley, Aunt Beth, and Ralph are going back to Georgia in the mornin' so it'll be good to visit with them before they have to leave. Brother Dan's taking me to breakfast in the mornin'. I'll be fine. Just drive carefully, Carlie. Promise me you'll be careful."

I got up from the porch swing and determined that this should be like taking off a Band-Aid. If I did it quickly there would be less pain. Doug had already loaded my things into the car. He stood and hugged me as though he'd never see me again. I tearfully whispered, "Until Friday." He whispered back, "I'll be there."

I cried as I drove out of Sharon, Tennessee. But they were happy tears. I thought I understood the future. I had no idea.

CHAPTER TEN: The More Things Change... The More They Stay The Same

CARLIE

November 8
University of Georgia

I arrived early for class and looked down at my phone to scan the ever-familiar pictures. My favorite was the one with his elbows on the table and the one of us sitting under the apple tree together. Oh, and that one of him sittin' on the porch swing. I was in love, yes. But life had to go on. He would go to work today. I would go to school. It was comforting to be in Dr. Chesterton's classroom. She was my favorite professor by far. She had inspired me to be a writer and many times had encouraged me to press on when I got rejection letters from publishers. She entered the classroom and said, "Carlie, can you come to my office for a moment?"

A million things went through my mind. Did she think I plagiarized the last writing assignment? I didn't. I went to the VA Hospital myself and interviewed three Vietnam veterans. I made sure my quotes were exacting. Was she disappointed in my grades? Couldn't be. I had a solid B. My palms were sweaty.

"Carlie, have a seat. We have a few minutes before class and...well...I couldn't wait to tell you the news. You did it! Girl, you knocked it out of the park."

"Did what?"

155

"Remember when I told you about seeing my old college roommate last spring at an Auburn reunion, the one who works at Harper Collins?"

"Yes, I believe so."

"I sent her your manuscript and nothing ever came of it."

"Yes, I remember that too. I've gotten very good at being rejected."

"Carlie, they've changed their minds. They want it. They want to publish it. They want to change the name to 'A Single Girl's Guide to Ordinary.' But they want it. Your life is getting ready to change, Carlie, change for the better."

"Wow, you can't be serious. I'm speechless. I mean, I wrote that two years ago and no one seemed to give a care. You even said yourself that it just wasn't the time to publish something about thirty-something single women. Now this."

"Yes. Well, things change. I told you there are waves. Trends. Now is the time. They said your interviews with working class single women combined with your sense of humor was exactly what they were looking for. They want to meet you, Carlie. There'll be the usual re-writes. They have to confirm the interviews you did with the women. There'll be some paperwork and other challenges. You'll need a contract negotiator. But all in all, it's a go."

"Gosh, I don't even know what to say. Thank you, Dr. Chesterton. What am I supposed to do now?"

"Cancel any plans you have this weekend. Saturday morning we're going to the Big Apple. I want to introduce you to some friends I know in the writing business and on Monday morning we'll meet with Joan at the publishing house. I'll be glad to help negotiate a reasonable contract. I've done it before. We should be able to get a Monday evening flight home."

"I have a problem with my job. I mean, I usually work week-ends and also I don't have the money for travel."

"Carlie, I'm not sure you understand what I'm saying. Thousands of people have spent the last twenty years trying to get this kind of break. They're gonna give you an advance on the book. I've got some part-time office work I can give you here if you need money. Quit your job. You're a writer now. They'll pay your travel expenses."

"Wow, I mean, great!"

"I'll buy the airline tickets online today. If you would, fill out this form with your personal information. I've been teaching here for fifteen years and I've always wanted to see one of my students become a published author. I'll e-mail you our flight schedule as soon as I can. Here are the copies of what Joan sent me on Friday about the details. They'll talk money on Monday. But don't worry, we'll negotiate a good deal. You can't expect much with it being your first book. But if it sells big, well, if it sells big, Carlie Ann Davidson will be a household name. Plus, you're graduating in just over a month and having a book contract in hand means you'll be a hot commodity on getting a job with maybe a magazine or newspaper."

I rose from the uncomfortable chair. "Dr. Chesterton, I have to hug you. You helped to make my dreams come true. I'll never be able to thank you enough. Really."

"Carlie, go out there and be a literary success. That will be all the thanks I need. See you on Saturday. Look for my e-mail."

I didn't listen well during class. I hardly listened at all. Dr. Chesterton was talking about humor writing and everyone in the class was laughing, except me. I was thinking about flying to New York City…and about kissing Doug Jameson under the apple tree in his mom's backyard. I was thinking about my name being on the cover of a book at Barnes and Noble…and about the way Doug looked so sweetly at Aunt Charlotte when she explained her detailed freezing methods. I was wondering what to wear to a meeting at a publishing house…and remembering Doug's funny comment to Shannon when she was in her pajamas. The biggest thing I was wondering? How to tell the man I loved that I wouldn't be waiting for him this weekend. That I'd found someone new…someone from my past…someone I had almost forgotten. My dream.

I was nervous walking into the dollar store. "Hey Sherry! Is Mrs. Lawson around?"

"She's gone to the bank. Be back in a minute. Girl, how was your big trip to see your Tennessee man?"

"It was great. I mean, it was sad about his mom's funeral. But yeah, he's a great guy. I think this one might be a keeper, Sherry!"

"Well, look at you!! Carlie done found her a man. Too bad he's so far away, eh?"

"Yeah, that's a bummer."

Mrs. Lawson walked in whistling as always. But I could never figure out the tune. She was less than 5 ft. tall and round in the face. She reminded me of Mrs. Santa Claus. Cheery and without a lot of make-up. "Well, look what the cat drug in! Good to see ya, Carlie. Sorry I wasn't here on Saturday. I asked Hope to fill in so I could go down to Macon for my grandson's third birthday. I hope your trip to Tennessee was...well, worth it."

"Oh, it was. He's a great guy and he said it really helped for me to be there during the stress of the funeral and all. Can I talk to you a second?"

"Sure, Carlie. Come on back to the office."

The office was tiny and overly decorated with dusty plastic roses from the seventies. In ten years I had never seen the surface of Mrs. Lawson's desk. But she was a good woman. She always tried to work with our schedules. She gave us each $10 on our birthdays. She was a boss and a friend.

"Mrs. Lawson, you've always been more than fair with me. You've been a friend, not just a boss."

"And you're quitting."

"How'd you know?"

"I know these things. I'm surprised you've been here as long as you have. Let me guess. It has something to do with this banker in Tennessee."

"Actually, no. I kinda got a big break, Mrs. Lawson. My book is gonna be published by a company in New York City. I know. Weird, isn't it? And well, with me graduating from college in less than a month and with working on the book business, I just won't be able to work like I have been."

"A book? Congratulations, Carlie. It couldn't have happened to a nicer girl. I'm proud of you. Proud of the woman you've become. When you first came to work here you were like a puppy that'd been kicked. I didn't know why. I didn't ask. But I always knew you had the potential to be a Grand Champion. You just needed a little healing. You're all healed up now. Time to go out there and make it happen."

I started crying and reached across the tiny desk to give her a hug. How is it that the last month had been the happiest of my life and yet the most tearful?

Doug had texted me that he had a late afternoon trip to a farm south of Jackson, but that he'd call at 8:00. I tried not to plan my words. I didn't want them to seem scripted.

November 8   8:10 pm

"Hello."

"Carlie, I'm sorry I'm a little later than I said. I got tied up and there was some trouble with the negotiations and all."

"Hey, no problem. Did it all get solved?"

"Yeah, we came to an agreement."

"Of course. You probably melted them with your suave and sophisticated laugh and your adorable puppy-dog eyes. They didn't have a chance."

"Yeah, I can't tell you how many times my puppy-dog eyes have brought fat men in overalls to tears."

"I miss you, Doug. It doesn't matter that we've talked on the phone maybe, what? Five times since I left. But the phone is not the same."

"I know. But now we can begin the countdown to Friday. Only four days left."

"I need to talk to you about somethin'. I'm not gonna be able to do this weekend. I'm so sorry, heartbroken even. I hope you'll understand."

"What happened?"

"Well, it's good news. Unbelievable news in fact. Harper Collins is gonna publish my book. It's a book I wrote two years ago and my professor gave it to them a while back and now they want to publish it. She and I have to fly to New York City Saturday morning."

"Carlie, that's great! I don't even know what to say. This is unreal. Wow! Congratulations! The Big Apple! A publishing contract?"

"But I'm gonna miss you terribly. I want to see you. Would the next weekend work?"

"Oh absolutely, unless I end up getting a call back from MGM about starring in that new movie. But yeah, if that doesn't work out, I'll definitely be there."

"Aren't you funny? This could still end in a train wreck. Just cause they're publishing it doesn't mean people will actually buy it. And if they don't buy it, how interested do you think Harper Collins will be in giving me another chance with another book? Yeah. It could definitely go south."

"Are you kidding? It will be a wild success and we'll all say we knew you back when."

"Back when I was unloading gallons of Hawaiian Punch?"

"Right."

"That stopped today too. My professor told me to quit my job and she would get me some work at the university so that I'll have the time I need to get this book thing worked out."

"Gosh, I never even got to see you in your yellow smock with your name tag."

"I'll ask Mrs. Lawson to take a picture of me. I told her I'd work 5-9 Monday through Friday of next week as my last hurrah. She's kinda pushed right now with Thanksgiving coming up and I hated to see her in a pinch."

"That's why I like you, Carlie. I like you for a thousand reasons but that's probably one of the biggest. How many people fly to New York City to sign a book contract with Harper Collins and then come home to stock the shelves at Dollar General with canned sweet potatoes?"

"What can I say? I'm highly committed to carbs."

"You're committed to the people there. You know they helped bring you to where you are and you're not gonna leave them in the dust. That says a lot about you. It's way more impressive than just writing a good book."

"If I didn't know better, I'd think you kinda like me."

"You're growing on me."

"I wish I had a dime for every time I've been under that apple tree in the last two days. I keep staring at the picture. You looked so comfortable leaned up against the tree with your arms around me. I felt like nothing could hurt me. And the deer in the field and the way they rarely come out that time of day. I don't know. I never wanted to leave that moment."

"Yeah. And I look forward to us making new moments. Just not this Friday. So, it's now an eleven-day countdown. I can live with that but don't forget to come back home 'cause I'm not sure I can wait more than eleven days."

"That brings up an interesting subject we probably should talk about, Doug. The subject of waiting."

"Okay."

"Well, I've done a little research on line. Do you know the percentage of people between the ages of twenty and twenty-nine who have never had sex?"

"Wow, you get right to the point, don't you? Believe it or not, I don't know. We never covered that in my Intro to Marketing class. If we had, there would have been a lot more marketing majors."

"8 percent."

"Okay. And you're wondering if I'm in the 92 percent or the 8 percent. That's probably a fair question. What would you guess?"

"Well, there's no doubt that your Christian faith would say that sex is for marriage, that you would hold that as absolute truth. But I also know that all of us sometimes violate the standards of faith even if we live to regret it. So, I would definitely say that you believe sex is for marriage but that I don't know whether you've violated those standards in a moment of weakness."

"Well, what did the statistics say about people over thirty?"

"Among people thirty to forty, 4.8 percent haven't had sex."

"Hmm. So somebody that's say thirty-two would be even less likely to have waited."

"Are you asking me if I've waited, Doug? I mean, it's not like you haven't wondered. I've wondered about you. When I saw the way Sandra looked at you…well…of course I wondered. Anyone would have wondered."

"I'm not asking you, Carlie. But if you want to tell me, I'm all ears."

"I'm in the minority, Doug."

"So am I. I'm not tryin' to prove I'm better than anyone or holier than the masses. I just really do believe it's a system that works. When I was a teenager my dad said, 'Doug, any dog can bed down a lot of females. But only a real man can love one woman for a lifetime.' I never forgot it. It hasn't been easy and I'm not saying I haven't had moral failures. Sandra and I went further than we should have on a few occasions. I crossed some lines in college that I shouldn't have. But if you're asking if I have well, you know…no."

"Well, okay then. I guess we got that cleared up."

"Actually, I'm glad you brought it up, Carlie. I mean, I've been wonderin', you know…it's probably good that we talked about it."

"Yeah, good to know we're on the same page."

"So tell me more about the book. What's the title?"

"Well, they wanna call it, 'A Single Girl's Guide to Ordinary.' It's kind of a funny look at being a single thirty-something woman, the challenges, the rewards. I even interviewed other single women and some of their comments are hilarious. I was pretty proud of it when I finished it a few years ago. I'm probably a little less passionate about it right now. But hey, I'm not complainin'."

"Well, it's amazing that you're gonna be a published author. I'm impressed, Carlie. The book must be really good."

"Thanks. I hope so. A lot of people are pullin' for me. I know you've had a big day and need your rest. Plus, I've gotta go to my parents' house. I still haven't told them the big news."

"I'm sure they'll be proud of you. I'll talk to you tomorrow. Same time?"

"Sounds good. Bye, Doug. I miss you."

"I miss you too. Bye."

The next eleven days were a fast-moving blur. I went to New York City with Dr. Chesterton and signed a book contract. I finished my job at Dollar General by stocking canned pumpkin pie filling and endless bags of marshmallows. I talked to Doug on the phone every day. Happiness.

Tomorrow Doug drives to Commerce to meet my parents and Clara and to stay in the Rockfords' guest room which is covered with pink wallpaper. And to tell me that he thinks about me all the time and couldn't wait to see me. I won't be able to sleep tonight.

November 19

My last class dismissed at 3:00. I told Dr. Chesterton I'd meet her to go over some changes in my manuscript. We had already made a lot of changes. But the publishers wanted me to do some re-writes on Chapters 3 and 4. They gave me some guidance and told me to submit the changes within a week. They wanted to push forward in an attempt to get the book released in January. "January is the time when single women will be ready to have a good laugh and get a fresh start. We'll do a big push to make this book happen by January 15. So get us the changes. Time is money, Carlie."

I knew time was money. I also knew that the man I loved would be driving into town at 8:00. All writing would cease at that point. This wasn't up for discussion. Dr. Chesterton was pleased with the changes I made. "I think they'll like this, Carlie. Let's change some wording here and move that paragraph to the end." We worked on the book for about three hours and then agreed to deem it perfect. "Let's submit it, Carlie. I'll send it to Joan and she'll get back with us about whether it's a go. I think it is better than it was before. We should get good news."

"Thank you, Dr. Chesterton. I can't thank you enough."

"It's my honor to help you."

November 19 6:00

I've got just enough time to get cleaned up, do my hair, and put the chicken spaghetti in the oven. I told Doug to eat a late lunch and we could have supper together when he arrived. He's going to the Rockfords' house first to drop off his things and then coming to our apartment for supper. Clara had agreed to meet him for five minutes and then excuse herself to her parents' house. All is moving along like clockwork.

November 19   8:15

Dinner is ready. Warm and bubbly chicken spaghetti. Crisp salad. Green beans and crescent rolls. Table is set with an ivory tablecloth, new blue cloth napkins, and old white china plates my grandma had given me for my thirtieth birthday. Toothpaste globs meticulously cleaned out of the sink. I changed clothes at least seven times. I decided on blue jeans and a plain black button-down shirt. Finally, the doorbell rang. I opened the door and neither of us said a word. We had talked on the phone every day for two weeks. We had laughed about small town parades and barbecue cook-offs. We had talked about bank loans and favorite books and ridiculous movies. We'd even cried a few times about his mom, about life. But what we had really wanted was this...this moment. I didn't expect to start crying. Doug was wearing khaki pants and a navy blue sweater. I had never seen a better looking man in my life. He reached out to hug me and I could hear his heart beating. I thought about what Agnes Robertson at the Commerce post office said, "Gosh, you hardly know this guy. You met him how? Through e-mail? Ridiculous." No, Agnes. You're ridiculous. This is love.

"Carlie, Honey, why are you crying?"

"I don't know. It's funny really. I mean, I guess I've just missed you. And our lives...well, they're moving at such a fast pace and I've looked forward to this moment so much...just sitting with you again." I started crying even more as Clara came out from her bedroom. Clara seemed

167

embarrassed to be interrupting this obviously emotional moment. Her beautiful red hair was pulled back in a pony tail. Her clear ivory skin was perfect. She was about 5'6 and was lovely in every way…well, except that she didn't have presence.

"Uh, I'll just go on over to my parents' house now, Carlie."

"Wait, Clara. I'm okay. Just a little emotional, I guess. I want you to meet Doug. Clara, this is Doug Jameson. Doug, this is my roommate, Clara Johnson. She's been my friend since high school."

"Clara, I'm glad to finally meet you. I've heard so many great things about you and I'm glad you've been such a friend to Carlie."

Clara just turned red and stared at the dingy cream-colored carpet. "Uh, nice to meet you too, Doug. I'm gone now. Won't be back till mornin', Carlie. Have a great time."

"Tell your parents I said 'Hello.'"

I felt terrible for Clara. She is so great with little kids and so "not great" with adults. Where was her Doug? How would he even find her in this horrible little apartment? And why hadn't I tried harder to search for Clara's knight in shining armor? When I heard her car pull out of the parking lot, I realized these were questions for another day.

I wiped my eyes one last time. "Dinner's ready!" I walked toward the stove to retrieve the pan. "How was your trip, Doug? I mean, no problems or anything, right?"

Without saying a word, he grabbed my shoulders, turned me around, and put his hands on my face and kissed me. I had missed him more than I had ever missed anyone in my life. Signing the book contract didn't even come close to the joy of this moment. I would never forget it. The smell of chicken spaghetti. Dentyne on his breath. The Irish clean smell that had become a distinct memory of him.

"I missed you, Carlie. I don't know if you'll ever understand how much I missed you."

"I think I have a pretty good idea. I mean, there I was in New York City. The publisher said, 'Let's go out for a late dinner to celebrate,' and all I could think about was getting back to the hotel room to talk to you on the phone. Yeah, I think I know how much you missed me, Doug. The feeling is mutual."

"So, what's the latest news on the book?"

"Scheduled for release on January 15, if we can get all the re-writes approved."

"Wow, great! I mean, will you be going on book-signing events after that?"

"It depends. They'll schedule some events not too far from home but the biggest thing is that they'll give it a month or so and see if the book can 'grow legs.'"

"And how does a book 'grow legs'?"

"Yeah, if you find that out, let me know."

We both laughed. I was new to the literary world. But I knew that the book could become a flop as easily as a success. I also knew a lot of that was out of my control. And somehow, I didn't care as much as I probably should have. Doug and I spent the whole evening eating and laughing and telling more stories of childhood. We made a hard and fast rule that he would leave for the Rockfords' house by midnight. He left at 12:47. Note to self: Be better at following rules.

Nov. 20
Breakfast With my Parents…Egads!

Doug rang the doorbell at 8:15. We were supposed to arrive at my parents' house by 8:30. He wore dark blue jeans and a tan corduroy shirt. His hair was still damp and when it was damp it was extremely curly. I laughed to myself because he looked like a little boy on a dairy commercial. Cute and cuddly. I just prayed my mom wouldn't chew him up and spit him out. I drove down the familiar tree-lined street where I had lived the first eighteen years of my life praying that he wouldn't turn his back on me after meeting my mother.

"Doug, I need to prepare you. My mother, well, she's very opinionated."

"Sounds like my mom. Don't worry. I know the drill. Be nice. Agree with her as much as I can and don't bring up controversial subjects."

"Wow, you're good."

"Look Carlie, I've told you enough about my mom that you know she was crazy and controlling and judgmental. Trust me. Your mom can't be any worse than mine was."

"Don't be so sure."

As we pulled in the driveway, I laughed out loud making note of the completely flawless way my mom hung the outside Christmas lights every year. No one was allowed to help her.

The strings of lights had to be measured and hung with perfection as the goal. A NASA engineer would have been proud of her precision.

About that time Mom came out onto the sidewalk wearing creased gray pants, a black sweater vest, and a starched white shirt. She had been a perfect size 9 since the eighth grade. She was sixty-one years old and still wore a size 9. This was one of her goals in life...and she had achieved it, though not quietly. "Carlie! Doug! We're so glad you're here!"

Doug extended his right hand and put on the biggest smile I had ever seen. "Mrs. Davidson, it's so nice to meet you. Thanks for inviting us to breakfast."

"Well, you're welcome. Carlie has spoken so highly of you, Doug."

I realized at that moment that Doug was the kind of man that women everywhere wanted to bring home to Mom and Dad. He had skills. Not over-powering. But just friendly enough to be considered engaging and worthy of serious consideration.

When Dad came through the entry way, I naturally went to hug him. "Daddy, this is Doug."

"Nice to meet ya, Doug. You've sure made our little girl swoon."

It didn't even bother me that Daddy said "swoon." He was almost sixty-five and no one expected him to wear gold jewelry or hip-hop jeans. He could say *swoon* if he wanted to. In fact, his word usage went perfectly with his navy blue Sansabelt pants and brown wingtip shoes. Daddy's pants were a size 32 waist when he was in high school. He wore a size 40 now. He wasn't like Mom. Thank God for small favors.

Mom had the breakfast table set perfectly: a freshly-ironed white tablecloth, white china with yellow flowers painted in the middle, real silverware that had been hand-polished, white roses from the flower shop downtown.

"Mom, it all looks beautiful."

"Oh Honey, this was no problem at all. Just something I threw together."

We all sat at our assigned seats and I was kind of glad Mom and Daddy hadn't invited my brothers. I wanted this time for Doug to get to know them without the background noise of my little brothers and their exciting lives.

Daddy had just spoken the "Amen" over breakfast when Mom began her questioning.

"Doug, Carlie tells us you're in banking."

"Yes Ma'am. I work mostly with rural and farm loans. The town where I live is similar to Commerce. Small. I really like it."

"Would you like to move up in the banking business? I mean, would you be open to going somewhere else if it meant a promotion?"

Shoot. Why did Mom have to do this? Why couldn't she just stick with perfecting the art of Christmas lighting instead of trying to perfect my boyfriend.

"Mrs. Davidson, I think it depends on the way a person defines 'promotion.' Every day I help people fulfill their dreams. I help farmers buy more land, farm more crops. I

172

can't imagine that another job would be a promotion…I mean, not really. I guess the answer is 'no.' I'm not interested in another job in another town."

"Well, that's certainly your prerogative, Doug."

I knew Daddy would change the subject. "So, what do you think about our little girl becoming a real writer, Doug?"

"It's pretty exciting. It couldn't have happened to a nicer person either."

"Yeah, that's what Mom and I have always believed."

Doug and I lived through two hours at my parents' house. We lived through Mom explaining why she can't eat hash browns because of the carbs. We lived through the photo albums of my third grade play. "Carlie was always a lot bigger than the other children. Bless her!" We lived through Mom re-applying lipstick and Daddy sneaking an extra biscuit while she was in the bathroom. We lived through the story of my family life condensed into two hours. I just hoped Doug wouldn't hold any of it against me. I wasn't the writer of it. I was only a chapter.

As we pulled out of the drive, Mom yelled, "Carlie Honey, come again and bring Doug with you! Be careful not to hit the mailbox this time."

I chose silence as we drove back up the tree-lined street.

"That went well. They were exactly like you had described, Carlie."

"Look, if you want me to drop you off at the Rockfords' house so you can hop in your car and race back to Sharon deleting my number from your cell phone as you drive 80 mph down the freeway, I'll understand. I wouldn't blame you."

"Are you serious? I thought I was gonna have to jump out of the car when you slowed down at a curve."

Doug was smiling. I knew he wouldn't leave me regardless of my mother's ridiculousness. He wasn't the leaving kind. Mr. Rockford had called him *solid.* And Mr. Rockford doesn't lie.

We spent the rest of the weekend laughing and grieving Sunday afternoon's cruel separation. It was a blissful time. This is what people meant by *falling in love.* I couldn't imagine anything better. It didn't even bother me when my Sunday School teacher's wife whispered in my ear, "Wow, he's cute, Carlie. How did you snag such a 'looker'?"

We ate lunch at the Rockfords' house. When we got home from church, Mrs. Rockford's crockpot roast and potatoes had filled the house with a savory aroma that reminded me of my grandma's house. Four red plastic placemats had already been set carefully on the kitchen table with plain white Corelle plates and a white paper napkin folded on the left. Coleslaw in a small crystal bowl was retrieved from the refrigerator. Brown n' Serve rolls were put in the oven. Homemade apple pie sitting on the counter. Sweet tea in big glasses. Sunday dinner in the south.

Mr. Rockford patted Doug on the back. "I wanted to take ya to the best place I knew to eat. So here we are!"

Mrs. Rockford smiled and said, "Stanley's always been my biggest fan. And I'm his too."

We stood in awe of the simplicity of their love and service to each other. Inspiring. I helped Mrs. Rockford clean up the kitchen while Doug and Mr. Rockford sat in the living room.

"Carlie, it looks like you're rather smitten with our Doug. And he with you."

"Yes ma'am. He's a wonderful man."

"He is. And you know we think a lot of you and your family. Always have. A lotta people think they understand love and can explain it. I mean, I watch those early mornin' shows on television and there's always somebody on there tryin' to explain why love works sometimes and why it doesn't. Silly, if you ask me. Love is a decision, Carlie. Deciding to put someone else's needs above your own. When both people do that, it's love and it looks like love and other people can tell it's love too. There's a mystery as to why a man is drawn to a certain woman and vice versa. That's a beautiful mystery only God can explain and he hasn't cared to explain it to the rest of us as of yet. But I know this. It's wonderful. It's wonderful in the beginning and for folks like Stanley and me...well, it's wonderful even in the end."

"Yes ma'am. It is beautiful."

November 21   2:45 pm

Doug had planned to leave Commerce by 1:00. But we weren't doing very well sticking to our plans.

"Carlie, I have to go. Can I come back in two weeks?"

"You can come back tomorrow. In fact, why don't you just stay to save you the trip back?"

"You're beautiful when you're funny."

"That's what all the rural bankers say."

When he laughed, his eyes closed for a second. I was memorizing his face but I didn't have enough time. Never enough time. I cried as he pulled out of the parking lot of my dumpy apartment building. I had no idea he wouldn't be back to Commerce in two weeks or four weeks or two months. Life wasn't going to help us stick to our plans.

CHAPTER ELEVEN: The More Things Change...The More They Stay The...Uh-Oh, This Time They're Really Changin'

CARLIE

November 22

I dreaded going to class because none of it meant anything to me anymore. Well, truthfully, classes had never really meant that much to me. Studying was never my strong suit. But it was even less important now. I wanted Doug Jameson. It was all I could think about. I wanted him physically. I wanted him emotionally. I wanted him in every way. Dr. Chesterton was constantly pushing me to be excited about the book contract and about graduation and about my future. But all I wanted was to wake up every morning next to him. It was crazy. I sat in my regular seat in Dr. Chesterton's class and tried to prepare my mind for British literature. I only had ten days of college left and I couldn't blow it now. I needed decent grades on my final exams. Doug would be here in three weeks for my college graduation. Mom had planned a huge party. It was all moving along like clockwork. Note to self: When life moves along like clockwork, be prepared.

"Carlie, I need to speak with you for a few minutes in my office."

"Sure, Dr. Chesterton." I walked down the ever-familiar hallway past the bulletin board filled with flyers about International studies programs. I had always wanted to do a travel study program, but I was busy working and I'd never even applied for a passport. I dreamed of going to Ireland. But I'd spent ten years stocking shelves of marshmallow crème instead. That's okay. It's not like my life was over. It was just beginning.

"Carlie, you may have a job offer. Joan sent your book out for some preliminary reviews and well, the reviews have been amazing. They're doing a rush on the book to get it on shelves by December 15. You're scheduled for some interviews in New York City around that time. *Today's Woman* is not only going to do a feature on your book for one of their spring issues, they want to talk to you about a job. The features editor said they needed a smart single southern girl to bring some humor and balance to the pages of their magazine. If you're interested, you need to be on a plane by the end of this week. Joan told them you could probably be there for an official interview Friday morning. You'll need to fly out Thursday afternoon. Well…what do you think?"

"Wow…I mean, Wow. I wasn't prepared for all this. But yeah, of course, I'm excited. Who wouldn't be?"

"Look, you need to call Joan as soon as you get out of class. She has a full docket of interviews scheduled for you and she'll solidify the meeting with *Today's Woman* on Friday. You're going to be spending a lot of time in New York City, Carlie. Your professors will work with you at this point on finishing up classes. I know Joan can make a way for you to be back for graduation ceremonies. But there's not going to be a lot of free time. Are you ready?"

"Sure. I mean, I guess. I mean, yes! And thanks, Dr. Chesterton."

What was I saying? I wasn't ready. I couldn't fathom working in New York City. Less than a month ago I was stocking shelves at the Dollar General Store in Commerce, Georgia. Now Dr. Chesterton says I could be moving to New

York City to work for a national magazine. The biggest question? How could I wake up every morning next to a rural West Tennessee banker if I were living in an apartment in New York City?

Joan worked out all the details. My professors agreed to let me complete my exams online and they all seemed genuinely excited for my opportunities with the book and the job. Joan said I would be in Commerce on the eighteenth for graduation and on Christmas Eve and Christmas Day. She couldn't promise anything more. I agreed. I agreed in the same way a cow agrees to be slaughtered. I was already in the chute and there was no place to turn around. How would I break the news to Doug that I might not ever come back?

November 22   8:00 pm

The phone startled me.

"Hello."

"How's the prettiest girl in Commerce, Georgia?"

"I don't know, but I could call her and get back with ya. Gosh, you're in a good mood."

"I am, Carlie. I got word today that I'm getting an award from the Tennessee Banking Association. Seems someone you know was awarded Loan Officer of the Year. I don't know for sure what that means, but hey, I oughta at least get a country ham out of the deal, right?"

"Oh, absolutely! And make 'em throw in a pound of country sausage! Wow! Congrats, Doug! You've earned it. Sometimes integrity pays and you're living proof of that. I'm proud of you. Really, they couldn't have chosen a better guy."

"Tell me you can go to the awards banquet with me on the thirtieth."

"Of this month?"

"Yeah, December thirtieth n Nashville. It's at the Opryland Hotel and it's beautiful that time of year."

"Oh Doug, I don't think I can swing it. Things have changed, well, a lot, even in the last twenty-four hours."

"Really? What's goin' on?"

"Well, I'm leaving for New York on Thursday afternoon. Seems they're doing a push to release the book on December 15 rather than January 15. The publishers have filled the month of December with interviews and promotional gigs. And I have an interview with *Today's Woman* magazine on Friday morning."

"An interview about the book?"

"Not exactly. Seems Harper Collins sent out all these promotional copies of the book and things…well, they're lookin' good right now. *Today's Woman* is interested in interviewing me for a job."

"Wow. Well, hey, congratulations Carlie. I mean, that's amazing. I'm sure you'll be gettin' more than just a country ham out of that deal, yes?"

Doug was trying to sound supportive but I wasn't buying it.

"I guess. Anyway, the problem is I'm not gonna be home much for the next few months."

"That is a problem, but I guess it's the price of fame, right? I mean, it sounds like your book is 'growing legs.'"

"Yeah, Joan thinks it is. So I was thinkin' maybe you could come to New York for New Year's Eve. Is that even a possibility?"

"I don't know. The awards deal is on the thirtieth. Let me look into it. Plus, isn't a hotel room in New York City pretty expensive?"

"Yeah, I guess so. I'm stayin' in a room that's leased by the publishing house. I could see what's near there."

"Well, between the plane ticket and the hotel room...I mean, that's probably a little steep for me right now, Carlie. I doubt American Airlines would accept a country ham as payment."

"I totally understand. Plus, I don't even know if I'm gonna get the job with *Today's Woman*. Shouldn't count my chickens till they've hatched, y'know?"

"I'm sure they'll want you. Who wouldn't want you?"

"Thanks, Doug."

"Carlie, I've got an early morning, so I better be hittin' the hay. I'm happy for you. It looks like everything's workin' out real well. I'm sure your parents are real proud."

"Hey, well, I'm happy for you too. Loan Officer of the Year is no small matter. Congratulations. You deserve it."

"Thanks. I'll talk to ya later."

"Bye."

Once again, I sat on the edge of the bed and cried into the pink paisley pillow. I couldn't go with Doug to his awards ceremony in Nashville. And I knew he never goes to bed at 8:30.

CHAPTER TWELVE: Thank God I'm A Country Boy...With A Woman In New York City. Yeah, That Doesn't Sound Right.

DOUG

I don't get it. I meet a nice girl who works at the Dollar General and within a month she's someone else. I thought we'd spend New Year's Eve eating Doritos and drinking Sonic limeades. What could I have been thinking? She's never gonna live that life again. Next thing I know she'll be dating a New York City dentist.

A knock at the door. "Hello, Doug?"

"Sandra? Hang on a second."

"No problem! Sorry I'm comin' by unannounced!"

I opened the door and there stood Sandra dressed in a black suit and carrying a briefcase.

"Doug, I'm so sorry for just droppin' in like this."

"Don't apologize. Come on in."

"I'm in a bit of a quandary and I was hoping you could help me."

"Sure. What's up?"

"Well, you might think this is silly but I've applied for a job at Obion County High School. They needed a biology teacher and Daddy's not gettin' any better and I decided maybe research is not my thing and besides, you know I've always liked kids. And truthfully, I don't really wanna leave West Tennessee." Sandra sounded nervous and embarrassed.

"Sandra, I think that's great! And no, I don't think it's silly at all. Teaching is an honorable profession."

"Well, you can actually help me, Doug. I need some character references. I was sittin' down tonight tryin' to think of local people who could be my references. I wrote down Mrs. Burcham from our Honors English class and Brother Dan. But people around here know you well. You have a good reputation. We've known each other our whole lives and I was wonderin' well, if you'd be willing to put in a good word for me."

"Sure, Sandra! What do I need to do?"

"Well, here's the form and the envelope already has a stamp. You're supposed to mail it to them directly."

"I'd be glad to and for the record, I think you'll be a wonderful high school teacher."

"Thanks. How's Carlie, Doug? I mean, I guess you've talked to her a lot. Marcie Jenkins told me that she has a book publishing contract. Wow!"

"She does. In fact, I just got off the phone with her. She has an interview with *Today's Woman* magazine on Friday morning in New York City. And the book is now comin' out on December 15. Early reviews have been positive. Looks like it's all goin' her way right now. So, of course, I'm proud of her."

"Well, I guess. Sounds like a really big deal."

"Yeah, I think it is."

"Well, Doug, I guess I better go. I can't thank you enough for takin' care of that for me."

"No problem, Sandra. Please tell your mom and dad that I said hello." I stood and walked to the door thinking it probably wasn't appropriate for us to be alone in the apartment together. But Sandra never moved from the leather couch.

"You should come over sometime, Doug. I know it would mean a lot to my dad. He's not doing well. He's not getting better. I don't know how to deal with it. I don't know how to face...well, how to face..."

Sandra started crying uncontrollably. I handed her a Kleenex but I knew she needed something more than that. Something I couldn't give. Something I felt obligated to withhold.

"Death? Are you saying you don't know how to handle death? That's okay. None of us do. Believe me, I could write a book about my lack of preparedness regarding the death of a parent. I'm sorry for what you and your mom are going through, Sandra. I really am. It's not easy to lose a parent. There's nothing I can say that will make it any better."

"I know. I don't see how you survived losing both parents."

"God didn't give me a choice."

"At least you have Carlie. You have someone to love you. You're not alone. I'm alone, Doug."

"I'm sorry, Sandra. I really am."

"I believe you. I'll get out of your hair. I know you weren't expecting a drop-by visit from a crying maniac woman from your past." She walked to the door and looked at me as though there was something more she wanted to say. Something she was afraid to say.

"Don't worry about it. And I'll get this in tomorrow's mail. I hope you get the job. I think you'd like teaching high school students."

"Thanks, Doug. You're one of the most supportive people I've ever known."

"Thanks."

Sandra walked down the metal stairs and I knew it would have been good manners to walk her to her car. But I didn't. It would have been chivalrous and I didn't need Sandra Miller to think of me as chivalrous. Without thinking, I quickly dialed the phone.

"Hello."

"Shannon?"

"Hey Doug! Great to hear from you!"

"I hope it's not too late to be callin', I feel bad I haven't really talked to you much since the funeral."

"Oh Doug, are you kidding? You've been crazy busy. Don't worry about it. Besides, I've been talkin' to Carlie and I can hardly believe all the good news about her book. Wow!"

"Yeah, it's pretty amazing. She's gonna be really busy in New York City. Even has a job interview on Friday. How are you and Dave? I mean, I guess you're gettin' excited about Thanksgiving, huh?"

"Doug, I've known you your whole life. You didn't call at 9:30 on a Monday night to chat. What's wrong?"

"I'm confused. I started dating a thirty-two-year-old college student who was working at the Dollar General in a small town in Georgia. Now that she's my girlfriend, well, all this stuff starts to happen and now she lives a life that makes mine look pretty conventional."

"Is she complaining?"

"She doesn't have time to complain, Shannon. She's packing for the Big Apple. She's preparing for a promotional tour. She's following her dream."

"Maybe she has dreams she hasn't told you about."

"Maybe. But if she gets this job at *Today's Woman*, you think she would really give it up to come live on a farm with me in West Tennessee? Would you ask a famous author to spend every Sunday eating with Uncle Bart and Aunt Charlotte? You think she would have fun at Buster and Michelle's tenth anniversary bologna cook-out? Right. Me neither. She has the chance for something more."

"Define the word *more.*"

"I don't even know how to define it. I just know she's talented and I don't wanna stand in her way. And I don't wanna be in her shadow either."

"Doug, you could never be in anyone's shadow. You're not a nineteen-year-old kid. You're a man. You know who you are. And I think you know who Carlie is too. She doesn't discard people."

"I know. But I don't wanna be like an old pair of shoes she keeps because they remind her of a simpler life. I want someone who will enjoy life in Sharon, someone who won't think it's a step down from something better."

"She's crazy about you, Doug. You know that. A job in New York City doesn't change that."

"Sandra came over tonight."

"You're kidding. What was that about?"

"She just needed a reference form filled out. She's applying for a teaching job at Obion County High."

"She decided to stay in the area?"

"Well, her dad's real sick and I think the research jobs are limited right now anyway."

"Or maybe she holds out hope that a young banker will give her another chance."

"I don't know."

"Would he? Would he give her another chance?"

"What? No. Of course not. You know how I feel about Carlie, Shannon."

"Yeah, I get that. But when one woman is on her way to New York and the other woman is a teacher who lives four miles away, you're saying it's crazy for me to think that could be a difficult situation."

"I'd never call you crazy."

"Be careful, Doug. Don't give up on a good woman because she's inconvenient."

"I'm not giving up on a good woman. Maybe I'm setting her free a little. I don't know. I don't know what I'm doin'. That's why I called you. I thought maybe you and Dave could tell me what to do."

"Are you serious? 'Cause if you're serious, here's what I would tell you. Carlie's a catch. She was a catch when she worked at the dollar store. And she's a catch now."

"I know. That's the worst part. I know you're right."

"Don't be in a rush to decide. Let her find a little fame. See what happens next. You don't have to know tomorrow, right?"

"I guess. But I'm lonely."

"You miss your mom and dad. That's normal."

"Well, yeah. But it's not just that. I'm tired of feeling alone. Talking on the phone is not the same as being with someone."

"I get that. But think of the long-term, Doug. Don't do something stupid because you didn't want to wait for the right one."

"I know. Why don't you and Dave come over and we'll play cards. That would cheer me up."

"Gosh, I wish we could. I do wish you lived closer. Dave is at a meeting but when he gets home, I'll tell him you called. Why don't you come stay with us sometime?"

"Yeah, I would say I'd stay on the way to Carlie's. But I can't see I'll be going there anytime soon."

"What about graduation?"

"I'm not sure. She'll only be there one day. She comes in Friday night, graduates Saturday morning and flies back to New York on Saturday evening. Plus, all her family will be there and it'll be chaotic. I may sit this one out."

"Doug, be careful."

"Yeah. I gotta go. Tell Dave I'll talk to him soon. Bye."

"Bye."

I drank a double dose of Nyquil and crawled under the tan flannel sheets. I was Loan Officer of the Year for the State of Tennessee but I could hardly stand to hear myself think. I prayed for morning to come quickly. My prayers were answered. Well, I doubt prayer had anything to do with the sun rising.

November 23   6:45 am

While eating a bowl of Frosted Flakes I had a revelation. Must have been the sugar rush. I'm not calling Carlie tonight. She needs to get ready for her trip. I need to give her space. No, that's not the reason. I don't wanna hear about the new airport security, or the difficulties of getting a taxi in New York City. I don't wanna hear about which radio shows she's going on or what Joan said about what so and so critic said about the book. I liked it when Carlie talked about the kids comin' in the store to buy supplies for their school projects. I liked it when she talked about books she'd read or funny things Clara did with the kindergarteners. I even liked it when she said she hadn't saved for a rainy day. I knew I *had* saved for a rainy day. I knew I could swoop in and save her…if only she'd let me. But Carlie Ann Davidson doesn't need saving anymore.

November 23   5:00 pm

Cell phone rings.

"Hello."

"Doug Honey, come to supper. Uncle Bart brought home leftover barbecue from the Elk's Lodge Luncheon. I made coleslaw and orange Jell-o. I'm gonna make Jiffy cornbread muffins in a few minutes. Please tell me you'll come."

"Sure. I'd love to. I have to do about thirty more minutes of paper work. Can you hold off till 5:45?"

"Absolutely. I'll put the cornbread in at 5:30. If your Uncle Bart gets hungry, he'll just have to nibble on a Ritz cracker. See ya soon, Darlin'."

"Thanks, Aunt Charlotte."

November 23   5:43 pm

I can't believe Uncle Bart still has that John boat for sale. The "For Sale" sign has faded and the inside of the boat has rusted from pools of rain water. Chester says, "Bart's too proud of that boat. Ain't nobody gonna pay no Cadillac price for a Hyundai."

Uncle Bart and Aunt Charlotte live in the all-American lower middle class home. Two bedrooms. One bath. A few shingles missing from the roof. Gray vinyl siding which had been chewed by a vagrant Black Lab. Plastic over the windows to conserve energy. But always warm and filled with food smells, some good and some, well, marginal. But Mom was wrong. Uncle Bart and Aunt Charlotte weren't under-achievers. They'd gotten everything they'd ever wanted.

Aunt Charlotte wiped her hands on an apron covered with yellow daisies as she walked onto the front porch. The wooden porch always creaked a little when she stood on one side as though it would give up the ghost at any moment. But it stood. It stood strong just like Aunt Charlotte, regardless of adversity. "Doug Honey! Good to see ya! Get yerself in this house. I jest put the cornbread in."

"Thanks, Aunt Charlotte."

"Bart, your stupid coon done ate the cat food again! Get those stale hamburger buns and lead him back into the cage. So help me, Doug, I'm gonna kill your uncle if he brings one more creature onto this place. We got three cats, two of 'em with stomach trouble, two wild coons, a crippled Labradoodle from Michelle's last batch, and two parakeets that don't sing no more. We're like the island of misfit critters."

"You've got a lot of compassion, Aunt Charlotte."

"Thank ya, baby. You're lookin' good, Doug. Must be love."

"Well, thanks. I've been workin' out down at the community center. Yeah, I feel pretty good."

"When is Carlie comin' back to see us?"

"I don't know. She's pretty busy. She's spending a lot of time in New York working on the book and all."

"Well, tell her that if she'll come, I'll make her some of them deviled eggs that she liked so well."

"I'll tell her, Aunt Charlotte."

The evening with Uncle Bart and Aunt Charlotte went exactly as I had expected. After eating dry barbecued pork, Uncle Bart fell asleep in the rose-colored recliner. Aunt Charlotte cried over my mom several times. And a cat peed on the hall carpet. Some things never change.

November 23   9:00 pm

Entering an empty apartment again. Tired of living alone. Tired of feeling alone. Where's the Nyquil? No. I don't need it. Mindless television. A book I got from Mom's house about suffering. Finally, sleep.

November 24   12:34 am

Phone rings. Who could be calling at this hour?

"Uh, hello."

"Doug, he's gone. He's gone." I could hear Sandra sobbing as she spoke the words. I knew her pain. I had been there.

"Where are you, Sandra?"

"I'm at the hospital. He died at 11:30. Mom's not taking it well. I'm sorry, Doug. You're the only person I knew to call."

"No problem. I'll be over in five minutes."

I put on old jeans and a blue sweatshirt. Didn't even bother combing my hair or brushing my teeth. It didn't matter. I had to enter through the Emergency room entrance as every other door of the small hospital was locked. I hadn't seen Sandra without make-up in years. She looked like a 15-year-old wearing jeans, a gray t-shirt, and her hair in a pony tail. She certainly didn't look like a doctor. She ran to hug me. I knew it was more than just grieving. But I didn't know what to do about it. I re-directed my attention toward her mother.

"Mrs. Miller, I'm terribly sorry. He was a great man. And he loved you. He loved both of you. What can I do to help?"

"Oh Doug, how are we gonna make it without him? I just don't see us making it." Mrs. Miller stumbled to find a chair. I got them two cups of coffee from the nurse's station. Sandra and Mrs. Miller cried in that wailing way I had seen people do at funerals. I was unprepared.

"Look, let me drive you both home. You'll need your rest. The next few days will be tiring."

"Okay. Thank you, Doug Dear. It was sweet of you to come."

I led both of them to the truck and took them home. While unlocking their front door, Sandra spoke quietly to her mother,

"What would we do without Doug? I should have never gone to California." I made no comment other than to say again what a great guy Mr. Miller was and how everyone in town thought he was the most conscientious mail carrier they'd ever had. When we entered the house, I was at a loss. "Look ladies, the best thing you can do is try to sleep. I'll be back early in the morning with sausage biscuits. I'll call the church prayer chain tonight and Aunt Charlotte will organize everyone."

Sandra wiped her eyes and said softly, "Thank you. I knew I could call you and you'd make everything alright. Thank you, Doug."

"Try to get some sleep. Trust me. You have to sleep." I walked out the front door before Sandra had a chance to hug me. I was feeling uncomfortable about the constant hugging.

I called Aunt Charlotte on the way home and she burst into action.

November 24   8:30 am

By the time I arrived at the Millers' house, there were already several cars. The sausage biscuits I brought were lost in a sea of blueberry muffins, egg casseroles, and pigs in blankets. Uncle Bart and Aunt Charlotte sat at the dining room table visiting with Michelle. Brother Dan was in the living room with Sandra and her mother. It was an all-too-familiar scene.

I spent the whole day at the Millers' house or at the funeral home. I'm not sure why. Maybe I wanted to live up to what Sandra said about me. I was "always there." I was consistent. A rock. I would never leave them in a bad situation. But my heart wasn't in it. And that was the plan. To leave my heart out of it.

November 24   7:30 pm

Cell phone rings. I walked out to the screened front porch.

"Hello."

"Doug, are you busy?"

"I'm fine. Carlie, how's it goin'? Tomorrow's the big day, right?"

"I guess. How are you doin'? Have you found out any more about your award ceremony?"

"No, I've been busy. I'm over at the Millers' house right now. Sid Miller died last night and the whole community has been here helping Mrs. Miller. It's a bad time for 'em, Carlie. Real bad. He was only fifty-five years old."

"Oh gosh, I'm sorry. I knew he had been really sick. How are they doin'?"

"As expected. It's sad. He was a great man. He really was. He lived in this community his whole life. He made a difference too. He'll be missed."

"Well, I won't keep you, Doug. I know you're busy. Tell Sandra I'm really so sorry."

"Yeah, she was really close to him. Visitation is Friday morning and the funeral is at noon. I'm gonna run up to the office now and try to get a few hours of work done."

"You didn't go to work today?"

"No. I told them I'd help with the arrangements and it took all day to get everything settled."

"They're blessed to have someone like you around."

"Thanks. Have a good trip tomorrow, Carlie. Knock 'em dead in the Big Apple."

"I'll try. When will I be able to talk to you again?"

"You'll be busy with the interview and all the book stuff. I can't imagine you'll have time to talk on the phone much."

"Doug, tell me the truth, are you leaving?"

"I'm right here in Sharon, Carlie. It's where I've always been. It's where I'll be tomorrow."

"You know what I mean. Are you leaving *me*?"

"Wait. You're the one getting on a plane to fly to New York...and you're asking if *I'm* leaving?"

"I may be in New York tomorrow but I know where my heart is. I'm not sure you know where yours is anymore."

"And you think going to New York for the rest of your life is gonna help me decide?"

"No one said I'm going for the rest of my life. It's just an interview, Doug. It's not a job offer. Besides, if you became the King of England, I'd still know I wanted a relationship with you. It wouldn't make me toss you aside."

"You're not a man, Carlie. You've no idea what it's like to be a man. I'm happy for you. I am. But if you're asking if I'm gonna wait in the wings for you...If you're asking if I'm gonna spend my life savings flying to New York once a month hoping you'll give me a little attention between interviews with Al Roker and Diane Sawyer...The answer is 'no.' I'm not. I can't do that."

I could hear Carlie crying and it was the worst sound I'd ever heard in my life. Worse than hearing Aunt Charlotte cry over Mom. Worse than hearing Sandra cry over her own father. I hadn't loved them. Not like this. I was getting ready to speak when I heard the click of the phone from the other end. And she was gone. I sat on an old green lawn chair and put my head in my hands. Not one of my better days.

Sandra walked out onto the porch slamming the screen door behind her. "Doug, are you okay?"

"Yeah, I'm fine. Just need to get to the office and take care of some work. I'll see you at the funeral home at 10:00 on Friday, Sandra. It looks like everything is ready. Now you just have to get through tomorrow without him. It won't be easy, your first Thanksgiving. But you're up to the challenge. I really do have to go."

She touched me on the sleeve. "Wait! Doug, I'm sure you know this already. But Mom and I...well, we appreciate everything you've done. You took charge and we needed that. It's nice to have a man around. Thank you. What are you doing tomorrow? I mean, what are your Thanksgiving plans?"

"I'll be at Uncle Bart and Aunt Charlotte's tomorrow afternoon. Nothing too exciting. Buster will fry a turkey in the back yard. The standard fare."

"Mom told Mr. Groeden not to schedule any visitation on Thanksgiving Day. Said people would feel obligated to come

198

and change their family plans and Daddy wouldn't have wanted that. He was selfless that way. So, I guess, well, we'll just be hanging out here at the house tomorrow, if you want to drop by or something."

"I know it'll be hard having Thanksgiving without him, Sandra. But you'll make it. You and your mom will help each other. And for the record, your dad...He really was a stand-up guy. He won't be forgotten. I'll see you at the funeral home Friday morning."

"Yeah, see ya then, Doug."

With that I walked off the porch and into a pit of sadness. It had nothing to do with Sid Miller's death or the fact that my parents were dead or the realization that I didn't have a date for an awards ceremony. I entered a pit of sadness because I jumped too quickly into a relationship with a girl I barely knew, a girl who so quickly outgrew me. For the first time in my life, the town of Sharon had a noose around my neck. And I was suffocating.

I drove past the office. I called Jessica on my cell phone and we drove to Jackson where I drank myself stupid. Jessica and her friends talked about designer hand bags and the "Twilight" movies while I drowned my sorrows in Jack Daniels. The problem? Jack Daniels didn't drown the sorrows good enough. He just put them on life support. They would be fully revived in less than twenty-four hours. And life would be even more complicated than before.

CHAPTER THIRTEEN: Things, They Are A Changin' (For Real)

CARLIE

November 24

When I hung up on Doug, I drove to the grocery store and bought a half gallon of Blue Bell Homemade Vanilla and a bottle of chocolate syrup. It had been several months since I'd done something so ridiculous and sinful. I even lied, telling the check-out lady that my grandma was celebrating her eightieth birthday. It was 8:30 on a Wednesday night and the check-out lady should have said, "Honey, thou doth protest too much." But she didn't. She just smiled and said, "$7.23 ma'am."

I couldn't eat as much as before. I had lost eleven pounds and had gotten out of the habit of depending on food as a friend. But now I had lost my best friend and the only man I had ever wanted to sleep with. Life seemed much more hopeless than before. I wondered if the people at Harper Collins knew that their rising star was sitting on an old blue couch in northern Georgia eating ice cream like there was no tomorrow. But there was a tomorrow. A tomorrow in New York City. I fell asleep at 12:20 after watching four straight episodes of "Seinfeld." I was George and everyone knew it.

November 25 Thanksgiving Day 11:00 am

Atlanta airport was crazy. I thought it would be less crowded on Thanksgiving Day. But, no. There must have been tons of people like me who were glad not to be with family on Thanksgiving Day, who were relieved to be able to say,

"Mom, Dad, I'm sorry I'll miss the dry turkey, but I need to travel that day for work." Yeah. I wasn't alone. And my new gray dress pants felt tighter now after last night's episode. I felt bloated and dehydrated and no amount of concealer could hide the terrible bags under my eyes. I had done something stupid. And it hadn't even helped. While sitting in an uncomfortable chair at gate 22, I started crying. I would never kiss Doug Jameson again. I would never wait while he opened a door. I wouldn't sit on the front porch with him. I would never hear him pray over the food or cry over his mother. It was over. He would marry Sandra within the year and they'd have beautiful little redheaded babies with curly hair. And everyone in town would say they were perfect for each other. And everyone in town would be right. Two beautiful well-educated people with beautiful children.

I went to the airport bathroom and threw up. I'm sure everyone in the bathroom felt terribly sorry for me. A tall fat single girl with no prospects and a stomach virus traveling on Thanksgiving Day. If only they knew that I was on my way to New York City to do something really important. Or that's what people kept telling me.

November 25   5:30 pm

While on the plane, I tried to fix my ailing appearance. I stopped crying and determined to think about the interview. At baggage claim, I saw a young intern from the publishing company holding up a sign that said, "Carlie Ann Davidson." I introduced myself, retrieved my bag, and we were soon in a taxi heading for my new life. Thanksgiving dinner? Room service meatball sandwich.

CHAPTER FOURTEEN: Paying the Piper

DOUG

November 25   11:30 am

The hangover was maddening.   Woke up on my couch at
11:00 with my clothes on and a foggy recollection of a bald
bartender and a nauseous ride home in the back of Jessica's
Trans Am.   I guess Jessica found my apartment key in my coat
pocket.   She called my cell phone five times this morning.   I
deserved every annoying beep.   I should have never called her
last night.   Now she thinks I'm interested.   How could I
explain that I just wanted a driver for my drunken binge?   That
I didn't wanna be alone?   Yeah.   There was no decent
explanation.   That was the kind of thing a selfish eighteen-
year-old would do.   I threw up twice and asked God to forgive
me for all of it.   The excessive drinking.   Using Jessica.   And
for acting like I cared desperately about Sid Miller's death.
Truth?   I didn't care about anything anymore.   I was numb.

November 25   1:00 pm

A shower and two bottles of water helped a lot.   When I pulled
my truck onto the side of the gravel driveway, Buster already
had the turkey fryer goin' in the front yard.

"Hey there, Doug!   It's gonna be a good 'un.   Yeah, this here's
a real beauty of a gobbler!"

"I'm sure, Buster, I'm sure."

"You brought pecan pies?   Those are my favorite, man."

"Yeah, mine too."

"You can carry 'em inside. Charlotte's got all the desserts laid out on the coffee table. Mrs. Miller and Sandra brought some kind of red velvet cake. Somebody brought it to their house for the grievin' so I reckon they decided to share."

Oh no. It would be just like Aunt Charlotte to invite grievin' folks to a Thanksgiving dinner celebration.

"Hey Doug, Sweetie, come on in the house. You look tired, dear. Are ya tired?"

"I'm fine, Aunt Charlotte."

"You'll never believe who I invited to Thanksgiving dinner, Doug?"

Oh, I'm sure I won't. Let's see…a grieving widow and her lonely single daughter? "Who, Aunt Charlotte?"

"Sandra and Mrs. Miller! I told 'em it wasn't right for them to be over there in that big ol' house all alone on Thanksgiving Day. Why, no! Sid would have never wanted that. I knew Sid Miller well enough to know that he'd a wanted them over here enjoyin' Buster's fine fried turkey with the rest of us."

"Yes ma'am. You're probably right."

"I know I'm right. Now set those pecan pies on the coffee table and come on in and visit with Sandra a while."

Sandra had not gotten the memo about our family's casual dress code for holiday dinners. She wore a black skirt and a bright red jacket with some kind of scarf. Her hair and make-up looked like the hair and make-up of a girl who was going on a date. I looked like a man who wasn't going on a date.

203

Like a man who would never go on a date again. I looked exactly the way I felt. Unshaven, tan t-shirt, and faded blue jeans.

"Hey Sandra, Mrs. Miller, welcome to the finest Thanksgiving dinner in Sharon."

"I believe it! We were thrilled that Mrs. Charlotte invited us. It's so hard, y'know, missin' Daddy and all."

"I know. Believe me, I know."

"Oh…yeah…sometimes I forget that you're, well, you're missin' both of your parents. I'm sorry, Doug."

"Thanks. Uh, I've been meanin' to ask how the job search is goin'. How did that work out at Obion County High?"

"It looks good, Doug. The principal said they oughta know for sure the first week of December."

"Yeah, well, I'm sure you'll get it. You're definitely over-qualified. Those high school kids will be lucky. Real lucky."

November 25 2:00

The gobbler's end was far less glorious than its hopeful beginning. I sat with seventeen family members and friends in a small house eating dry over-cooked turkey, delicious cornbread dressing, canned cranberry sauce that made the ever-familiar sucking sound when it landed on the fake crystal serving platter, sweet potato casserole that was more like dessert than vegetable, canned corn, green bean casserole, coleslaw, and brown n serve rolls. Oh, and after two large pieces of pecan pie, I proudly rode the wave of sugar rush like a professional surfer. Thanksgiving in the South.

CHAPTER FIFTEEN: Little Fish In A Big Pond

CARLIE

November 26   10:30 am

The waiting room at *Today's Woman* was exactly as I had imagined. Beautiful modern red furniture. Horribly ugly paintings on the wall which were supposed to be cutting edge. Lovely thin women wearing expensive clothing scurrying here and there searching for information needed to meet deadline.

"Carlie Ann Davidson."

"Yes, I'm Carlie."

"Follow me, Carlie. Mrs.Thomas is ready to see you now."

"Mrs. Thomas, this is Carlie Ann Davidson."

"Nice to meet you, Carlie. Have a seat." The office was tiny and cluttered with file cabinets and piles of paper. It was nothing like a big editor's office in a movie. I realized now that that really big clean oak desk is just a movie prop, not reality. Mrs. Thomas was a working woman, not a movie prop.

"Carlie, I don't have much time and I'm not one to beat around the bush. We love your book. My staff thinks it's fresh and honest and well-written. You're not a cold over-achieving kind of person which is good because that is completely out right now. You're real. People like real. Real sells magazines. Dr. Chesterton sent a glowing reference.

Said your work was probably the best she'd read in fifteen years of teaching. Okay. So, you can write. That's been established. What I want to know now is can you work with us? Can you be on a team? You can't know the answer to that until I tell you what that means. It means working weekends sometimes. It means working late. It means being committed. It means doing stories sometimes that you don't love. Are you ready to give us all that in order to work with the best national magazine on the stands?"

"Yes ma'am. I certainly am prepared to give it my all. I don't do things half-way. I'm not afraid of hard work. My only question would be concerning all this book promotion set up by Harper Collins. It seems like I'll be busy the next few months with that."

"Certainly. But we understand that, Carlie. We want that. Every time someone interviews you, it will be said that you're a writer for *Today's Woman* magazine. That's work as far as we're concerned. Valuable work. Profitable work. And if this book does what we think it's gonna do, well, you could do a lot for our magazine. And we tend to be generous with people who do a lot for the magazine. But with that said, we expect you to be working on stories while you're doing your promotional rounds. We'll start you on a story as soon as you get moved. We expect you to drop our name when you're making the talk show rounds. We may also want you to sort through piles of story submissions we have and help us uncover the best new ideas."

"Yes ma'am. I'm ready."

Mrs. Thomas scribbled something on a piece of paper and said, "Here's where we're prepared to start you plus a moving stipend, of course. Think about it and get back with me. You're hired, Carlie. You have a job if you want it. But you have to decide if you want it. It can't be that you *kinda* want it. You have to know."

I looked at the paper, thought about ten years of stocking shelves, and said, "I want it, Mrs. Thomas. I do."

She stood, extended her hand, and said, "Welcome to the family, Carlie. You won't regret it. This is a smart career move. You won't get any better experience or better exposure. Diane will help you find temporary housing. We want you here as soon as possible. What about the week after Christmas? Is that doable?"

"Yes ma'am. I'd already told Joan I'd be back and ready to do more promotional work on the twenty-sixth."

"We're good to go then. Joan is sending over some info. She said you can stay in their provided housing until the first of the year. We'll help you find a place as of the first. By the way, be prepared to see half that salary go to housing. It's not cheap here, Carlie. You'll still need to be tight with your money."

"I understand how to be tight with money. Really. You have no idea."

"Okay then. Diane, show Ms. Davidson where her desk will be. And get Joan from Harper Collins on the line."

Diane never spoke. She dialed the phone at the speed of sound, patched Joan through, and led me by the arm to a big open room where several men and women had back-to-back desks. Some were on the phone. Others were on the computer. And some looked like they were working on a group project for school. It looked like a place of chaos and creativity. Did those two things always go together? My desk faced a window, which made me happy. I'd always loved windows and light. But all I could see was city. Diane asked proudly, "Isn't this a beautiful view?" I nodded. But I knew that it wasn't. A beautiful view was a group of deer in a quiet cornfield.

"Everyone, this is Carlie Ann Davidson. She's starting after Christmas."

Some people waved or smiled. A few people were on the phone and motioned a welcome hand gesture. But within five seconds, they were all back to work. Time was money. Yeah, and money was...well, I wasn't sure yet. Thankfully, my hotel was within walking distance of the magazine offices.

I had never spent much time in a big city and was confused by the subway schedules and the never-ending noise. I felt self-conscious trying to hail a taxi so I didn't bother. I wasn't even sure if I had the money to be riding around in taxis. After the meeting at *Today's Woman*, I walked into a little bakery and dropped $10 on one blueberry muffin and a macchiato. Unbelievable. I didn't understand the way the bakery line worked or where to find a napkin. A wave of insecurity poured over me. Unstable hormones convinced me that everyone in the bakery was staring at the tall fat girl. That they all knew I was a small-town southern girl and that I didn't belong here. I wore "newcomer" like a sign around my neck.

I felt like Hester Prinn in "The Scarlet Letter." I know. The Hester Prinn comparison is a bit of an overkill. Note to self: Blueberry muffins and sugary coffee don't stabilize crazy hormones very well. The most painful part of the bakery experience was knowing that I could get a roast beef sandwich and a bag of Sun Chips for $4.99 at Sammy's Sandwich Emporium in Sharon, Tennessee. Sometimes Sammy even threw in a free sweet tea. I think he was trying to lure us into buying a dog bed or a winter coat.

November 26   11:00 pm

Can't sleep. Composing a letter to Doug on the computer:

Dear Doug,

I'm sorry I hung up on you. I was hurt. But that's no excuse. I never stopped to think about what all the changes in my life meant for you. I kept thinking it would be the same, only way better because I wouldn't be stocking shelves anymore. I realize now that the girl you were interested in did stock shelves. Maybe that was part of her appeal.

And you're right, Doug. You haven't moved. You're in Sharon. You're Loan Officer of the Year for the State of Tennessee. You're movin' into your mom's house in January. You're stable and that's a good thing. An honorable thing. It's not like you joined the circus and asked me to understand. But I have joined the circus, Doug. At least, it feels like that. Today's Woman offered me the job today. They're moving my things in early January.

I'm moving from Commerce, Georgia, to New York City. I don't know if it was the right decision or not. But it's already made. I have to believe God opened the door and I just walked through it. I dread breaking the news to Clara. She's been such a good roommate. She could easily afford to stay there by herself. But she probably won't. My new desk has a window view. But it's all just dark gray city below. Nothing like the view from the apple tree. I understand why you can't do this. Maybe I even respect you for it. But that doesn't keep me from crying several times a day. I wish things could have been different. Maybe I hold out hope that someday they will be. I'm still the girl you met at Cracker Barrel in Chattanooga. Don't forget that, Doug. Congratulations on being Loan Officer of the Year. You deserve it.

Carlie

I did what everyone knows you should never do. I pushed "send." I didn't re-read it. I didn't alter it. I didn't wait till the next day. I sent it. I said good-bye to the only man I'd ever loved and then I fell asleep in New York City.

CHAPTER SIXTEEN: Life Without Carlie

DOUG

November 26

The funeral was the standard Sharon funeral. The same people who were at Mom's funeral came out to grieve Sid Miller. I went through the grieving motions as best I could. Sandra asked me to speak and I told about the time her dad taught me to fly fish. I explained that he was the best Little League coach I ever had because he showed me how to choke up on the bat more and because he never yelled at me when I got distracted in left field. I even got a little emotional when I talked about sharing a cabin with him at youth camp. How he always prayed for us by name and believed we'd do great things. Sandra said it was the best part of the funeral. I knew she was biased.

I skipped out on the church lunch explaining that I had a headache. Sandra cried a little and told me she'd miss me. I slept all afternoon on top of my brown bedspread. I didn't even take my shoes off. Depression was setting in. Sid Miller prayed that I would do great things. But I hadn't.

I got an e-mail from Carlie. Basically, she said good-bye. She traded me in for her dream just like Sandra did five years ago. I was such a nice starter boyfriend but when life offered excitement or challenge or opportunity, a loan officer from Sharon couldn't compete. I understood that. But it still hurt. Did I write back? No. There was nothing left to say.

December 23

I decided to go to Dave and Shannon's for Christmas. Aunt Clarice was coming in from California. It would be good to get away and take my mind off, well, off of everything. I hardly remembered the last month. Working and sleeping. Sleeping and eating. Driving down Dave and Shannon's street made me sad though. Kids and dogs and family. I didn't have any of it. That's why I was on my way to spend Christmas with my cousin. I was Dave and Shannon's "Christmas Project 2010" and everyone knew it.

Dave had strung lights on their mailbox and around the front deck. It was endearing in a far less-than-perfect way.

"Doug! Hey man, come on in from the cold! Shannon just made cider."

"Thanks, Dave. And thanks for inviting me to stay with you for Christmas. Really. I appreciate it."

"Yeah, I didn't want you to come but Shannon pretty much insisted."

"I had a feeling."

"Doug, I know things have gone, well, not so great lately. Just wanted to tell you that I'm sorry."

"Thanks. I figure it's nothin' some late night card playin' couldn't cure."

"Look, if gettin' beat at every game known to man is considered great therapy, well then, yeah, you're at the right place, brother!"

Shannon greeted me with a big hug. "Are you boys already trash talkin'?"

I could smell the cider and the tree looked like something out of a Norman Rockwell painting. It wasn't that it was perfect. No. It just looked like home.

"Shannon, the house looks beautiful. You're an amazing woman. I really think you could have done better than Dave. Why didn't you listen to all of us when we tried to stop you?"

"Aren't you funny? How are you, Doug? And don't say, 'fine' cause I won't believe you."

"I've been better. It's been a month now. It doesn't get easier. I keep thinkin' it'll get easier."

"I'm sure. I've talked to Carlie several times. She's in the same boat."

"I didn't know you guys still talked?"

"She's my friend. I felt a bond with her from that very first night. That doesn't change because you decided you didn't want to date her anymore."

"Oh, is that what she said? That I broke it off with her?"

"Well, yeah. I mean, Doug, you did. You said you didn't want to go to New York to see her. What was she supposed to do?"

"So you think I should have gone to New York and stood in line behind all the people who wanted to spend time with her? I mean, that's how you define a great relationship?"

"A great relationship is being with someone you love, Doug. It's not about location or standing in line. The minute she got opportunities in New York, you were done with her. And no, I don't think that makes sense. I wanna think Dave would have run after me. I wanna think he wouldn't have let me slip through his fingers so easily…just because it got difficult."

"Moving to New York is what doesn't make sense. She never even considered me, never thought about future plans, or what it would take to have a relationship with me. Did she think I would just quit my job and follow her up there? That I would be her wing man for this new exciting life? She knows me better than that, Shannon."

"Doug, she's thirty-two years old. She graduated from college. She can't just sit in an apartment in Georgia waiting for you. She had to make a plan. She had to start making a living. This opportunity came up and well, anyone would have taken it. They made her a decent offer. And it was the only offer on the table, Doug."

Shannon was right and I hated that. I never made an offer to Carlie. I didn't tell her that I wanted to rent a moving truck and move her things into Mom and Dad's old house. How I'd already thought about using my rainy day fund for a honeymoon in Ireland. I didn't tell her that I bought one of those coffee machines that makes the coffee she likes. I never told her I planned to turn my old bedroom into a writing space for her, that I'd already thought about painting the walls that odd color of green she likes, that I could build a computer desk by the window so she'd have a view of the apple tree and the back property. I never told Carlie how desperately I wanted to wake up next to her every morning, how I'd dreamed of her being the first…and the last. Sadly, Shannon was right. New York City was the only offer on the table. And Carlie so quickly said, 'Yes.'"

"Shannon, you may be right. Let's change the subject, shall we?"

"We shall."

Spending the next few days with Dave and Shannon was equal parts wonderful and terrible. Watching them hold hands while playing cards or sharing a kiss after breakfast gave me hope that someday this could be my life. But watching them also made me grieve what was lost. I didn't try to drown my sorrow in Jack Daniels this time. Dave helped me find a better path. Late night Texas Hold 'Em and five-hour games of Risk. Dave and Shannon prayed with me every morning over coffee. They were like a breath of fresh air. Why couldn't I convince them to move to Sharon?

December 27

It was as good a Christmas as I could have expected. Aunt Clarice's last-minute decision to stay in California to tend to her ailing poodle was a gift of sorts. I was scheduled to go back to work on the twenty-eighth and I knew I had to leave. Plus, my lease was up on January 15 and I needed to have all my stuff moved to the farm before then. As I was pouring my last cup of coffee, I heard a loud knock on the door. Dave greeted someone and then closed the door promptly. "Shannon, come look! Flowers!"

He opened a large card that came with the flowers. "They're from Carlie."

I walked from the kitchen and leaned against the door facing. I didn't wanna act too interested. But who was I kidding? Dave and Shannon both knew the truth.

Shannon glowed as she admired the huge bouquet of white lilies and red roses. "Read the card, Dave."

"Dave and Shannon, I'm sorry these are late. I hope you had a Merry Christmas! Thank you for being so kind, for taking me into your home and into your lives. I hope we will always stay in touch. Make note of my new address below and come see me anytime. Please bring your blueberry muffins. There's a bakery near my new apartment but they charge $6.75 per muffin. Of course, that goes against my rural sensibilities. Shannon, I owe you a lot for your counseling services. Maybe someday I will be able to pay up. I thank God that He brought you both into my life. Happy New Year, Carlie"

Dave was uncomfortable and never made eye contact with me. He cleared his throat a few times. "Well, they really are beautiful! And yeah, she's right. You do make killer blueberry muffins, Shannon."

Shannon touched a white lily and said, "How thoughtful!"

I walked back into the kitchen and drank my coffee black, never saying a word to Dave and Shannon about the flowers. I smiled about Carlie's comments about the bakery muffins. Yeah. That wasn't her style. She would make them in her own kitchen or eat a Pop-Tart. I started to ask Dave for her address. But my pride held me back. Shannon placed the flowers on the kitchen table and never spoke of Carlie again. I drove to Sharon and couldn't stop thinking of her.

December 27   5:00 pm

Aunt Charlotte and Uncle Bart had invited the whole family to their house for an after-Christmas get-together. I got into town in time to take a long nap before going by Jim's Grocery

216

to buy a coconut cake. No one expected me to make homemade coleslaw or creamy potato casserole. They knew I'd just go buy a cake or a pie. When I arrived, cars were already parked in the small yard. Somehow that felt comforting.

Michelle was on the front porch smoking a Marlboro like it was her last. "Doug, guess what Uncle Bart made me do. Go ahead, guess."

"I have no idea."

"He made me move my van because he said I was obstructing the view of the John boat from the street. Can you believe that?" She laughed quietly and I could tell she wasn't really mad.

"Well, hey Michelle, there's probably an after-Christmas run on rusted-out John boats…and you shouldn't let your Dodge Caravan stand in the way of Uncle Bart's surprise anniversary cruise for Aunt Charlotte." We both laughed out loud. We knew Uncle Bart wouldn't even take Aunt Charlotte out to eat in Jackson. He said the same thing every time someone suggested it, "If I wanted to see all my money go up in smoke, I'd a jest thrown it in the fire."

"How are you doin', Doug? You makin' it okay?"

"I'm good. Dave and Shannon send their love. It was nice stayin' with them a few days. Good to get away, y'know?"

"Yeah. Look, I'm not one to get in anyone's business. Shoot, I can't even take care of my own business, Doug. Molly's pregnant again and we still have two from the last litter. Buster's hours are bein' cut back at the plant. Jimmy's decided he's gonna win some kind of rubber band shootin' competition and we all have red marks on our arms. But for the record, I mean, in case you were wonderin'…I liked her, Doug. Carlie. She was different. I don't know. I guess I just wanted to tell you that."

"Thanks, Michelle. Yeah, she was different all right. Let me know if you want me to try to find homes for the puppies. You never know when the general public might take a renewed interest in buying old rusty John boats and Labradoodles."

Michelle smiled as she threw the cigarette butt into a small metal can on the porch railing. "We can always hope, Doug. We can always hope."

The dinner was nothing like a Norman Rockwell painting, unless Norman Rockwell painted an old man feeding a raccoon from the table. Little Jimmy shot Aunt Charlotte in the behind with a rubber band while she was getting cornbread out of the oven. While doubling over with laughter, she chased him down the hallway armed with a dirty yellow fly swatter and a massive slur of verbal threats. That was the entertainment for the evening. Buster and Michelle sprung for a spiral ham which was delicious. Chester and Ida brought hash brown casserole. Aunt Charlotte made cornbread muffins and opened several jars of Mom's green beans. Brother Dan brought a raisin pie and a Jell-o salad. I never understood why they called it a Jell-o salad. I don't think adding fruit cocktail to strawberry Jell-o makes it a salad.

Aunt Clarice called from California and spoke to everyone individually, even telling Brother Dan he needed to wear a clerical collar the next time he spoke at a funeral. Yeah, Mom would have had plenty to talk about on the way home from this event. But I didn't feel an ounce of criticism. I was glad they all loved me.

December 27   9:00 pm

I dreaded making the call all day. What was I supposed to say? How could I help her understand my unusual situation? I felt like a sixteen-year-old boy asking Marsha Groeden to the prom, knowing full well she'd probably get drunk in the parking lot and leave me looking like an idiot.

"Hello."

"Sandra?"

"Hey Doug! Good to hear from ya!"

"Yeah. Well, I hadn't even congratulated you on the new job yet. Brother Dan said you're really excited about it. I'm happy for ya. You'll make a great teacher. When do you start?"

"My first day with the students is January 3. Yeah, I'm real excited."

"Sandra, I need a favor and I was wonderin' if you could help me out a little."

"Are you kidding? Of course, I'd love to help you with anything."

"I got this award thing…it's kind of…"

"Yeah! I read about it in the Messenger. Congratulations, Loan Officer of the Year! I would have sent a gift but I wasn't sure what one sends to a prominent local banker. Cigars? Wine?"

"Food. Food's always good."

She laughed with enthusiasm. "I'll have to remember that."

"Okay. Well, there's this big awards ceremony in Nashville on the thirtieth. Some of the folks from this branch will be goin' and lots of people from around the state will be there. It's at the Opryland Hotel and well, I was wonderin'…I mean, they gave me two free tickets to the dinner. And the food is supposed to be pretty good. They announce the awards after dinner. Probably be the most boring evening of your life, but at least it would get you out of Sharon. You interested? I mean, strictly as a friend, y'know?"

"Absolutely! I'm always up for boring awards ceremonies, Doug!"

"Okay then. I'll pick you up at 3:30 on Saturday. Will that work?"

"I'll be ready. I take it this is a formal deal?"

"Not formal like a tux or evening gown thing. I'm wearing a dark gray suit. I don't know what a woman would wear. Probably just any kind of dress."

"I'll figure something out, how 'bout that?"

"Yeah, don't go to any trouble though. It's no big deal."

"Of course it's a big deal, Doug. It's a really big deal. You should be really proud of yourself."

"I'm just supposed to go and I'm going."

"Well, I'm lookin' forward to a night out on the town…even if it does mean listening to bankers introduce each other."

"Thanks, Sandra. I'll see you Saturday and thanks for doin' this especially so last minute."

"No problem. See you Saturday."

"Bye."

I called a friend and asked her to go with me to an awards banquet. But that one phone call complicated my life far more than I could have ever imagined.

CHAPTER SEVENTEEN: Big Girl In The Big Apple

CARLIE

December 26   8:30 pm
On a plane to New York City

That was the worst Christmas of my life. Some mothers would have spent the whole time being happy for their little girl. They would have said things like, "We can't believe our little girl got a job with a national magazine! We're so proud!" or "Everyone's just so happy for you, Carlie. You graduated from college. You're moving to the big city, following your dream!"   But Mom was never one to waste time on happiness. "Do you think they're wearing that style of jacket in New York, Carlie? I seriously doubt it." "Whatever you do, don't wear those hideous brown shoes when you're in New York." "Have a professional do your hair color, Carlie. Do you really think the people at *Today's Woman* buy their Ash Blonde at Walgreen's for $4.78?"

I don't know, Mom. I don't know where they buy their hair color. I don't care. I was seated in 17B and almost laughed out loud because I was proudly wearing the hideous brown shoes. Rebel child that I am. I know it must have killed Mom not to get on the plane with me so she could remind me to wear eye shadow, and not to wear the outdated navy jacket, and that Doug probably broke up with me because I tend to be a carb eater. Shoot, she'd be running the whole city within two weeks.

The next two days would be spent doing radio interviews. Joan prepped me very little. "You've got presence, Carlie.

Use it. Be real. Be funny. Talk about the book the way you'd talk to a friend. You can do it. Say the title at least three times. Relax and enjoy the ride." I did like talking with people on the radio. And the radio personalities seemed to enjoy me and my southern accent. I was appropriately self-deprecating and the callers informed me that it was charming. The bottom line? I had nothing to lose. If the book flopped, it would be because Harper Collins chose a stupid book written by an unknown southern woman with a big behind who stocked shelves for a living. I couldn't take responsibility for that. And I wouldn't.

December 27   9:00 pm

I saw my new apartment today. It was the size of my parents' walk-in closet and the floor was covered with green tile from a public school bathroom. For what I'm paying in rent, I could have bought a lovely home in a nice neighborhood in Commerce. But I don't live in Commerce anymore. I live and work in New York City where ice cream is twice as expensive and I get lost on the subway and Mrs. Thomas thinks all single people live together before getting married. The worst part? The old blue couch my grandma gave me is never gonna fit in that efficiency apartment. But I'll survive. I am woman, hear me roar...and all that worthless jazz.

Joan said the radio interviews went well and that book sales have been brisk. I don't know what that means. I'm working on a funny story called, "Messies vs. Cleanies" for *Today's Woman*. I already have five paragraphs written. Life is good. But it's far from perfect.

December 28   7:00 am

On the wrong subway again. Thankfully, I wore the hideous brown shoes as they are by far my most comfortable shoes for running through New York City trying to find my office.

December 28   7:53 am

At home at my desk now. Another gray day in the Big Apple.
E-mail from Joan said we move to television after the first of
the year. I'm supposed to be ridiculously happy. But all I can
think about is how enormous I'm gonna look on a television
screen. If I wear black, I'll look thinner. But black tends to
wash me out. If I wear bright colors, my face will look better
but my body will look like a big fat round carnation, all fluffy
and ridiculous. This is a lose/lose proposition.   Yeah. I
should have thought about the word "lose" a few months ago
and maybe I wouldn't have eaten so many blueberry muffins
and drunk so many sugary coffee drinks.

I need to get online and see what Oprah's wearing these days.
She and I are about the same size. But my pasty white skin
will make me look so much bigger than Oprah. Plus, she may
be wearing an outfit that costs $2000. I only have $698.76 in
my account right now and I need to go to the grocery store and
re-fill my subway card. Mom told the Commerce Garden
Club I'd be meeting a lot of famous people in New York City.
But I missed people like Mr. Porter and the Rockfords. I even
missed my brother borrowing my bread machine. I should just
give him that bread machine. I don't need the carbs. And I'd
have to store it at the foot of my bed anyway.

December 31   11:00 pm
New Year's Eve

A pint of Ben and Jerry's. A promise that my things will be
moved into my tiny apartment on January 2. Working on a
new story about women who are sworn to singleness.
Women who really want to be single.   Funny interviews.

224

Some great quotes. Realistic? Not on your life. Bed by
11:22. Happy Almost New Year.

CHAPTER EIGHTEEN: Lookin' For A Country Girl...And A Country Ham

DOUG

December 30

I bet Mrs. Miller is gonna be all happy that Sandra and I are going to Nashville. She'll probably compliment my suit and say we make a lovely couple. I dread that whole process. Yeah, the porch light is already on and it's just 3:27 in the afternoon.

"Doug, come in Dear."

"Thank you, Mrs. Miller."

"Don't you look handsome? You sure do. Sandra has just been beside herself about what to wear. She shopped in Jackson, even went to Memphis yesterday. You won't be disappointed, Doug. She's a real beauty."

"Yes ma'am, she is."

About that time Sandra walked into the living room wearing a black dress with sparkly things all over it. Her hair was pulled back loosely. She was beautiful. Sexy even.

"Sandra, you look beautiful."

"Thanks, Doug. You're not so bad yourself."

"Now stand by the fireplace so I can get your picture. You two make a lovely couple."

See, I knew that's exactly what she'd say.

"Mom, please, we're not seventeen."

"I know. But a mom can take pictures if she wants, can't she?"

"That's fine, Mrs. Miller." Why was I always so easy-going about stuff like this? I didn't want to have my picture taken. But I did. Path of least resistance, I guess. And where had that path taken me? Yeah. Nowhere.

The awards banquet was exactly like I thought it would be. Dressed-up people introducing people who introduced people who thanked people who introduced other people. When it was over, I whispered an apology to Sandra. She smiled and whispered back, "This is the most fun I've had in six months."

The Opryland Hotel was beautiful with all the lights and Christmas decorations still up. But I wasn't happy. And thousands of lights never bring a man happiness. After the banquet, Sandra asked if we could walk around a while and I agreed. It was the least I could do after putting her through such boring dribble. A few people approached us and congratulated me on the award. Susan Mathis, our branch manager, patted my arm and said with a smile, "I had a feeling you two would eventually get back together."

Before I had a chance to say that we weren't together, that I was planning to paint my old bedroom green, that my real love interest was a famous writer in New York City…Sandra had already smiled and said, "Thank you, Susan."

I was silent as we approached the elevators to go to another level.

"What's wrong, Doug?"

"This was a mistake. I'm sorry, Sandra. I should have never asked you to come. It wasn't fair to you. I thought we could come as friends but that was stupid. You don't need a friend. You have friends. And, well, I don't need someone other than a friend right now."

"You don't? I thought everyone needed someone, Doug. I thought everyone needed someone special they could confide in. Someone to encourage them, look out for them, take care of them."

"Yeah. But that's the problem. I've already found that person, Sandra."

"Then why isn't she in an elevator with you at the Opryland Hotel?"

"Fair question. And I don't really have the answer. To quote Facebook, 'It's complicated.' She's busy in New York City. But that's not even the complete answer."

"Marcie Jenkins told me you and Carlie were a thing of the past. But she got it wrong. You're still hung up on her. And these expensive shoes are killing me. Let's call it a night, Doug."

"I really am sorry. I hope you know that...that I never intended to use this evening to hurt you."

"Yeah. I get that. You needed someone to come with you. I was a convenient person to ask. Too bad you never had a sister, huh, Doug?"

We were in the parking lot within ten minutes. Awkward silence was an understatement. Less than ten words were spoken during the first hour of travel down Interstate 40. Sandra even nodded off a few times. We agreed to make a bathroom stop when we saw the big Shell sign. I checked my rearview mirror and moved toward the right lane.

"DOUG! STOP! He's coming!" But it was too late. The noise was deafening. Glass everywhere. I couldn't tell if we were on the road or in a ditch. My left arm was bleeding and my vision was blurry.

"Sandra? Sandra!"

"I'm here, Doug. My leg! What happened to my leg?!" Her head was bleeding profusely and she started screaming in pain.

God, what have I done? The truck was completely dented in near her right leg. I managed to open the door but I fell to the ground. Dizzy.

"Help! Someone help us!"

And that's the last thing I remember. Lying on the grass watching the underside of the truck drip oil and seeing smoke come from the engine.

I woke up a few hours later in a hospital in Dickson.

"Mr. Jameson. Mr. Jameson, do you know where you are?"

It felt like a really bad hangover. The worst hangover of my life. "No. Where am I?"

"You're in the hospital here in Dickson. You were in a very serious car accident, Mr. Jameson. Do you remember the accident?"

"Uh, yeah, a little."

"We wanted to check for internal injuries. You broke your left arm and you're a little banged up. You had a slight concussion. We'll have to watch you overnight. But you should be fine. You're a lucky man, Mr. Jameson. And your wife will be fine too. Don't worry. But she'll have to go through some serious rehab."

My mind was still foggy. "My wife? I'm not married."

"Oh, I'm sorry. The woman who was with you...she's on another floor. Her leg was injured pretty badly and she has some facial lacerations, but she'll make it. And you'll be doing so well that you'll be able to help her in no time. Don't worry. Really, she'll be fine."

I didn't know what to say. I'd injured Sandra Miller in more ways than one. I'd tossed her aside because I wanted Carlie. Then I nearly killed her on I-40. Now I'd be left to help her recover. That was the least I could do, right?

They released me from the hospital early the next morning and I took the elevator to Sandra's room. I wore my gray suit pants even though the knees were torn. The nurses found a t-shirt for me to wear. I didn't plan what I was going to say to Sandra. It hurt to see Mrs. Miller and Brother Dan in the hallway outside her room. I'd really done it this time.

"Mrs. Miller, I'm sorry. I can't say it enough."

"I know, Dear." Mrs. Miller looked ten years older than when I had come to pick up Sandra the day before. Her husband died less than a month ago and now I had put her daughter in the hospital. How much more could she take?

I reached out to hug her. "I don't even remember the whole thing. They told me she's gonna be okay, but they're just now releasing me. I haven't been able to come up here and see her. Can I see her? I mean, is she taking visitors?"

"Yes, but don't stay long, Honey. The doctor wants her to get plenty of rest. Her surgery is this afternoon."

I would have paid all the money I had to not have to walk into that hospital room. But I wasn't a child and I couldn't run from what I'd done. I thought about what my grandpa always said, "Own up to your mistakes. No matter how bad."

Her eyes were closed and her face was badly cut and swollen.

"Sandra? Sandra?"

"Oh Doug, I was hoping you'd come."

"Of course. Sandra, of course I'd come. I'd never leave you here. I'm sorry. I'm so very sorry. I don't even remember what happened. I know you saw something. They tell me it was a big truck. But it was my fault. I know it was my fault. And I'm sorry. So sorry."

"Don't worry about it, Doug. I'm gonna be fine."

"What are they gonna do to you?"

"They have to put a rod in my leg and do some repairs on my knee. I'll be in a wheelchair a while, a walker after that, but I'll walk again. I'm sure of that."

"I'll help you, Sandra. Anything you need, I'll be there. Just name it." I reached out to hold her hand.

She managed a small grin. "I know. That's why it hurts so badly."

"Your leg?"

"No. That you don't want me. Because you really are a stand-up guy...the kind of guy who'll bring me dinner, who'll bring me books from the library, re-arrange my pillows. You'll probably drive my mom home and get me situated and bring us groceries on your way home from work. That's the kinda guy I always wanted, Doug. The sad thing? I had him once. But I was determined to break free of a small town. And by the time I knew better, it was too late."

"If I were such a great guy, you wouldn't be in this hospital bed right now."

"It was an accident. People have accidents all the time. No one thinks less of you. You don't owe me anything. Don't take care of me out of guilt."

"What about your insurance coverage?"

"Yeah. Now there's a story for the front page of the paper, Doug. A broke unemployed doctor of bio-ethics...who didn't see the need to get insurance 'cause I was gonna be gettin' a job any day now. Yeah. Brilliant."

"Sandra, tell me you have something, some kind of health insurance."

"Bupkus. And that would be the second stupid thing I did…or didn't do."

"We'll work it out with the hospital. I'll do what I can. I know my truck insurance covers injuries to some extent. I'll have to see what's available. I have a small savings account and if needed…"

"Doug, you don't need to spend your money. I should have known better than to be uninsured. I did know better."

A friendly older nurse came in and said calmly, "I'm sorry, Sir, but you need to leave. Ms. Miller, they've moved your surgery time up to 11:00. We'll be doing your prep now."

"Thanks. Doug, pray for me before you leave, would you?"

The nurse smiled and said sweetly, "That'll be just fine, Honey." Mrs. Miller and Brother Dan walked in quietly. I carefully held Sandra's bruised hand and said, "Lord, we pray for Sandra right now. She's hurting and we hurt for her. We pray you would use the doctor's hands to repair her leg and knee. Thank you for our safety. Thank you for Sandra's forgiving attitude and sweet spirit. We pray you would walk with her through the difficulties of this process. In Jesus' name, Amen."

Mrs. Miller sobbed quietly and hugged me like I had done her a favor. Didn't she understand that I was the reason she was in this hospital room looking at her broken daughter? Forgiveness must run in the family.

CHAPTER NINETEEN: Starting Over...Again

CARLIE

January 1   10:30 am

Phone rings.

"Hello."

"Carlie? This is Shannon."

"Shannon! Great to hear from you. Happy New Year!"

"Happy New Year to you too."

"Tell me you and Dave are down in Times Square and you want me to meet you there."

"Hey, I wish. Did you celebrate with the masses down there last night?"

"I celebrated by eating ice cream alone and going to bed at eleven-something. Yeah, I'm a real party animal."

"Dave and I wanted to thank you for the flowers. They're still beautiful. We were so surprised."

"You're welcome. Did you go anywhere for Christmas?"

"We stayed here. My mom was supposed to come but she had a last-minute veterinary emergency. Doug came for a few days."

"Really. How's Doug? I mean, I guess he's the same, huh? 'Cept now he has that award. I hope they gave him a country ham 'cause he was laughin' and jokin' about how he really wanted a country ham instead of a plaque. And how that's the least that they could do for Loan Officer of the Year."

"Yeah. Carlie, I called to tell you something. I don't know why. I just thought you should know. It's Doug. He's been in a serious car accident. Coming back from the awards ceremony in Nashville, he was hit by a big truck on Interstate 40. His truck is totaled."

"Oh no! Is he alright? Is he hurt?"

"He broke his left arm. A few bruises, but he's fine. It really is amazing. Sandra wasn't quite so fortunate. She had surgery on her leg and knee yesterday. She'll be laid up for a while."

"Sandra was with him?"

"I'm sorry, Carlie. He just needed someone to go with him to the banquet. He says it was a horrible mistake. In fact, he and Sandra had just had a heart-to-heart talk before they got in the truck. He told her he shouldn't have asked her to the banquet because she could never be more than a friend. There was absolutely nothing between them. Really."

"I'm sorry about the wreck. As far as Doug and Sandra, it's really none of my business. But I am sorry she's hurt so badly. That won't be an easy recovery. Thankfully, well, I guess Doug will be there to help her...help her get better."

"I just thought you might like to contact him or something, Carlie."

"I still love him, Shannon. I dream about him at night...and daydream about him every day. But, no. I can't contact him. I can't feel like I chased him and wore him down. He needs time to decide what he wants. Who he wants."

"You're probably right. I have a tendency to wanna jump in and fix things. I need to let it go. Carlie, anytime you need a break, please come see us in Chattanooga. I'll make blueberry muffins on the spur of the moment. I promise."

"I'd sure love to be there right now, Shannon. You have no idea."

"Is everything okay? I mean, you like the job and everything?"

"I do. They say the book is selling well and the interviews have been fine. I'm going on the Today Show Wednesday morning. Can you believe it? I get to meet Matt Lauer."

"Of course, I believe it, Carlie! We all knew you were talented and special."

"Even when I drew a Triceratops that looked like a chocolate chip cookie?"

"Oh yeah, even then! Especially then! Wow! That's pretty exciting about being on the Today Show! We'll be sure to watch or TiVo it."

"Thanks. It's not that I'm not thankful. I'm thankful for my job and the opportunities I have here. I am. But I'm lonely, Shannon. I live in a city with millions of people and I feel utterly alone. I've gone twice to this small church near my apartment but I haven't connected with anyone yet. The people at work are friendly but I don't wanna throw myself on 'em. I don't know. This is supposed to be the most exciting time of my life. But sometimes I think, 'Really? This is all it is?'"

"I know. I'm sorry. I'm still praying."

"Thanks. I haven't given up hope."

"Yeah, it's way too soon to give up. I've gotta go. Call anytime, Carlie. Anytime, day or night."

"You too. Bye."

CHAPTER TWENTY: Lonely Days Of Winter

DOUG

January 3
Volunteer Community Hospital, Martin, Tennessee

"Good Morning! How's my favorite patient?"

"Ready to run a marathon."

"Well then, let me get your running shoes."

"It looks like you're carrying a decaf cappuccino which would help my running immensely, Doug."

"You're in luck."

"The doctor says I can probably go home today."

"That's great! I have a rental car and can pick you up whenever you get released."

"Actually, Brother Dan is bringing Mom this morning and they'll just take me home."

"Oh, okay. Yeah, that makes sense. You're not scared to ride with me are you, Sandra?"

"Of course not. But I also don't want you to think, well, that you're responsible for me, that you have to do everything for me. Other people are available."

"Yeah, I get that. Something looks different. Do you have on make-up? And your hair? You've given up that greasy pulled-back look…which is sad 'cause it was workin' for ya, Sandra. Really."

"Aren't you funny? Yeah, one of the nurses helped me look a little more presentable this morning. Washed my hair and I feel like a new woman."

"I bet." Sandra no longer looked like a battered woman. She looked healthy and beautiful. I couldn't help but notice that the hospital gown was pulled tight around her chest. Interesting.

I tried to sound optimistic. "So what is the plan for today?"

"Well, let's see, Doug. Mindless TV. Ridiculous magazines. And all the Jell-o I can eat."

"That a girl. Whatcha watchin'?"

"Today show. Turn it up and we'll learn what's goin' on in the world?"

We watched news of a bomber in Scotland, a dog who had rescued a woman from a burning building in Jacksonville, but I wasn't prepared for what came next:

"And for all you single women, we have some expert advice and humor coming up next. The author of 'A Single Woman's Guide to Ordinary' makes her first appearance on the Today Show to talk about life, love, and laughter for the modern single woman." Carlie waved at the camera and smiled in a most natural way. Her hair was a little different. Beautiful. Her body looked amazing contrary to what she would have thought. Pink sweater with a multi-colored scarf. Long black skirt. Black boots. I was mesmerized.

Finally Sandra spoke. "Wow! Carlie's on TV! Pretty impressive."

"Yeah. I'm happy for her. We don't have to watch it if you don't want to." I wasn't about to confess that I was recording it on TiVo at the apartment. That Shannon had called me and told me to watch it.

"Are you kidding? Of course, we're gonna watch it, Doug. It's back on. Turn it up."

"We're pleased to introduce you to a new author who's quickly making a name for herself. Carlie Ann Davidson's 'A Single Woman's Guide to Ordinary' has only been on the market a few weeks but it's becoming an internet sensation. Carlie, we're glad to have you here this morning."

"It's my pleasure to be here, Matt."

"Okay. So I'm reading your background last night and I'm thinkin', 'Impossible.' Is it true that only a few months ago you were shelving groceries at a store in Georgia while finishing up an English degree?"

"Absolutely. I worked at the Dollar General Store for ten years and if you could see me wield a case of Hawaiian Punch...well, you'd be pretty impressed."

He smiled sincerely. "I'm sure. How did you get interested in this subject, Carlie? What made you think you could write this book?"

"Well obviously, I'm single but I'm not one of those women trying to prove I'm happy about it. I'm not really that happy about it, Matt. So, if you know someone...I'm open to suggestions."

He laughed so genuinely, "Are you asking for referrals?"

"Oh, absolutely! But they have to be tall. I'm 5'11 and not all men can handle that. You're definitely tall enough for me, Matt. But I know you're happily married and you may not like a woman with such a big caboose."

Again, his laugh was genuine, "Have you always been funny and how did you find the other funny women you interview in the book?"

"Every woman interviewed for the book has a few things in common: They're southern, single, and willing to talk about it. Most of them I knew personally. Others were recommended to me by friends. We just started chatting and enjoying similar experiences. The book was truly a project of love." Carlie then looked directly into the camera, "Women, please go out and buy the book. Really. I need the money. Buy it so I don't continue wearing hideous shoes my mom hates. Heck, you can buy the book even if you're a man. I won't mind."

"Yeah, I'm sure you wouldn't," he said with a smile. "Carlie, the book talks a lot about love or the lack thereof. At the time of the writing, you were thirty and unattached. Two years have passed and you're telling me you still haven't found love?"

Carlie's face grew deathly serious. "I'm not saying that."

"Oh, so who's the lucky guy?"

"Well Matt, here's the deal. I can love someone but that doesn't mean he loves me back."

"I'm sorry about that, Carlie. Let's go a different direction then. Your book makes it obvious that you're proud to be a southern girl. Yet you recently moved to New York City to take a job with *Today's Woman*. Have you been out with any of the men here in the city? And what do you believe are the differences between small-town southern men and men from the big city?"

"It's funny you asked that question because a very nice man from work took me to dinner last night and showed me around. But truthfully, I don't think he was that impressed with me. I was home by 8:30. Is that a bad sign? As to the differences, men in the rural South tend to shoot their own dinner...and I think that's frowned upon in Times Square."

Matt bowed his head in laughter and then held up the book and extended his hand to Carlie. "You are a delight, Carlie Ann Davidson. The book is 'A Single Woman's Guide to Ordinary.' Available now. Back in a moment with weight loss tips for the New Year."

The silence in Sandra's small hospital room was deafening. I was hurting so badly that I wanted to throw up. She had gone to dinner with another man. She thought I didn't love her. Matt Lauer thought she was funny and engaging and adorable and I'm sure he wasn't the only one. Carlie lived in New York City now and she was famous or almost famous. She looked even more beautiful than the last time I saw her. And I thought her big rear end was perfect. I always had. I didn't need the world to tell me she was wonderful. I knew that even when the world ignored her completely.

Depression was setting in. I hadn't shaved in two days and was sitting in a hospital room in Martin, Tennessee, with a woman who didn't have insurance. A woman I was now obligated to care for. A woman I wanted to love but couldn't.

Sandra finally broke through the silence. "She was great, Doug. Really. She has a gift."

"Yeah. She did well. Funny too. Great to hear that the book's doin' well."

I excused myself to the bathroom and we never mentioned the interview again. I went to work and told Sandra to call me when she was home. Told her I'd bring dinner from Sammy's Sandwich Emporium and did she want Sour Cream and Onion Chips or Sun Chips. Susan Mathis stuck her head in my office door and asked how Sandra was doing. I told her she was going home today. Susan bragged about the amount of work I had managed to get done at the bank despite the difficulties of the wreck. But I think she knew I was only going through the motions. She was trying to give me a pep talk without calling it a pep talk.

There's not much to write about the cold months of January and February. I grew a beard. I paid two high school kids from church to pack and move all my things from my apartment to Mom and Dad's house on January 12. Most of those boxes are still in the garage. I donated my furniture to Good Will. I ate supper on the cream-colored couch every night. I took dinner to Sandra and Mrs. Miller every night for three weeks straight and they always asked me to stay and I always said that I couldn't. The ladies from church volunteered to do some of the nights but I refused. I owed Sandra and Mrs. Miller and everyone in town knew it. I was weary of everyone's constant questions, "How's Sandra,

Doug?" "I heard Sandra is improving. When will she be walking?" "You guys were sure lucky. What happened?"

When the hospital bills came, we filed a claim with my truck insurance and then I wrote a check for thirty-two thousand dollars. Twenty thousand dollars was the cash I'd inherited when Mom died. Twelve thousand was half of what I had saved. Mrs. Miller cried saying that I was terribly generous. I wasn't generous at all, just indebted. It was settlement money, not generosity. I knew it wouldn't even put a dent in her bills. I'm sure Sandra knew I was using the money to *put her away* of sorts. To be done with it all. To be done with her. I stopped bringing dinner but called Mrs. Miller on the phone every few days. Sandra started walking with a walker on January 30 and was teaching biology at Obion County High on Feb. 7. According to the local news hounds at the barber shop, Sandra and the new football coach were hand-in-hand at the church Valentine banquet. Aunt Charlotte said, "They make a lovely couple even though she still has a horrible limp and he's from Michigan." February was one of my best months at work. I already put eighteen hundred dollars in savings. Time for spring.

March 14   8:00 pm

Phone rings.

"Hello."

"Doug, how's it goin' old man?"

"Good, Dave. Real good."

"Is that right? What's goin' so good?"

"Well, I finally got the garage door fixed. I painted the fence by the driveway, put twenty head of cattle in the back field, work is pickin' up, and it'll be spring soon. No complaints here. How are you and Shannon doin'?"

"We're great. I mean, no cattle or garage door news…nothin' exciting like that, but hey, we're makin' it. Gettin' ready to make a little road trip up to Nashville this weekend."

"Sounds like fun. What's the occasion?"

"A book signing."

"I guess Shannon talked you into that one, huh?"

"Look, Buddy. I'll cut to the chase. Shannon asked me to call you. I don't know if you've been keepin' up with Carlie and the book thing but it's goin' well, I mean, sellin' like hot cakes. Been on all the talk shows and everything. They say she'll have another book out within six months."

"Good. I'm happy for her."

"She's gonna be at a book signing in Nashville on Saturday afternoon. And well, Shannon thinks you should go."

"Shannon thinks I should drive to Nashville, stand in line with a bunch of single women, to get the autograph of the woman who wrecked my life? Tempting…but no thanks."

"Wrecked your life? How'd she wreck your life, Doug? Sounds like you've done a pretty good job of wrecking your own life without any help from Carlie Ann Davidson."

"I'm hanging up, Dave. Thanks for callin'."

"Wait, wait. I'm sorry, Doug. Really, I was out of line and I'm sorry. I admit it. You haven't wrecked your life. Not even close. But you haven't taken chances either. You haven't moved forward and I think you know that. Yeah, I'm happy for you on paintin' the fence and havin' some cattle now. I am. But there's more to life than order, Doug."

"I know that. You think I don't know that? You think I don't go to bed every night wishin' things were different? You think I don't ask God every day to make things different? Dave, if you called to tell me that I'm lonely, believe me, I know. I've known for a long time."

"Then quit bein' stubborn, Doug. Look, we all know you haven't gotten over her. You're not gonna get over her. It's impossible. It's one of those great mysteries of life. I remember it myself. You may not know this but Shannon broke up with me about a month before I was gonna ask her to marry me. She wasn't sure about our relationship, said she needed some space, the whole Dr. Phil scenario. That lasted almost a month and it was the longest month of my life. I lost ten pounds because I was physically sick almost every day. My friends said I would meet someone else, that I should move on with my life, but I knew they were all crazy. They didn't have a clue. They didn't understand that I didn't want anyone else. That I could never want anyone else. I get it, Doug. I do. So quit with the pride and stubborn routine and just go to Nashville and be done with it. If she rejects you flat out you will have at least tried. But the way it is now, well, you're just going through the motions of living."

"Was Shannon writin' on cue cards for you during that whole speech?"

"No. She was using a variety of hand motions. Did it work?"

"I don't know. Let me think about it. So when Shannon broke up with you, how'd you get her back?"

"I brought flowers to her apartment one day and told her that she should do what she thought was right, that I was willing to never see her again, that I had put my faith in God and I would live with her decision no matter how painful, that I wasn't going to stalk her or beg."

"Wow, I never knew you were so mature."

"Well, I didn't tell you what was on the card."

"I'm waiting."

"It said, 'I love you more than any man has ever loved a woman.'"
"And that was it? I mean, she actually fell for that? She threw her arms around you and agreed to marry you on the spot?"

"No. She said she cried for two days and ate ice cream. But yeah…three days later she called and told me she loved me too. It was the happiest day of my life."

"That sounds like a chick flick on the Hallmark Channel."

"So be it."

"Put Shannon on the phone."

"Doug, don't be mad at me. You know Dave and I love you and that's why we called."

"Dave called because he loves *you*, Shannon. His love for *you* made him call."

"Okay. Point made. Love is a wonderful thing. It makes men do things they wouldn't normally do. So go to Barnes and Noble on Saturday and be done with this. Meet us for lunch at Olive Garden."

"I'll get back with ya."

"And Doug, shave the beard before you go see her."

"Wait, how did you know I had a beard? You haven't even seen me."

"Like Aunt Charlotte doesn't have a phone. I love you, Doug Jameson. I'm not givin' up on this."

"I know. Love you too, Bye."

"Bye."

CHAPTER TWENTY-ONE: Winter Showers Bring Spring Flowers...Or Somethin' Like That

CARLIE

March 14

Another gray day in New York City. Does the sun not shine here? Or is it just so hard to see through all the shadows of gray buildings? A mystery. Tired of going through endless e-mails.

Ring.

"Hello."

"Carlie, everything is set for Thursday."

"Great. So, what's the plan?"

"You'll leave JFK at 8:37 and arrive in Birmingham at 11:49. Signing is from 5:00-7:00 Thursday night and then to Huntsville for Friday evening. You'll leave for Nashville Saturday morning. That's scheduled for 2:00-5:00. Your flight from Nashville to Atlanta leaves early Sunday morning. Wanda will go with you and keep everything running smoothly. Let me know if you have any problems."

"Thanks, Joan. Really. Thanks for everything."

"Don't mention it. It's my job. Besides, these personal events are a big part of the book business. Women love you, Carlie. You're the girl next door."

"If the girl next door craves blueberry Pop-Tarts, then yeah, that's me. Truthfully, I used to be the girl next door. Now I live in a big city and I don't know anymore. The crowds and the noise are causing me to lose some of my small town charm."

"I doubt that."

"Joan, can I ask you a personal question?"

"Shoot."

"Are you happy with your life? The fast pace, the crowds, the commute, the crazy busy world of publishing. Are you happy with all that?"

"If you mean am I happy every moment of every day? No, of course not. But yeah, I like what I do. And the New York thing...well, I've lived here all my life, Carlie. I can't imagine a slow-paced small town way of livin'. It would get boring after a while."

"Yeah, I've heard other people say that. But it's not boring. Not to me. I like sittin' around a coffee shop and not feelin' like someone is waiting to get my seat. I like grass and open space and people who are never in a hurry. I like seein' my old eighth grade teacher at the grocery store and watchin' dogs run through town never worrying if they'll find their way back home 'cause they will. They just know how to do that...find their way home."

"Carlie, are you homesick for Commerce?"

"I don't know. Maybe. I'm lonely. I mean, I'm always in a crowd but I'm never really with someone."

"You need a date, Girl."

"Got any suggestions?"

"Well, since you made that big virginity revelation on The David Letterman Show, I don't know if that would make it easier or harder for you to find a date in the city. I still can't get over it. I mean, Carlie, you never... not even once? I don't understand it. Maybe that's how things go in small town Georgia. But around here, well, that's pretty rare."

"I guess. But it's not a small town southern thing, Joan. The whole virginity thing...it's not without a purpose. I mean, it's not just that I'm a prude or somethin' or I'm afraid of men. I'm not afraid of men. You know that, right?"

"I know. It's all tied up in the Jesus thing. Good luck with that, Carlie. But Jesus never kept a girl warm at night. Not that I know of."

"I'm not lookin' for someone to keep me warm tonight, Joan. I was thinkin' more in terms of someone to wake up with every morning for the rest of my life."

"Touché. Note to self: Never get in a battle of words with a Jesus lovin' articulate writer...She'll win every time."

"Ha Ha. I love you, Joan. I mean, in a clearly platonic way...I love you."

"I know you do. Have a good trip, Carlie."

"Will do. Bye."

"Bye."

CHAPTER TWENTY-TWO: Turning A Corner

DOUG

March 18 5:45
Aunt Charlotte and Uncle Bart's house

"Doug Jameson, get in this house! You're just in time. The macaroni and squash casserole just went in the oven and I made sun tea this afternoon, which was no easy job on such a cloudy day as this one's been. Have a seat and we'll have a little talk before supper. Bart, come get this gall darn coon out of the living room!"

"Thanks, Aunt Charlotte. You don't have to invite me for supper. Sorry for just droppin' by like this."

"Lawsy, no, child! Don't you *ever* apologize for comin' by this house! Yur family, Doug. Close family."

"Truth is, I'm sort of confused right now. Not sure what to do. I never really got over Carlie, y'know. I tried but I couldn't seem to do it. I know everyone wanted me to get with Sandra but it wasn't gonna happen."

"Honey, we all know that."

Uncle Bart used a dried-up piece of leftover toast to lure the coon onto the back porch. Wearing overalls and a John Deere cap, he slammed the screen door and then sat down in the powder blue recliner which was broken and leaned to the left. "Hell, Doug, all of us knew you was crazy about that big friendly Georgia girl. It was the way you looked at 'er, the way she looked at you. So why ain't you two married and makin' babies by now?"

"Yeah, well, that's a little complicated. She's famous now, Uncle Bart. I mean, she's been on TV and everything. She's a writer and she lives in New York City."

"We know that. You think we're not cultured? We've seen 'er on the mornin' shows, Doug. Read about her in the papers. Yer sayin' you have to marry a non-famous woman, that you're too good to marry a famous one? Gosh, what's wrong with people yer age? Hell, who cares if she's famous or she works at the dollar store? Do you love her?"

"I do."

"Then tell her."

Aunt Charlotte chimed in from the kitchen as she poured sweet tea in three plastic Dollywood cups, "It's not that easy, Bart."

"It ain't? Well, thank God no one told me that, Charlotte. I knew I loved ya so I bought ya a hamburger when you was workin' at the Dime Store downtown. You 'member that?"

"Like it was yesterday."

"Doug, we got married three months later. We ain't been too miserable, have we, Charlotte?"

"We've been happy, Bart. And I thank ya for givin' me forty-three good years, real good years."

"Shannon and Dave told me that Carlie's gonna be in Nashville tomorrow. A big book signing event at a bookstore there."

Aunt Charlotte put four pieces of Wonder bread on a small paper plate and placed a tub of Parkay on the kitchen table. "And you're goin'?"

"I can't decide."

Uncle Bart scowled as he carefully rose from the broken recliner, "We may not be highly educated folks, but this don't take a rocket scientist, Doug. If you love that girl, go after 'er and that's all I'm a gonna say on this matter. Charlotte, you wanna jar of dill pickles from the shed?"

"That'd be good, Bart. Get a jar of pickled beets too."

And that was the end of that subject. We sat on the same yellow kitchen chairs they'd sat on for forty-three years. We ate macaroni and squash casserole and pickled beets. We talked of the weather. Unseasonably cold. Aunt Charlotte informed us that the football coach from Michigan was divorced but that his first wife was certifiably crazy and they had no children. And that Mrs. Miller said she liked him real well even though he wasn't a Methodist. He was Lutheran and that would have to do. Michelle managed to find homes for all seven of the Labradoodle puppies. The three of us deemed it an out-and-out miracle from the hand of God. Chester's cataract surgery was now scheduled for Tuesday morning so he brought his last will and testament to the barber shop and asked them all to witness his signature. Aunt Charlotte's only comment, "Lord, if that cataract surgery goes south, I pray we don't inherit the noisy parakeet. That's jest what we need 'round here."

March 18 10:30 pm

"Hello."

"Shannon, this is Doug. I'm sorry for callin' so late. I'll see you and Dave tomorrow."

"Hallelujah! Our prayers were answered."

"Maybe. But what if I told you that God used Uncle Bart to answer your prayers and not Dave's smooth-sounding speech the other day?"

"I'd say, 'God works in mysterious ways.' And I've learned not to question his methods."

"When do you wanna meet at Olive Garden?"

"Be there at noon and that'll give us plenty of time to get to Barnes and Noble by 2:00."

"I'll be there. And yes, I shaved my beard…and I'll brush my teeth, and take a shower, and make my bed. Anything else?"

"Go ahead and make fun. You'll thank me one day."

"See you tomorrow. Bye."

"Bye."

March 19 2:08 pm
Already a line out the door at Barnes and Noble

Dave tried to be light hearted. "Doug's in love with a rock star, Shannon."

I could hardly hear the conversation between the two of them over the pounding conversation in my own head. Carlie was just on the other side of that door. It had been almost three months since the last time I'd seen her in person. Did she still think about me? Or had she moved on? I stopped to re-tie my shoes. Dave accused me of stalling. There were mostly women in the line though there were a few men who looked uncomfortable.

Dave was clearly not uncomfortable as he visited with the folks in front of us. "This Carlie Davidson, she's kind of an overnight sensation, isn't she?"

A young college girl laughed, "She's hilarious! And yeah, she makes some good points too."

"Well, this good lookin' guy right here, he actually went out with her...several times. They were close."

"Are you serious?"

"Dead serious. You can ask him about it."

A young dark-haired college girl wearing a sorority sweat shirt acted as though she had struck gold. "Did you actually date her? The author?"

I couldn't believe Dave started this and I was determined to end it quickly. "No. Not the author. When I dated her, she was just a college student working at the dollar store."

"But it was *her*, Carlie Ann Davidson? That's who you were goin' out with?"

"Yeah. For a while."

I was thrilled when the store personnel opened the door and a balding older guy announced that they were going to move us all inside so that Ms. Davidson could share a few words before she signed the books.

We filed in like cattle. Standing room only. I tried to act like none of this mattered to me one way or the other. If Uncle Bart were here, he would just walk right up to the front and hand her a hamburger and that would be the end of it. For the first time in my life I wished I were like Uncle Bart.

A tall man in his mid-thirties and dressed in a black suit spoke into a hand held mic, "It's our pleasure today to introduce a young woman who has taken the literary world by storm. Her book, 'A Single Woman's Guide to Ordinary,' has delivered her down-home southern humor into mainstream America and mainstream America has welcomed it. We're honored she's here with us in Nashville. She's been on the Today Show, the David Letterman Show, and many other national television and radio shows. Let's give a big Nashville welcome to Carlie Ann Davidson!"

The crowd clapped and cheered and the man happily hugged Carlie as though he were an old friend...or not. She had cut her hair shorter but was as beautiful as ever. Black pants. Blue jacket. She still looked like Carlie, the old Carlie. The Carlie who smelled like vanilla and loved biscuits and gravy.

"Wow! I mean, Wow! You guys are great. Thanks for comin' out today. Thank you! And thanks for that introduction, Philip. Philip Glenn is a literary critic who lives here in Nashville and I'm blessed to call him a friend. Thank you, Philip." She looked back and smiled at him in that kind way that she smiles. My stomach was churning. I wanted to punch Philip Glenn in the stomach. I hated him and Matt Lauer...and everyone else who thought she was wonderful.

Where were they six months ago? I remembered when I was the only man who knew how wonderful she was. Well, me and Chester.

"I don't know what to say. It's been a crazy three months. First of all, to answer the most frequently asked question, yes, I'm still single. Not necessarily lovin' that, but it is what it is. I'm proud to be from Commerce, Georgia, and I still love lemon meringue pie and barbecue and biscuits and gravy. Truthfully, I need to love gravy a little less. I dread tryin' on clothes and I'm workin' on workin' on a plan to start workin' on a schedule for workin' out."

The crowd laughed. They loved her, imperfections and all. Maybe that's why they loved her. She wasn't afraid to say what everyone else was thinkin'.

"I thank you for wantin' to buy the book today. Thank you for that. I can't wait to meet you! All of you."

And with that, Philip escorted her to the table and we all fell back into line. My courage was waning. Uncle Bart was wrong. It did matter that she was famous. It mattered to me...and to Philip Glenn and Dave Letterman and all the people she called friends now. I didn't want to eat Thanksgiving dinner with Matt Lauer in New York City. I wanted to eat dry turkey in Sharon, Tennessee, with Aunt Charlotte and Uncle Bart and a stray coon even. Dave and Shannon were enthusiastic as they visited with the group of college girls in front of them.

I whispered in Shannon's ear, "This was a mistake. I have to go." I walked to the door and never looked back. I was still in a foggy haze as I pulled into Sharon almost three hours later. I stopped at the BP station to fill up with gas and Brother Dan said I looked tired and had I been ill. I'd had all that time to think about why I ran. And I came to a conclusion. I didn't want to see her look at me like that, like, "Poor Doug. Still bankin' in Sharon. Still eatin' with his crazy relatives while I'm bein' wined and dined in New York City. There he is, penniless after he nearly killed his former girlfriend. And to think...I almost fell in love with that guy." Yeah. I just couldn't take that look.

March 19   7:30 pm

While checking e-mail, my heart skipped a beat. Carlie A. Davidson. It had been almost three months since I'd seen her name come up on the screen.

Dear Doug,

I was hoping you'd come today. Praying you'd come. I knew it was a long shot. But when I saw you in the back of the room, well, that's why my speech was so short and confusing. I was nervous and excited and self-conscious all at the same time. I'm glad you weren't injured badly in the wreck. You look great. I was disappointed you weren't able to stay. I leave for Atlanta in the morning. It'll be good to get down close to home. I'm not a very good New Yorker, Doug. I miss the gravy. ☺ I hope you are well and taking time to enjoy the view from the front porch. That's still one of the most beautiful scenes in all of my memory. You're blessed to live there in peace and quiet. Can you believe I haven't seen one deer in New York City? And people say this is the exciting life. Yeah, I'll never understand that. Tell all your wonderful family members "Hello" from me. Tell

260

Aunt Charlotte I haven't forgotten about the deviled eggs...or her kindness.   That I will never forget.

Love,
Carlie

CHAPTER TWENTY-THREE: God Watches Over Fools And Insecure Women

CARLIE

March 20   Book Store in Atlanta

A tiny part of me is glad that Mom and Dad are in Hawaii for Spring Break. I can just see or rather hear Mom at the book signing. "The sound system is weak." "This lighting is poor." "That outfit makes you look old, Carlie." It was a relief to not have to entertain her and her general lack of satisfaction with life.

"Carlie, I think this is the biggest crowd we've had yet."

"Yeah, I guess it's like sports and this is kind of a home game, home territory."

Sally Vanderbilt, the bookstore owner, was a stylish gray-haired woman about 5 ft. tall and wearing a bright pink suit. "Everyone, may I please have your attention? Excuse me. It's time for us to get started. It's a joy to have one of Georgia's very own success stories with us today. Carlie Ann Davidson grew up in Commerce, graduated from the University of Georgia, and is now back home to share her book 'The Single Woman's Guide to Ordinary' with all of us. You know her. You love her. Carlie Ann Davidson!"

"Thank you, Mrs. Vanderbilt. Really. I can't tell you how happy I am to be back home in the great State of Georgia!!!"

The crowd burst into applause.

"I'm here to talk about the book and about being single and finding a way to have a sense of humor about it. Yes. But I also want to make an announcement. This week I turned in my notice with *Today's Woman* magazine and I plan to move back to Commerce, Georgia!"

More applause.

"New York City just wasn't the place for me. It's a wonderful place. But truth is, I'm a southern girl. I'll continue to write from my heart. And I don't wanna forget my small town roots. Who knows? I might even write a book about marriage someday. But sadly, not any time soon."

Applause and laughter.

"Most of you know I worked at the Dollar General Store in Commerce, Georgia, for ten years and I'm proud of that. I worked with good people. When I worked at the dollar store, my job was to be helpful and friendly, to care about the people who came in. That's still my job. It'll be my job ten years from now. God gave me that job, not a book publishing company. So I want you to know that I'm gonna love you today and treat you the same way I would treat you if I worked at the dollar store and you needed help finding Liquid Plum'r. And yes, I still remember that it's on Aisle 9."

Cheers, laughter and applause.

"I'm more than willing to take a few questions before we start signing books. Would anyone like to ask a question? The microphones are set up near the front. Yes, yes ma'am. You're the first. Go ahead when you're ready."

"Your humor is wonderful. But you talk a lot about love in the book and some of those comments are pretty serious.

Your perception of real love and commitment. You're thirty-two and you're still single. Do you still believe there are men out there who would want to marry you having never slept with you? I mean, is that even realistic?"

"Good question. Thanks for bringing that up. If you're asking if I think it's common for a man to want to wait. No. It's not common. If you're asking if I still believe there are men out there who believe sex is for marriage and are willing to wait. Yes. I do. In fact, I know for sure there are. Thanks again. Okay, yes. Right here in the red dress."

"Carlie, you talk a lot about weaknesses. Your love for food. Your lack of organization. Your foot-in-mouth disease." Laughter everywhere in the room. "I want to ask about your strengths. What do you consider your strengths?"

"You guys are deep. Okay. Truthfully, my strength is that I'm not afraid to share weakness. I mean, is that a strength? I'm not afraid of the truth. I know God's love and forgiveness. So I'm pretty open. I also hate to spend money. So maybe some people would consider that a strength. I'm not very materialistic. But I always believe that women should buy books. Never stop buying books, people! Yes. Right here in the yellow."

"Are you dating someone right now?"

"Wow! You don't beat around the bush. Are you asking if there are men who love tall fat women? I mean, is that your real question?" Laughter erupts throughout the store.

"No. We think you're beautiful, Carlie. I'm asking if there's a special man in your life?"

"Sadly, no. But if you have a brother or somethin', grab my card and give him my number. Thank you very much! You're a great group! Thank you!"

I stood at the front and hugged hundreds of women and a few men and signed hundreds of books. It was tiring but more than wonderful. I loved hearing their personal stories and knowing that somehow God used my own story to resonate with theirs.

Wanda brought me back to reality. "Carlie, we're nearing the end of the line. I'll talk to Sally and then get your stuff together. She'll want to speak with you before you go."

"Thank you. That's fine."

A few minutes later I was downing a bottle of water and gathering my bag.

Sally had to reach up to hug me. "Girl, you were a blessing! Thank you, Carlie. We had a great day. You moved women's hearts and you didn't hurt our cash register either. Come back and see us anytime! Oh also, a man left a present for you at the back. I guess he was a secret admirer."

"Wow! That's a first. Thank you, Sally."

As we moved to the back door, a young bookstore employee named Hank handed me a large shiny white box.

"Thank you! Wow! This is a surprise."

"Open it, Carlie. Let's see who it's from."

"Okay. Hang on."

I opened the box and carefully pulled back the folded white tissue paper. And there it was. I couldn't believe it. God had answered my prayers. Tears started flowing immediately.

"Gosh, Carlie, it's a dress! Look, a beautiful, blue sequined dress! Isn't that a bit odd? I mean, beautiful but odd."

I still couldn't speak. Hank handed me a tissue. I wiped my eyes as I read the card:

"Please meet me at the Crowne Plaza across the street at 7:30. I'll be the one in the monkey suit."

"Carlie, you better be careful. You shouldn't meet a fan without checking him out first. This could be really dangerous."

"Wanda, he's not dangerous. I promise."

"How do you know?"

"It's a long story. But I know."

"You know this guy?"

"I do. And I don't care what we have planned for the evening. I'm goin' to the Crowne Plaza."

March 20   7:30
Crowne Plaza

I was relieved the dress still fit. I'd been lonely and filling my late nights with ice cream but I'd also walked more and worked harder than I'd ever worked. I guess it all evened out. I wore plain black flats as that's all I had with me. Plain silver earrings and my hair curled loosely.   Nervous was an

266

understatement. I stood by a palm tree in the lobby trying to look natural. Then I saw him get out of the elevator. He looked exactly the same. The same way he looked that day in the store. The unpretentious southern James Bond. Except this time I knew him. He knew me. But I knew we wouldn't hug, not right now.

"Carlie, thanks for coming. You look more beautiful than ever."

"Are you kidding? Thanks for coming all the way to Atlanta. Thanks for inviting me here tonight. And wow! Thanks for the dress, Doug. I mean, I can't believe you remembered. It was a complete surprise. The best surprise I've had in a long time."

"I bought it a long time ago. Thought I'd give it to you for Christmas, but well, things didn't work out for that."

I stared down at the red carpet. "Yeah, I guess."

"They have a table waiting for us. You ready?"

"Absolutely."

We sat at a beautiful table in a quiet little dark corner. Doug seemed nervous. Three red roses in a clear vase. The waiter showed us a fancy menu filled with expensive food. None of it looked good to me. I was tired of tiny plates of ridiculously over-priced food.

Doug spoke kindly to the waiter, "This may seem strange. But I don't guess there's anyone back there who could make us some biscuits and gravy. Maybe some grits and eggs?"

"Yes, sir. If that's what you want, we can make it happen."

I smiled. "Thank you, Doug. It's like you read my mind."

"Trust me. I'm not a very good mind reader."

"Sure you are. You bought me this beautiful dress. You drove all the way to Atlanta. You asked me to meet you here. I couldn't have planned anything more wonderful. When I saw you in Nashville yesterday, well, I was the happiest I'd been in a long time. And then when you left I was sad and confused."

"Yeah, I was havin' a rough day. It was great to see you and all, but I don't know how to explain it."

"But you came here. Were you at the bookstore today or when did you leave the package?"

"Yeah, I was there…in the back. I heard every word you said. So you're leaving New York City, huh? I'm sure *Today's Woman* and your publisher were sad. Why are you leaving?"

"I'm not a very good New Yorker. I have to stay through the end of May and I'm not sad I went. It was a good experience. But, I guess I miss a small town. Not everyone would understand that but I know you understand."

"I do. Here's the deal, Carlie. I need to apologize. I didn't exactly handle things well a few months ago. Truth is, when you were going to interview for the job in New York City, I thought that was a rejection of me as a man. I know now that that was crazy. But that's the way I saw it. So I decided that I would just let you go. I wouldn't even try to hold you back from becoming this famous writer in New York. I would just keep livin' my life in Sharon and move on without you. It was a solid plan."

"It sounds like a solid plan."

"Oh, it was. And part of it worked. You did become a famous writer in New York and I did keep living in Sharon. But there was one problem with the plan. I couldn't move on without you. I tried. Believe me, I tried. I even tried to like Sandra again. That seemed like a convenient way to make the original plan work. But it didn't. None of it worked."

I wiped tears and managed to say, "I understand."

"So here's the deal. I'm gonna lay it all out on the table. And then you can take some time to think about it. I can't leave Sharon, Carlie. It's my home. That farm, it's been in my family for generations. And I know that life…and I get that it's not for everyone. I eat questionable casseroles with Uncle Bart and Aunt Charlotte at least once a week. Old women at church are always in my business. The International Aisle at our grocery store consists of Pace picante sauce and Kraft taco shells. And it'll always be that way. It will. I know there are men who could wine you and dine you. I'm not one of those men. I don't pretend to be. I saw how that Philip guy looked at you at the bookstore in Nashville. I'm a man and I know that look. But the thing is…well, the thing is...I looked at you like that before you were famous. I knew you were wonderful before Matt Lauer laughed at your jokes or before people stood in line to meet you. I bought one of those funny little coffee makers that puts foam on top just like you like it. I don't know why I bought it other than it made me think of you and the day in the mall and how you said you'd always wanted one. You know my old room? The one where you stayed that time? Well, I moved all those trophies into the attic and painted the room green, that green you liked from the Italian restaurant in Athens. Yeah, and I can put a desk in there that will work with your computer. And if we need a separate phone line, I can do that, I don't mind...I mean, a business line for your work and all. I love you, Carlie. I've loved you all this time. And I'm gonna choose to love you for the rest of your life. I don't want you to move to Commerce in June. I want you to move to an old farm house in Sharon, Tennessee. I want you to be my first...and my last. I want you to be my wife. No man will ever love you as much as I love you. I can promise you that."

The stiff white linen napkin made a poor handkerchief as I wiped my eyes and nose. My tears would not stop flowing.

"You don't have to decide now, Carlie. If you need to think about it...I get that."

"Think about it? Doug, that's *all* I've thought about...every day since I met you. Even that first day at Cracker Barrel, I thought about it. But after your mom's funeral, well, I was sure. I love you too, Doug. I love you and I want to marry you. Yes! A thousand times yes!"

By the time the waiter brought our biscuits and gravy, we were both laughing and crying.

The waiter smiled. "Is this good news? Are we celebrating something today?"

"We are. This beautiful woman just agreed to marry me. So...well, bring us your finest coffee, how 'bout that?"

"Congratulations! I'll bring it right out."

"Carlie, I don't know how you feel about this." He pulled a ring from his pocket. "It was the ring my dad gave my mom. I want you to have it but if you think, well, that you want something bigger or something that's not used or..."

270

"Doug, it's perfect. It's absolutely perfect."

"Do you have to get right back to New York?"

"Not if you have a better offer."

"Drive to Sharon with me. I want you to be there when I tell Aunt Charlotte and Uncle Bart and the rest of the family."

"I'd love to. My parents will still be in Hawaii for a week. Do you think you could drive to Commerce next week-end and we could talk to them together?"

"Sure. But I've already talked to your dad."

"When?"

"I called this morning. I told him I wasn't sure if you'd have me, but that if you agreed, would he be alright with it?"

"And?"

"And he said he was glad to get rid of you."

"I bet!"

"No, actually, he wasn't a pushover, Carlie. He had some questions. Some legitimate questions."

"Like?"

"Well, if I remember correctly, he said, 'Doug, what does a rural banker make nowadays? In round averages.'"

"He did not!"

271

"He did. And Carlie, it didn't hurt my feelings. He wants to know if I'm serious about making a decent living. It wasn't so out of line."

"And you told him?"

"I did. Then he said, 'Carlie's kinda serious about this writing thing. If she kept goin' with it and kept bein' successful, I mean, are you okay with that? You think you're the kind of man who can stand in a crowd and be the author's husband?'"

"And? I'm waiting with bated breath."

"I said, 'No, I never thought I could do that. But the girl I fell in love with ended up being that person. So it's gonna be fine. I'll adjust. She'll adjust. I trust her not to believe her own press. I do. They love her today, but could throw her away tomorrow. She knows that. It's the fickleness of the business. But if you're wonderin' if I'll ever throw her away. No. I play for keeps.' And then he said that you do tend to be sensible and not worried about what people think about you. And how he thinks you secretly liked working at the dollar store because it challenged people's way of thinkin', especially your mother's."

"You guys really had a heart-to-heart, didn't you?"

"He asked about church and family and children. And did I think we knew each other well enough? He must have liked my answers. He gave me his blessing."

"And if he hadn't given his blessing?"

"I never thought about it. I knew that he would. I had confidence with your dad. I was much more worried about

272

your answer. I knew your dad would be thinkin' things like whether I pay my bills, commit felonies, attend church regularly, come home after work every night. Did I know how to treat a woman with kindness? Could I lead a family with love? I knew that with God's help I could. I had the 'parent questions' answered. But I wasn't sure if you'd found a life you wanted in New York City. If you had, well, I knew I wasn't the man who could give you that life. Then I went to Nashville and I saw you up there in the spotlight and the way that Philip guy looked at you and you looked so comfortable in that role...and I thought I had my answer. You'd found something better. I was crushed and physically sick. But that night I got your e-mail."

Doug's eyes grew watery and he wiped them slightly with his hand. "And what you said about us sittin' on the front porch together and how you'd never forget Aunt Charlotte's deviled eggs and how not seein' a deer in New York City didn't seem right. And that's when I knew. I decided then and there that I would step out on a limb and tell you the truth."

"Wow, you crafted this little plan quickly, Doug."

"I never looked back. After I read your e-mail, I got up from the computer and found Mama's ring in the jewelry box. I got on your website to find the Atlanta location. I said a prayer, went to bed and slept soundly, and borrowed this tux from a friend this morning. And there you have it."

"That tux is a rental? I mean, a borrow?"

"Of course. You didn't think I'd be crazy enough to buy one, did you?"

"Of course not. Everyone knows rural bankers don't even wear ties."

"I love you, Carlie."

"I love you too."

CHAPTER TWENTY-FOUR: Rainbow After The Rain

DOUG

March 22 6:30
Family potluck at the farm house

Uncle Bart and Aunt Charlotte were the first ones to arrive. They brought deviled eggs (as requested), macaroni and cheese, and pickled beets. Michelle and Buster brought ham sandwiches and Chips Ahoy. Chester and Ida were proud of their squash casserole and a pitcher of watery Kool-Aid. Brother Dan added fried chicken from the Pic Pac and a plate of brownies to the table. I was so happy to learn that Uncle Stanley and Aunt Beth were in town visiting Charlene. All three of them plus Charlene's boys were able to come. They contributed corn casserole, coleslaw, odd-shaped sugar cookies, and a gallon of sweet tea. I had convinced Dave and Shannon to drive up from Chattanooga, said that I needed them desperately and that we'd first have supper with the family and then we could talk. They came. I knew they would. Ralph went by to pick up Uncle Charlie.

"Can I have your attention, everyone? Thanks for comin'! I promise we'll eat in a minute. I just have a quick little somethin' I want to say. It's been a strange six months. You've all helped me. Really. After Mom died, you became even more important to me. After the wreck, you helped me pick up the pieces, in more ways than one. Thank you for lovin' me, for carin' about me. I called you here tonight because I'm makin' an announcement, a big announcement."

Chester hollered out, "Make an announcement that it's time to EAT!"

"Ha ha. Yeah, we'll get to that, Chester. We will. I promise. We have a surprise guest with us tonight. Everyone, please welcome my soon-to-be-WIFE, Carlie Ann Davidson!"

Carlie opened the guest room door, pointed to the ring on her left hand, and yelled, "Surprise" as she reached out to hug me. Aunt Charlotte started screaming and crying and fanning herself with a John Deere apron. Uncle Bart had to open the kitchen window so she could get some fresh air. Shannon started crying and hugging Charlene. Dave shook my hand and hugged me real hard. Uncle Stanley wiped his eyes and Aunt Beth said, "Your mama and daddy would be proud of your choice, Doug. She's a fine Christian woman." Carlie and I asked Brother Dan and Dave if they could do the ceremony together on June 12 in the back yard at dusk. They happily agreed. And that was the end...or rather, the beginning.

CHAPTER TWENTY-FIVE: Building An Eagle's Nest

CARLIE

June 12 7:30 pm

Despite Mom's desire to create an over-the-top Martha Stewart wedding, we managed to keep it simple. The weather was a balmy 75 degrees. Friends and family members sat on chairs from various church basements. Everyone faced the field behind the farm house. Michelle played the wedding march on a keyboard and when everyone stood, Daddy wiped a tear and walked me down the aisle. I stopped half-way to hug Mr. and Mrs. Rockford and they both cried. Mr. Rockford had stepped out in faith that day and given me Doug's card. But it was his abiding love for Mrs. Rockford that had motivated me to use it. God had orchestrated it all. I wore a simple long white dress. Doug looked at me exactly like he did that day in the formal wear store.

Doug wore the borrowed tux again and this time his friend, Joe, gave it to him as a wedding present. "Seein' as how you're marryin' a famous woman, you're gonna need this, Doug. You'll be goin' to all them fancy big city parties and you need to represent Sharon well." We both laughed and assured Joe that we'd be eating pinto beans in Sharon more than we'd be at fancy parties but that his gesture was much appreciated.

Brother Dan and Dave worked together beautifully to paint a picture of marriage. The groom and his bride. Christ and His church. Sacrificial love and blessing. Doug looked into my eyes and made a promise to love and protect me until death. I promised to honor and respect him. We acknowledged our need for God's help in such lofty endeavors. Dave's voice cracked with emotion when he said, "You may kiss the bride." And Doug did. He brushed back my hair with his hand and kissed the bride. Happily. Joyfully. He never shed a tear.

After the ceremony Uncle Bart and Aunt Charlotte handed us a message written on a faded pink note card, "Doug, your mama and daddy would be real proud of you today. We know that for sure. Carlie, they would have loved you like a daughter. We love the both of you like our own and we hope you know that. We want you to go on that trip to Ireland you always dreamed about. Maybe it'd be nice for your first anniversary. Charlene looked it up on a computer for us and we put the money in a special account down at the bank. Just ask Jolene at First State and she'll get it for you. That's our wedding present to you. Now don't worry. We got plenty of money. God knows Bart's still got the first dollar he made. Congratulations. We love you both, Aunt Charlotte and Uncle Bart"

We were touched beyond words. All we could do was cry and hug them both. Uncle Bart said, "Now let's not get all crazy 'bout this. Time for cake. Charlotte, stop blubberin' and let's eat some cake now." And that was that.

The honeymoon in the Smokies was perfect. More than worth the wait. We stayed in a tiny cabin and hardly saw another human being. We drove into Pigeon Forge for dinner every night. But we had breakfast and lunch on the porch of the cabin. Now I knew what the Bible meant when it said, "And the two shall become one." This oneness was sexual and physical and emotional and spiritual. When one of us hurt, the other one would hurt. When one of us celebrated, the other one would celebrate. Five days later we drove into our farm

278

house driveway in Sharon for the first time as a married couple.

"Doug, I have a wedding present for you."

"I know and I love it. Thank you. A million times thank you!!"

"Ha Ha. Not that. I mean, a real present."

"Trust me. There's nothing you could get me that could make me happier, Carlie. Nothing."

"Well, I bought it from a very close friend and had it delivered here because I thought it was something you definitely needed, something that we needed."

As Doug drove the truck up under the carport behind the house, he smiled in that same beautiful way he smiled on the first day I met him.

"Oh gosh, Carlie. How'd you know? It's perfect. Perfect."

There sitting at the end of the drive was a rusty old John boat just waiting to be launched into Reelfoot Lake…where the eagles nest…and mate for life.

THE END

Doug and Carlie's Love Conspiracy
Available March 2013

CHAPTER ONE: Matchmaker, Matchmaker

I'm a married woman. I know. It's shocking to me and everyone else I've ever known. I still remember what happened when I went to the Commerce, Georgia, post office six months ago to have my mail forwarded to my new home in Tennessee. Agnes Robertson said she was so proud to see my wedding picture in the local newspaper. Well, those weren't her words exactly. She said, "Carlie Ann, now don't you fret none 'cause everybody knows pictures add at least 15 lbs. to a girl's physique." I didn't tell Agnes that the word "physique" hadn't been used since 1958 exercise shows on black and white TV.

"Oh Mrs. Robertson, I'm not worried about the picture 'cause I'm so deliriously happy being physically intimate with my good lookin' husband every night. It doesn't give me much time for frettin'."

I shouldn't have said it. That's my problem. You know those things that people think in their minds but know not to say out loud? Yeah, I tend to go ahead and say them out loud. Sometimes it gets me in a lot of trouble too. Other times it makes me "endearing." Or that's what Doug says. Doug is my husband. Just think of the most wonderful person you've ever known. Yeah, Doug is ten times more wonderful than that person. I don't want to make such a big deal about him being good looking. I mean, he's a lot more than that. I guess it's just that that was the part that surprised me. And clearly, that's the part that surprised everyone else too. I married a man who isn't just good looking or gainfully employed. But solid.

Most people in Commerce, Georgia, thought I wasn't going to get married because I was 32 with no prospects in sight. And that's fine. I mean, getting married is not the most important thing in life. But it's not unimportant either. If you really want to be married, it hurts not to be. And I think it's really dumb when people act like it doesn't hurt or that marriage doesn't matter. That's why I'm a matchmaker now. Because I care a lot about marriage and mostly I care about women like me who think they'll never meet someone wonderful. I also help women re-define "wonderful." And gosh, there are a lot of women out there who need that kind of help.

I don't mean I'm a matchmaker for my job. I'm a writer by trade. I don't make money matchmaking. I'm kind of like Mrs. Grissom. She's a woman in Commerce who's an excellent baker even though she doesn't own a bakery. She bakes for the love of baking. She bakes because she loves to hear my dad say, "Jolene, this chocolate pie will make you slap your grandma." Yeah, I understand Mrs. Grissom's baking now 'cause that's the way I feel about introducing single people to each other. I just can't wait until a newlywed comes up to me one day and says, "Carlie Ann, this beautiful woman you introduced me to is so wonderful. She makes me wanna slap my grandma." Yeah, that will be a banner day.

My name is Carlie and I got married to Doug six months ago. It's a long story how we met. Doug's Uncle Stanley wanted me to meet him even though he lived seven hours from Commerce in a tiny town called Sharon, Tennessee.

But I didn't think it was such a great idea. I acted like it was because I thought there might be something wrong with Doug. But the truth is…well, the truth is…I thought there was something wrong with me. So that's why it scared me to meet Doug. It's such a long story. I was in college and working at the dollar store when we met. But then I got a book published and I went on TV and so I stopped working at the dollar store. But Doug's career has been gloriously consistent throughout our entire relationship. He's a bank loan officer. That whole journey is recorded in a book called, "Doug and Carlie."

Sometimes there is a certain grace extended to people like me who believe they are beyond help in the relationship department. I now live with my husband in a beautiful old farm house in Sharon, Tennessee. I'm thirty-three years old and Doug is twenty-nine. I love it when his Uncle Bart says, "Carlie, you done came up here to Tennessee and robbed the cradle." Then he always laughs real big and we're all scared he'll lose his dentures. His laugh speaks a lot of words into my heart. Those words are, "Carlie, we love you very much. We're glad you're in our family." Maybe that feeling right there is why I'm willing to devote a lot of spare time to matchmaking.

My first victim…uh, I mean, non-paying customer is my old roommate, Clara Johnson, from Commerce, Georgia. She doesn't know she's getting ready to be a customer. I thought it best not to share that information quite yet.

Clara is 31 years old and she's a kindergarten teacher. She's really pretty but she thinks she's really ugly. This is a very common feeling among women. If you don't know that, you don't know much about women. Look out, Clara. A big, determined, happily-married woman in Sharon, Tennessee, is on the look-out for your future husband. Oh, and all you wonderful single men in Sharon need to be on your guard. I'm watching, boys. I'm watching.

The real question was whether Doug was going to join me in my sideline business of matchmaking. I decided to carefully broach the subject at supper one night.

"So, Doug, what's news at the bank today?"

"Sad news. Maxine fell and broke her hip at the ballpark last night. Her grandson, Dusty Jr., hit a triple and Maxine started jumping up and down with such enthusiasm. Chester was there and he thinks she forgot about the grandstands bein' kinda dry-rotted. And Maxine, well, she isn't exactly a featherweight. She's still at Volunteer Community Hospital. They think she'll be gone from work for a few weeks. Mr. Smith called to check on her and do you know what she said?"

"I'm dying to know."

"She said, 'Mr. Smith, I could just kick myself because I had just figured out the new online banking system and now here I am laid up for several weeks. By the time I get back to work, you'll have to explain it all again.' But truth is, she still hadn't figured out the online banking system. I was helping her several times a day. But I didn't think I should tell Mr. Smith. He'll figure out soon enough. A group of us will go by and see her tomorrow."

"Well, Honey, that's real sad. I hate that for Maxine."

"How was your day, Carlie? Weren't you doing a conference call about the new book?"

"Yeah, and it went well. Everything is lined out perfectly. It's just that now I have to actually finish writing the book. And that means work. And you know what they say about work, Doug? Work is always best accomplished tomorrow."

Doug bowed his head slightly and smiled real big because he isn't rude or judgmental or harsh. Doug is a faithful worker. He isn't sporadic or overly-creative. He can be counted on. He likes me even if it is hard for me to get stuff done. He knows I'll write the book. He knows someday the barbecued chicken won't be as tough as it was tonight. He knows I care about Maxine and Chester and his Uncle Bart and Aunt Charlotte. He is gracious and remarkably patient.

"Doug, I have a question."

"Shoot."

"Well, I'm worried. I'm worried about Clara. I was wondering if we could invite her for the weekend sometime?"

"Sure. But what's the worry, Carlie? Has she been sick or something?"

Okay. Now here's a difference between most men and women. Doug assumed something was physically wrong with Clara. He never even thought about the fact that Clara was living in our dingy old apartment and that she might be dying of loneliness and that the kindergarteners might be a daily reminder of the fact that she didn't have children or a man or even any prospects. Whew! Doug was handsome but he needed enlightenment.

"Well, Doug, she called me yesterday. She got a new cat and now I'm really worried."

"She got a cat? And that's what you're worried about?"

"Oh, absolutely. I think it's the beginning of the end. See, when a shy lonely woman gets a cat, the universe begins to work against her in so many troubling ways. First, it's the cat

284

hair on the furniture and then it's the wanting to get a 'cat friend' for the current cat. Doug, within a year Clara could have 20 cats and be operating a failed recycling business out of her backyard. I'm serious. These things happen. We'd better intervene."

Doug smiled really big and started laughing. I knew what his laughter meant just like I knew what Uncle Bart's meant. Doug's laugh was saying, "Oh Carlie, you're so overly-dramatic and funny and obsessive…and I love you."

"Y'see, Doug, Clara wants to be loved. She needs to be loved. But she doesn't know how to start the process."

"And you think you're the person who can help her?"

"Oh, I know I can. I mean, we can."

"So I'm in on this too, huh? What role could I possibly play in keeping Clara from becoming a cat lady with a failed recycling business in the backyard?"

"Oh, Doug! I'm so glad you asked. With you being from here, you would come near knowing who the available men are and how we could work out the introductions."

"Oh no, Carlie. I'm not sure about this. Don't people usually end up hating the ones who try to fix them up?"

"Hate? No one could ever hate you, Doug. I'm asking you to step out and take a risk with me the way Uncle Stanley took a risk when he introduced us. He helped us find true love, remember? I think we owe it to Clara to do the same."

I had him and he knew it. Oh, I don't mean I was controlling him. Doug wouldn't be controlled nor would I even try. No, I had him with the love part. And Clara Johnson, a shy Kindergarten teacher from Commerce, Georgia, who was frightfully embarrassed to talk about pork chops with the pleasant-looking butcher at Pic Pac, was getting ready to be our first official beneficiary. Roll up those shirt sleeves, Doug. This won't be easy.

Doug and Carlie
Discussion Questions

1. What insecurities did Carlie possess at the beginning of the book? Can you relate to those insecurities?

2. Were you surprised that Carlie had spent 10 years working at the Dollar General Store? Why or why not?

3. If you were a close friend, what counsel would you have given Carlie at the beginning of the book?

4. Did you relate to any of the characters surrounding Carlie in Commerce or surrounding Doug in Sharon? Which ones?

5. What did Carlie learn about Doug through the loss of his mom?

6. How do you explain Carlie's ability to handle the "competition" (Sandra and Jessica)?

7. If you were in Carlie's situation, would you have gone to New York? Elaborate.

8. What were the similarities between Carlie's mom and Doug's mom? Do you believe that had an impact on the story?

9. After Carlie went to New York, there was a lapse of communication between Doug and Carlie. Whose fault was that? How did it impact both of their lives?

10. Which character did you like most? Why?

Made in the USA
Charleston, SC
09 February 2013